continued . . .

Bedeviled Eggs

BERKLEY PRIME CRIME, NEW YORK

MYS
CHILDS

THE BERKLEY PUBLISHING GROUP
Published by the Penguin Group
Penguin Group (USA) Inc.
375 Hudson Street, New York, New York 10014, USA
Penguin Group (Canada), 90 Eglinton Avenue East, Suite 700, Toronto, Ontario M4P 2Y3, Canada
(a division of Pearson Penguin Canada Inc.)
Penguin Books Ltd., 80 Strand, London WC2R 0RL, England
Penguin Group Ireland, 25 St. Stephen's Green, Dublin 2, Ireland (a division of Penguin Books Ltd.)
Penguin Group (Australia), 250 Camberwell Road, Camberwell, Victoria 3124, Australia
(a division of Pearson Australia Group Pty. Ltd.)
Penguin Books India Pvt. Ltd., 11 Community Centre, Panchsheel Park, New Delhi—110 017, India
Penguin Group (NZ), 67 Apollo Drive, Rosedale, North Shore 0632, New Zealand
(a division of Pearson New Zealand Ltd.)
Penguin Books (South Africa) (Pty.) Ltd., 24 Sturdee Avenue, Rosebank, Johannesburg 2196,
South Africa

Penguin Books Ltd., Registered Offices: 80 Strand, London WC2R 0RL, England

BEDEVILED EGGS

A Berkley Prime Crime Book / published by arrangement with Gerry Schmitt & Associates, Inc.

PRINTING HISTORY
Berkley Prime Crime mass-market edition / December 2010

Copyright © 2010 by Gerry Schmitt & Associates, Inc.
Excerpt from *Scones & Bones* by Laura Childs copyright © by Gerry Schmitt & Associates, Inc.
Cover illustration by Lee White.
Cover design by Annette Fiore Defex.
Interior text design by Kristin del Rosario.

ISBN: 978-0-425-23823-3

BERKLEY® PRIME CRIME
Berkley Prime Crime Books are published by The Berkley Publishing Group,
a division of Penguin Group (USA) Inc.,
375 Hudson Street, New York, New York 10014.
BERKLEY® PRIME CRIME and the PRIME CRIME logo are trademarks of Penguin Group (USA) Inc.

PRINTED IN THE UNITED STATES OF AMERICA

10   9   8   7   6   5   4   3   2   1

Acknowledgments

Heartfelt thanks to Sam, Tom, Niti, Jennie, Dan, and all the designers, illustrators, writers, and sales folk at Berkley Prime Crime. And a special thanks to all the booksellers, reviewers, librarians, bloggers, and wonderful readers who helped put *Eggs Benedict Arnold*, the previous book in this series, on the *New York Times* bestseller list. Wow. Who would have thought a funky little cozy about three middle-aged women would land *there*?

To Dr. Bob and twenty-five years of marriage. Yowza!

CHAPTER 1

"HE reads Mario Puzo," Suzanne murmured, focusing on a couple that was eyeing each other warily. "She likes Charlaine Harris."

"Could be a match made in heaven," said Toni, brushing her hands against her apron after hastily arranging a plate of sugar cookies.

"Only if you believe in a vampire who'll make you an offer you can't refuse," Suzanne quipped, as she glanced over the crowd of hopeful singles that had jammed the Cackleberry Club this Sunday evening.

It was the week before Halloween and Suzanne Dietz, café owner and slightly reluctant matchmaker, was holding her first-ever "read dating" event. The whole shebang was similar to speed dating, except that the singles, mostly middle-aged and divorced folks from the small midwestern town of Kindred, were searching for compatibility based on reading preference. It wasn't exactly a polite afternoon of tea and cookies at Hope Church, but it wasn't the slightly desperate and bumbling last call for alcohol at Schmitt's Bar, either.

"Uh-oh," said Toni, putting a hand up to scrunch the frizzle of reddish blond hair that bobbed atop her head like a show pony. "A World War Two buff and a romance reader just paired off."

"If she's into historic romances, it's a done deal," said Suzanne. Toni may have been a show pony, but Suzanne was both Thoroughbred and workhorse. With silver blond hair brushing her shoulders, eyes of cornflower blue, and a penchant for slim-fitting jeans and white shirts tied at the waist, she could have breezed through an elegant crowd at an East Hampton polo tournament. Instead, Suzanne was CEO, PR director, and chief purveyor of eggs and sundries at the Cackleberry Club. This heartwarming midwestern café, where all manner of egg dishes were whipped up for breakfast, had been launched some eight months earlier, right after Suzanne's husband, Walter, had died.

In the weeks following Walter's funeral, Suzanne, not one to put off decisions, had taken a long, hard look at her life, sorted through her various passions and penchants, and bet the house on the Cackleberry Club. Under the combined banners of sisterhood and over-forty BFFs, her best friends Toni and Petra had thrown in with her to help revamp a rickety little Spur station into a cozy café. Now, with the addition of a Book Nook and Knitting Nest, the Cackleberry Club had become a kind of crazy quilt magnet for knitters, book lovers, and breakfast lovers.

"One, two . . ." Toni called loudly, as she stepped to the center of the room, then blew an eardrum-busting toot on her silver whistle.

Which caused an immediate flurry among the "read daters."

"Nice to meet you" and "I'll give you a call" echoed throughout the café, as men popped up from their chairs like manic gophers dodging potshots, then quickly moved to the next table. Much clearing of throats and smoothing of hair, or what was left of it, ensued as they plunked themselves down to meet yet another potentially available female.

Suzanne figured that, with any luck, the read daters would enjoy the books they discussed and maybe each other as well. Maybe.

"I've got one more pan of blond brownies in the oven," Petra announced, as she tottered from the kitchen, bearing an enormous tray stacked with peanut butter cookies and lemon bars. Her white chef's hat bobbed atop her head as she hefted the tray and gazed out over the buzzing crowd. "Can you believe how hungry these men are?" she asked. "Our first two trays of desserts disappeared in something like three seconds flat. They didn't even bother to chew, they just . . . gunk . . . swallowed everything whole, like crocodiles. Really hungry, I guess."

"And for more than just food," Suzanne observed. She'd seen flickers of interest in the eyes of quite a few men, who ranged in age from fortyish all the way up to Methuselah.

"Typical," snorted Toni, coming up to grab the tray from Petra. "All men are hot to trot, aren't they?" Toni had a chip on her shoulder the size of Rhode Island, thanks to her on-again, off-again marriage to Junior Garrett, an overage juvenile delinquent who was known for his roving eye. Especially when it came to floozy female bartenders with tight angora sweaters and hot pink extensions clipped into their hair.

"Still," said Petra, "this was a grand idea." She nudged Suzanne. "You see Mrs. Moxley over there?" They all turned to gaze at a cheerful-looking woman with a head of white hair who was talking animatedly to a red-faced farmer in overalls. "She probably hasn't had a date since her husband died some twenty years ago."

"It's not really a date," Toni pointed out. "More like a . . . mixer."

"Even so," said Petra, a faint smile playing at her lips, "it's nice and sociable." Petra, as head baker and chef at the Cackleberry Club, was the third partner in the troika. Big-boned and bighearted, she had a clean, square-jawed face with shining brown eyes. Today, the green ivy–print apron she wore over her chef's jacket matched the bright green Crocs she wore on her size-ten feet. Petra, too, had lost her husband, only in a different but just as heartbreaking way. Donny suffered from Alzheimer's and now resided in the Center City Nursing Home. Though Petra visited him constantly, Donny was rarely responsive.

"You going to pass out those bars?" Suzanne asked Toni.

"Yup," replied Toni. "Then I'm gonna blow my whistle and move 'em on again."

"Excellent," said Suzanne, grabbing a lemon bar dusted with powdered sugar as Toni moved off.

"Those are for our guests," Petra said, scolding.

"Can't help it, they're so good." Suzanne laughed.

"Well, in that case . . ." said Petra.

Suzanne and Petra grabbed steaming pots of coffee and Darjeeling tea and wound their way through the tables, pouring refills and doing their fair share of eavesdropping.

"This really is a success," said Petra, when they met back behind the counter. Then she made a tiny grimace. "I just hope our Quilt Trail is this popular."

"Are you kidding?" said Suzanne, ever the civic booster, "you've been working with the historical society, planning it for months. It's gonna be like gangbusters!"

The Quilt Trail was a special event Petra had talked the Logan County Historical Society into sponsoring, and it kicked off tomorrow. Giant quilt squares, painted on blocks of wood, had been hung on the county's historical homes, barns, historic sites, farmer's markets, and quaint country restaurants. Self-guided maps had been readied to lead tour goers to these special sites via a meandering route through the most picturesque and remote parts of the county.

"Still," said Petra, as she measured Kona coffee into the coffeemaker, "I always . . ."

"Are you insane?" came the sudden burst of a woman's shrill voice. It rose above the normal buzz and clatter, instantly causing heads to turn.

Petra frowned and glanced over. "Jane?" she murmured. Jane Buckley was one of her best friends. And right now, Jane Buckley was beaucoup angry over something.

"You're the one who's crazy!" a male voice shouted back, matching and even exceeding Jane in volume.

You could have heard a pin drop in the Cackleberry Club. Then chairs scraped and necks craned as everyone tried to see what Jane Buckley and Chuck Peebler were shouting about.

"If I find out that you . . ." Chuck Peebler raged again, only to shrink back in his chair as Toni leaned down and blew her whistle directly in his ear.

"Time to switch!" Toni cried. "Move along, move along, just like the Mad Hatter's tea party!"

"Fast thinking," Suzanne breathed, watching everyone change partners again.

"Why was Peebler yelling at Jane?" wondered Petra.

"Maybe because she disagrees with his political platform?" Suzanne speculated. Chuck Peebler was a mayoral candidate running against the incumbent Mayor Mobley. Though popular opinion held that Peebler would be a breath of fresh air, after Mobley's dirty tricks and politics.

Except, perhaps, Jane?

Toni came tripping up to Suzanne and Petra, smiling broadly. "Pretty crazy, huh?" she trilled. "Kind of like our own version of *The Bachelor* or *The Bachelorette*."

"Seemed more like *Survivor* to me," Petra murmured.

TWENTY minutes later, the event was slowly winding down. Men and women shook hands, exchanged pleasantries, and exchanged phone numbers. More than a few bought books.

That was just peachy with Suzanne, who was hunkered in the Book Nook, ringing up sales like crazy. She watched mysteries, cookbooks, and even romance novels fly off the shelves. Maybe because interest had been piqued, maybe because she was discounting everything 20 percent tonight.

Whatever the reason, sales were good, and the evening had been a lot of laughs.

"You okay over there, Mr. Mayor?" Suzanne asked Chuck Peebler. He was lingering in the Book Nook, nosing through books on the Korean War.

"Sorry about . . ." Peebler began. Then, because he didn't look particularly eager to explain his earlier outburst, he amended his words to just, "Sorry."

Suzanne pushed the cash register closed and walked out into the empty café with Peebler. Toni was humming to herself and halfheartedly pushing a broom around. Petra had already gone home for the night.

"You need help?" Suzanne asked Toni.

Toni shook her head. "I'm cool, but the front door's already locked, so you two will have to go out the back."

"No problem," said Suzanne. She smiled at Peebler, who still looked slightly sheepish, then added, "We'll just scoot through the kitchen. Easier than unlocking the front door and resetting the security system."

Peebler nodded, as he followed her through the swinging door. "Sure. I'm parked back here anyway."

Suzanne juggled her jacket, her purse, her keys, and a handful of Quilt Trail brochures as she pulled open the back door. "Know what I think?" she said, eager to forgive his earlier transgression, "I think you're going to be elected in a landslide. Everyone in Kindred is fairly convinced that Mayor Mobley is up to his armpits in more than a few dirty deals."

"That's why I'm running," said Peebler, holding the door for Suzanne.

"So a good thing," echoed Suzanne. She strolled out into the backyard where her dog Baxter was pulling himself up to greet her. Suzanne grimaced, worried about the cool autumn weather playing havoc with Baxter's arthritis. "Baxter," she said, concern coloring her voice. "You okay, fella?"

But Baxter had spun around and was staring directly into the dark woods where leaves rustled and shifted in the night wind and a twig suddenly snapped.

"Did you . . . ?" Suzanne began, turning back toward Peebler. Then her words were interrupted by a kind of mechanical twang followed by a strange swooshing sound.

Peebler's hands flew up in protest as he let loose a harsh gasp and began to crumple.

Suzanne uttered a sharp cry as Peebler continued his

downward, slow-motion progression, wondering what on earth had happened to the man! Heart attack? Stroke? She put out a hand to try to lend some sort of assistance and was suddenly stunned to see a gleaming metal shank protruding directly between Peebler's eyes. And just before Peebler fell forward onto the dry earth, she saw a thin trickle of blood ooze slowly down the side of his nose, like some unholy form of war paint.

Dumbfounded, Suzanne lifted her head and stared into the twisted tangle of buckthorn and scrappy poplars that backed up to the Cackleberry Club. She figured that was where the arrow had zinged out from. And the terrified, fleeting thought that burst like a cartoon bubble in her brain asked, *Am I next?*

CHAPTER 2

LUCKILY, Suzanne's survival instinct kicked in big time. Grabbing Baxter by his collar, she dragged his furry, protesting, sixty-pound body back inside the Cackleberry Club. Once the dog's tail had cleared the sill, she slammed and bolted the back door, her heart thundering in her chest, her breath coming in rattley gasps.

Is that it? Am I really okay?

A couple of hard thwacks against the back of the building told her no.

Ducking down below window level, Suzanne let loose a low moan. Then, because she wasn't out of danger yet, she pulled it together and screamed, "Toni! Douse the houselights now!"

Suzanne was deeply fearful that the shooter could see inside. The windows in the Cackleberry Club were large, allowing maximum light and visibility, especially in the kitchen. Usually, that was a good thing.

But Toni, smart cookie that she was, did exactly as she was instructed. The terror in Suzanne's voice must have answered any questions about the seriousness of her request.

Another thwack sounded against the side of the building. Then another.

Suzanne didn't know if the shooter was coming after her

now or was just trying to scare her to death. But if he had intimidation on his mind, it surely was working!

The door from the café flew open and Toni flew in, crying, "If that no-good Junior is out . . ."

"Get down! Get down!" Suzanne screamed again, gesturing frantically.

There was another thunk against the back of the building and Toni slid into the kitchen like a major leaguer sliding into home plate.

"It's not Junior," Suzanne whispered, as Toni crawled closer to her. "Chuck Peebler's been shot!"

"What?" Toni's eyes were big as saucers. "When?"

"Ten seconds ago. He's lying outside in the dirt. Dead, I think."

Still Toni was confused. "But who? How?"

"An arrow through his . . ." Suzanne stopped, hiccupped, couldn't seem to go on. What she'd just witnessed was too terrible for words. In fact, she wanted to believe it was a nightmare and that she'd wake up soon. But the voices in her head screamed, *This is reality, baby, and you're in deep doo-doo. Better do something!*

Toni scuttled closer to Suzanne and Baxter. "What are we gonna do?"

"Do you have your cell phone?" Suzanne asked.

Toni patted her apron pocket then shook her head. "I think . . . in the Book Nook? Want me to, um, make a run for it?"

"No, no, sit tight," said Suzanne. She glanced up, saw the wall phone illuminated by a sliver of light that shone in from the yard light, decided she'd have to make do. Her head whipped back and forth, then she spotted what she was looking for. "I've got another idea," she told Toni.

"Yeah?" Toni didn't sound all that convinced.

Slowly, quietly, Suzanne began to ease her way toward the far corner, crawling on her stomach the way she'd seen guys in war movies move toward enemy lines.

Baxter whimpered, then let loose a couple of sharp yips, as if warning her to remain still.

"Baxter, be quiet!" Suzanne hissed, pulling herself forward with her elbows. "You're not making this easy."

"You sure you know what you're doing?" Toni muttered, slipping her arms around Baxter's neck to comfort him.

But Suzanne had already swiped a hand out and grabbed the broom in the corner.

"Ah," Toni murmured, as Suzanne scurried back on her knees, dragging the broom. "Smart girl."

Using the handle, Suzanne knocked the receiver off the hook. It banged and bounced on the floor, dancing on the old kinked up cord, and causing everyone's heart to skip a beat. Holding their breath, they listened for footsteps, or heaven forbid, more thunks, but heard nothing. Carefully, gently, Suzanne snagged the receiver and pulled it toward them. Success!

From there it took only a few moments to press 911 with the end of the broom handle and get a dispatcher on the line.

"This is nine-one-one," came the dispatcher's voice in Suzanne's ear. A woman's voice, calm, but sounding very professional. "What's the nature of your emergency?"

"A man's been killed," said Suzanne, her words tumbling out. "At least I *think* he's dead. And somebody's still out there shooting at us!"

"The three of us," Toni added.

"You're being shot at with a gun?" came the swift reply.

"No, an arrow," said Suzanne. "Several arrows. Multiple arrows."

"Please confirm your location," said the dispatcher.

"The Cackleberry Club," said Suzanne. "Out on Highway 65."

There was only the briefest pause, and then the dispatcher responded, "Stay on the line with me. Do not hang up. Help is on the way!"

MINUTES later, Sheriff Roy Doogie and his deputy Wilbur Halpern arrived in a blaze of flashing lights and loudly wonking sirens. Suzanne and Toni peeped their heads up gingerly and peered out the back window. Baxter, smart guy that he was, stayed curled up on the kitchen floor.

A knock rattled the back door and then a deep baritone voice asked, "Suzanne? Are you okay?"

Through the window, Suzanne could see a flashlight beam dance across the backyard. She made a motion to stand up, but Toni yanked her back down.

"How do you know it's really Doogie?" Toni asked, her voice trembling. "It could be someone pretending to be the sheriff."

Suzanne looked askance. "I don't think the killer would come back with lights and sirens and official-looking cars."

"You never know," said Toni, scuttling across the floor. "You ever see those deer-hunting rigs guys put on their pickup trucks? Lights and racks and all those crazy doodads?"

But Suzanne was already sliding the bolt. Then she cracked open the door and whispered, "Doogie?"

"Holy bull dingers!" came an exasperated burst of static. "What kind of mess did you get yourself in now!"

"It's Doogie, all right," said Suzanne, yanking open the back door. She'd recognize that ornery temper anywhere.

Sheriff Roy Doogie, in all his khaki bulk and duly sworn glory, stood on the back stoop, glaring in. His jowls shook above his fleshy, pink neck. His service revolver was drawn and clutched in his right hand. "What the Sam Hill's going on?"

"That's what's going on," said Suzanne, pointing at the dark, crumpled heap across the yard that was . . . that had been . . . Chuck Peebler. "Chuck Peebler's been shot dead!" As if to punctuate her sentence, Deputy Wilbur Halpern's bouncing flashlight happened to land on Peebler's still form at the exact same moment.

"Jumpin' Jehoshaphat!" Doogie exclaimed. He thundered down the back steps and strode heavily toward Peebler, then dropped down onto one knee. "Keep that light shined right here, Wilbur," he instructed his deputy.

The deputy complied and Sheriff Doogie sat back on his heels as he checked Peebler's respiration, then carefully studied the man's face. A shiny, metal shank with black and orange flanges stuck out from Peebler's forehead. His blue eyes were stuck wide open as if he was riding the down side of a steep roller coaster; his mouth was open in surprise. The only detectable movement was the small amount of bright red blood that continued to trickle down the side of Peebler's face, like a slowly dripping faucet.

When Doogie loosened Peebler's collar and placed two fingers against his neck, Suzanne forced herself to stifle nervous laughter. Even she could tell the poor man was dead as a doornail. Then Doogie turned back to look at her and said, as if surprised, "You're right, he's dead."

Suzanne crept down the back steps, Toni following in her wake, drawn by the macabre scene of a dead body sprawled on their back lawn. Baxter remained inside the Cackleberry Club, peeping through the screen door, keeping his distance.

"The arrow killed him, I guess," said Toni.

Doogie sighed, then pulled himself up, no easy task for a man who far preferred glazed doughnuts to steamed vegetables. He brushed dirt and leaves from his khaki-covered knees and asked, "What happened?"

As if in answer, the bray of another siren suddenly filled the air. Now the ambulance was heading their way.

"It was horrible!" Suzanne told him, her words tumbling out. "There was this weird twangy sound and when I turned to look at Peebler, he had this metal thing protruding from between his eyes." She touched an index finger between her own eyes and shivered. "The end of the arrow, I guess."

Doogie cast another glance at Peebler, as if to confirm Suzanne's story. "Shot clean through," he muttered. "Like his head was a ripe melon." He winced slightly. "Let's hope Peebler didn't feel too much pain."

Suzanne shivered, knowing she would have felt extreme pain if her melon had been so rudely lobotomized. She was pretty sure she would have even experienced a shred of cognition mixed with horror as she faltered and buckled like Peebler had, just like a cheap card table.

"But who would do this?" Toni sputtered.

Young and eager to help, Deputy Halpern stepped forward to answer. "Could have been an accident. Maybe a hunter. It's deer season, you know."

"Too early for that," said Suzanne.

Halpern shook his head. "No, ma'am. Bow hunting runs from mid-September till end of December."

"So maybe an accident after all," Doogie offered, shrugging.

Suzanne was quick to interject. "Sheriff, no way was this an accident."

"You don't know that, Suzanne," said Doogie.

"Shine your light near the back door," said Suzanne. "Check the wall."

Deputy Halpern shone his light on the back wall of the Cackleberry Club, then ran it slowly across the whitewashed boards.

"Well, I'll be," Doogie responded as the beam danced against the wall, revealing two visible arrows stuck into the weathered wood. Three other arrows lay on the ground.

Wilburn Halpern bobbled the light as he rushed toward the back wall, tripping over his own feet at the last minute.

"Wilbur, you be careful!" Doogie yelled. "And for gosh sakes don't *touch* anything. This is all crime scene evidence. We gotta bag it and tag it."

"Sure thing, Sheriff," said Halpern.

Doogie turned toward Suzanne and sucked air through his front teeth. "Someone after you, Suzanne? Something you're not telling me?"

"No, no," Suzanne answered softly. "I think the shooter was aiming for Peebler. I was just in the wrong place at the wrong time."

"But it's not the wrong place," said Toni, looking all discombobulated and wild-eyed. "It's the Cackleberry Club. It's the right place, because it's *your* place."

"Toni does have a point," Doogie muttered, gazing at Suzanne with the hooded eyes of a slumbering rattlesnake. Doogie only looked a little slow moving. In reality, he was dogged, surprisingly analytical, and sharp as a tack.

"I really don't have any enemies, Sheriff," Suzanne insisted.

Doogie eyed her. "You mean as far as you know."

Suzanne shook her head as if to dismiss Doogie's words. "I'm pretty sure the shooter was aiming at Chuck Peebler. I'd lay money on it."

"Huh," muttered Doogie.

"Maybe something to do with the election?" Toni asked, her voice rising in a squawk.

"It is awfully strange," Suzanne agreed, "seeing as how the election is just two weeks away."

Toni edged forward to stare at Peebler. "Kind of looks like our incumbent Mayor Mobley doesn't have much to worry about now. I mean as far as opposing candidates go."

Doogie rocked back on his heels, looking thoughtful. "And here I was kind of hoping the town would get a chance to boot Mobley out of office."

Suzanne glanced sharply at Doogie. In the hotly contested mayoral race, the now-deceased Chuck Peebler *had* been the odds-on favorite to edge out the incumbent Mayor Mobley. Peebler had been perceived as, pardon the expression, the straight arrow of the two. Mobley was widely recognized as a greasy-palmed deal maker.

They all turned as the ambulance screeched around the building and bumped to a halt. Two paramedics jumped out from either side, then ran around to the back and pulled out a gurney. It clanked across the hardpan, white sheets fluttering.

"Don't hurry on this fellow's count," Doogie told them.

"He's a goner. I'm guessing he was dead the minute that arrow split his frontal cortex."

"Now you're a coroner," Suzanne muttered.

"Seen enough of death," Doogie muttered back.

"You want us to shoot a couple of pictures for you, Sheriff?" asked one of the paramedics. "We've got a camera in back."

"That'd be real helpful," said Doogie. "Then bag his hands and zip him into a body bag will you?"

"Sure thing, Sheriff," replied the paramedic.

"Wilbur," said Doogie, "you go into the woods back there and see what you can find. Try to rustle up some sort of evidence."

Deputy Halpern nodded tersely, as if he'd just been tasked with storming an enemy bunker at Anzio. "Sure thing, Sheriff." He ran toward the wooded area, managing to trip only once on a tree root.

The woods and fields directly behind the Cackleberry Club were also owned by Suzanne. The fertile acreage had been purchased as an investment by her late husband Walter. The land and farmhouse were now rented out to a farmer named Ducovny, who grew record-breaking amounts of soybeans and unbelievably tall stalks of corn in the nutrient-rich black soil. Ducovny also kept Suzanne's horse Mocha Gent and a mule named Grommet, in the fading red, hip-roofed barn that sat on the property.

"Why the heck was Peebler here in the first place?" Doogie asked, gazing at the dead man as the paramedics worked on him. "Don't tell me you guys are open for supper now?" Doogie looked mildly interested. Like maybe Suzanne and Toni might offer him a tasty plate of meatloaf or pork chops.

"For read dating," Suzanne explained.

Doogie screwed up his doughy face and let loose a dubious, "Hah?"

"It's like speed dating," Suzanne explained, "except you judge your compatibility with someone based on the kind of books you both like to read."

"For Doogie that would have to be comic books," said Toni, giving Suzanne a nudge and emitting a high-pitched, nervous laugh.

Doogie chose to ignore Toni's comments. "Anything unusual go on here tonight?"

That put a damper on Toni's mirth. Her eyes slid over to Suzanne and they exchanged meaningful glances.

Their exchange didn't go unnoticed by Doogie. He stuck out a big paw, waggled his fingers, and said, "Come on, what gives?"

"Nothing, really," Suzanne told him, her mind suddenly searching for the right words. She knew whatever she said could easily be misconstrued. "There was just a teeny little altercation between Chuck Peebler and Jane Buckley."

"Buckley," said Doogie, thinking. "She's that librarian at the art museum, right? At Darlington College?"

"Actually, she's the registrar," said Suzanne.

"Regis-what?" Doogie asked, confused.

Suzanne realized museums were not Doogie's natural haunts. But she knew this wasn't the time for a remedial lesson on the finer points of academia.

"You're right," said Suzanne. "Jane's the librarian."

"So what were she and Peebler arguing about?" asked Doogie.

"Probably an altercation over a book," interjected Toni.

Doogie cocked a wary eye at her. "Were you there? Did you hear them?"

"No," Toni said in a small voice.

"Then butt out," said Doogie. He turned toward Suzanne and shifted his attitude into super-cop. "Spill it, Suzanne. What did they say to each other?"

"I didn't hear the whole argument," said Suzanne. "I just know there was a heated exchange and then Jane told Peebler he was insane."

"And then he called her a crazy lady," said Toni. "And I think everybody pretty much heard that."

"Got a list of names?" Doogie asked. "Of your read-dating guests?" He said the words *read dating* like he was referring to cow poop.

"You can have a list, yes," said Suzanne.

"What else went on?" asked Doogie. He'd pulled a spiral notebook from his pocket and was scratching notes in it now. "What else were they scrabbling about?"

"Not sure," said Suzanne. But she sure had an itch to find out.

An earsplitting crack caused them all to spin around as Wilbur Halpern, deputy extraordinaire, stumbled out from the dark and flipped, headfirst, over a waist-high wild blackberry bush.

"Ouch," said Toni, as the deputy sprawled on the ground.

"You okay?" asked Suzanne. It seemed like Wilbur had taken an awful tumble.

Wilbur gave a feeble wave as he staggered to his feet. "I'm good."

"Find anything?" Doogie hollered.

"Not a doggone thing," Wilbur yelled back as he brushed leaves off his khaki trousers and carefully plucked thorns from his shirt. Suzanne noted that a few leaves were still stuck in his curly brown hair.

"Boy couldn't find his butt crack at high noon in the hall of mirrors," Doogie muttered under his breath.

"It is awfully dark," allowed Suzanne. Honestly, Doogie could be an awful sourpuss. And was this situation not totally weird? Standing in the backyard of the Cackleberry Club, a dead body sprawled on the ground, Doogie grousing, his deputy rustling around in the dark.

"I'll have to come back here in the morning and take a closer look." Doogie sighed. "Wilbur, grab the yellow tape out of the vehicle, will you?" As was typical of law enforcement, Doogie pronounced it "ve-hi-cle," hitting hard on three distinct syllables.

Suzanne grimaced. Nothing would scare away paying customers faster than fluttering yellow tape with the words *Crime Scene—Do Not Enter.*

"Sheriff, you're not really going to hang that awful black–and-yellow tape on our café, are you? Our customers will freak . . ."

"Just the backyard," said Doogie. "So you better make sure all employees enter through the front door until I clear them."

"Employees?" said Suzanne. "You mean Toni and Petra?"

"You suspect *us*?" shrilled Toni.

"Whatever." Doogie shrugged. "You got other people working here, too, don't you? You're a big hoodoo enterprise now, what with all your little nooks and crannies and books and yarns."

"We have a busboy who helps out," said Toni. "And once in a while Kit Kaslik pinch hits as a waitress. 'Course most of the time she's workin' as an exotic dancer out at Hoobly's, so I think you can rule out any concealed weapons . . ."

Suzanne placed her hands firmly on Toni's shoulders. It was their super-secret, nonverbal, BFF code that basically meant *Time to shut up, sweetie.*

Thankfully, Toni did.

"I'll have the tape pulled down soon's I can," Doogie told Suzanne. He hitched at his belt, shifting gun, flashlight, keys, and what looked like a thermos bottle. "But I have to follow procedure."

"Excuse me, Sheriff?" said one of the paramedics. He was a thin-faced man whose nametag read Pauley. "This here's some wicked-looking arrow."

Suzanne recognized the paramedic as Sid Pauley. Pauley had once worked at a local hardware store, mixing paint and measuring out lengths of rope and chain. Now that the big Save Mart had set up shop on the edge of town, edging out local businesses, Pauley had probably found steadier income as a paramedic.

Doogie walked over and made an acknowledging sound. "Arrow cut clean through," he told Pauley. He shook his head in a sort of tacit acknowledgment of the grim reaper. "You fellas know anything about bow and arrow hunting?"

The other paramedic, Dick Sparrow, leaned in to take a closer look. He snapped on latex gloves and, with practiced fingers, gently lifted Peebler's head, letting it loll in his hands as he inspected the protruding arrow. Then he lowered Peebler's head back down to the ground and touched an index finger to the metal part between the dead man's eyes. Sparrow looked up at Doogie, concern mingled with interest. "That's no ordinary arrow, Sheriff," he observed. "It's from a crossbow."

CHAPTER 3

"A crossbow," said Petra. She was standing at her enormous black industrial stove, dropping silver-dollar-sized pancakes onto the sizzling grill. It was Eggs Mornay Monday at the Cackleberry Club, so she was also stirring a pan of cheese sauce, adding fistful after fistful of freshly grated Swiss cheese. Suzanne and Petra had just filled her in on last night's bizarre incident.

"A crossbow with a carbon arrow," said Toni, as she laid out large oval-shaped white platters, the better to accommodate the Cackleberry Club's generous servings. "At least that's what one of the ambulance guys thought."

"Sounds nasty," said Petra, as she flipped a line of golden pancakes. She turned, gave a little grimace, and focused on Suzanne. "So what did Doogie think? Possible hunting accident?"

"Not unless someone was hunting white-tailed deer at night," said Suzanne. She dreaded the idea of someone skulking around the Cackleberry Club, stalking prey through a night scope. Or maybe she'd just seen too many movies where crazy Bruce Willis–type international hired killers peered through scopes and assassinated heads of state. Then jumped off rooftops and hang-glided away like bats in the night.

"What about that herd of wild boar that's been tromping around the countryside, ripping up gardens and scaring people silly?" asked Petra. "Maybe some hunter had been trailing them. He thought he was going to nail one, but made a terrible mistake." She nodded to herself, liking her theory. "The hunter hit Peebler instead, then got scared and ran away." She looked up with a slightly hopeful look. "It *could* have been a hunting accident."

"Something tells me," said Suzanne, "that our shooter didn't have a pig roast in mind."

"What's really important," responded Petra, "is that you and Toni had a guardian angel watching over you. That neither of you were injured or killed."

"Or Baxter," said Suzanne. The loss of her four-legged, furry companion would have been too much to bear. Especially since it hadn't been quite a year since Walter's death.

Petra heaped hash browns onto platters, added short stacks of pancakes, then placed two maple-flavored pork patties next to each stack. Satisfied with her arrangements, she wiped her hands on her apron. "Murder?" she asked, glancing up at Suzanne, voicing the one word they'd all jigged and danced around.

"That's the notion swirling in Doogie's brain," said Suzanne. She nodded toward the back door. "He's out there right now, scuffling around in the dust, searching for clues."

"Working up a hefty appetite, too, I'll bet," said Petra. Petra was an imposing gal of fifty who enjoyed fly-fishing, knitting, quilting, and feeding people, not necessarily in that exact order. Her passion for food had come early in life. She'd been the only nine-year-old kid on her block who preferred reruns of Julia Child over episodes of *Scooby-Doo*.

Toni balanced three platters of food on her left arm, then

grabbed another with her right hand. She gave Suzanne a worried look and asked, "Have you told Petra about Jane?"

Suzanne shook her head while Petra, who'd begun sifting ingredients for another bowl of pancake batter, suddenly froze.

"What about Jane?" Petra asked in a chilly voice.

Toni answered. "I think Doogie's going to be taking a hard look at her. Especially after last night's little shouting match."

Petra's brows knit together. "You told Doogie about that? Why on earth would you even mention it?"

"We kind of had to," said Toni. "Doogie wanted to know what Peebler was doing at the Cackleberry Club and . . ."

"You didn't have to tell him about their silly little squabble," Petra interrupted. "You could have said that Peebler was here for the read dating event and just left it at that." She shook her head. "I'm positive their little tiff was completely unrelated to the murder. Jane would . . . Jane would *never*!"

Suzanne tried to be diplomatic. "Petra, I know Jane is very dear to you."

"Yes, she is," Petra said, sniffling. "She's one of my closest friends. When Donny was first diagnosed with Alzheimer's, Jane never left my side. She went with us to all the doctor's appointments and even drove us to the Mayo Clinic for a second opinion."

"But Peebler's death, which really does look like murder, is a black mark against the Cackleberry Club," Suzanne told her. "And we don't want *that* hanging over our heads. So the sooner everything's cleared up the better."

"Still," said Petra, "Jane's my friend, just like you and Toni are. You know I'd never give Doogie any reason to suspect either of you." Petra stopped talking and clutched her stainless-steel bowl, deciding to take her anger and frustration out on the dry ingredients. As she attacked the batter-to-be with a balloon whisk, her swirling circles carried so much force Suzanne was afraid she'd dent the metal.

Suzanne tried her best to comfort Petra. "Jane and Peebler were arguing, Petra. And believe me, everyone heard them. So it's better Doogie learned it from us first. That way we can run interference."

Petra's circles got smaller and her breathing relaxed. "I suppose you're right." She glanced up. "Sorry, didn't mean to fly off the handle like that."

"Hey," said Toni, "we're friends, remember? No need to apologize."

"Thank you," said Petra, as the bell over the front door jingled, signaling the arrival of more customers.

"Dang, it's a busy morning," said Toni, bumping her hip against the swinging door that separated the kitchen from the café. "And I better deliver this stuff before it goes cold!"

Alone with Petra, Suzanne asked, "You okay?"

Petra nodded vigorously. "Better now, yes."

"We'll get this thing figured out," said Suzanne.

Petra lifted a corner of her white apron and touched it gently to her eyes. "Promise?"

"Promise," said Suzanne, meaning it.

OUT in the café, Suzanne grabbed a couple of coffeepots and started pouring refills. French roast for most, Sumatran for the more daring of the coffee drinkers. As she slipped between tables, she noted that every seat in the house was occupied, including the wobbly stools lined up against their vintage marble-and-wood counter. If another hungry body arrived, they'd just have to cool their heels on the front porch.

But something funny was going on, too. Many of the customers had finished eating, but were lingering longer than normal over their cups of coffee. There was also a low buzz of conversation and more than a few furtive eye darts.

Oh man, they're talking about Peebler. About the murder. Well, that's not good.

Hurrying to the front door to greet an elderly couple who'd just arrived, Suzanne said, "It'll be just a few minutes for a table." Then decided a bit of friendly chitchat would make them feel welcome as they waited. "What brings you to the Cackleberry Club this morning?" she asked in a breezy tone.

"We heard on the radio about . . ." the man began excitedly, until his wife gave him a determined elbow jab in the ribs.

"Breakfast," the woman finished in a brisk tone.

Suzanne groaned inwardly. The Cackleberry Club's unfortunate connection to the murder was being broadcast across small-town airwaves. In other words, via word of mouth.

Toni, who'd heard the exchange, strolled past Suzanne and said in passing, "By lunchtime we'll have 'em lined up outside the door. Folks are just getting curiouser and curiouser."

Suzanne nodded in agreement. What happened to the good old days when a murder kept people *away* from a place? Ah, but those days were probably long gone, given today's penchant for ripped-from-the-headlines stories and lust for true crime with all the gory details tossed in for good measure.

When a table of four finally left, Suzanne quickly

cleared away dirty dishes, wiped it down, and set it up for the elderly couple.

"Here you go," said Suzanne, offering the husband and wife a set of menus.

"You got eggs for breakfast?" the old man asked.

"Absolutely," she told him. "There's our special Eggs Mornay as well as eggs Benedict, toad in the hole, frittatas, Eggs in a Basket, and even Slumbering Volcanoes."

"Why so many kinds of eggs?" asked the woman.

Suzanne gave a slow reptilian blink. *Don't get out much?* was the answer that bubbled up inside her brain. Instead she said, "Well, this *is* breakfast and we *are* the Cackleberry Club."

Zipping back to the old brass cash register to ring up a check, Suzanne noticed that the ruffled pink Depression-era candy dish, normally filled with mints, was empty. And the stack of Quilt Trail brochures that also sat there had been reduced to a single copy.

Gotta get some more, Suzanne told herself, snatching up the colorful tri-fold brochure and sticking it in her apron pocket. Then, ten minutes later, when things were finally under control, Suzanne stepped into the Book Nook and dialed the number for the Logan County Historical Society.

Arthur Bunch, the director, answered the phone himself. "Logan County Historical Society."

"You're in early," said Suzanne. There was dead air for a moment, then she continued, "Hey, Arthur, this is Suzanne from the Cackleberry Club."

"Oh hello," said Bunch, sounding cheery now.

"Just wanted to tell you that we're down to our last copy of the Quilt Trail map. Looks like you might have a hit on your hands."

"Sure hope so," replied Bunch. "I've been putting in twelve-hour days but loving every single minute. The buzz we're getting over here is terrific. I think lots of folks are planning to drive the trail!"

"It's a great thing for the county," said Suzanne, "to showcase all our historic buildings." She hesitated. "I hate to add to your workload, but we sure could use some more of those brochures. We've been talking the Quilt Trail up like crazy and, of course, Petra's completely gung ho."

"I'll get some to you as soon as possible," said Bunch. "Wait a minute, are you by any chance serving cranberry almond scones today? The kind with Devonshire cream?"

"It's our autumn special all this month," Suzanne told him. "Along with wild rice soup and pumpkin pie."

"Then I might just bring those brochures over myself," enthused Bunch. "And I won't even feel guilty about deserting my post, I'll just consider it multitasking."

Arthur chuckled loudly and Suzanne could almost see his trademark bow tie moving up and down his wiry throat in the process. Arthur Bunch was a gentle soul, with his bow ties and serviceable, tweedy suits. He could have almost been cast in a 1950s sitcom as the good-hearted neighbor or even the slightly bumbling but well-intentioned dad.

"See you soon, Arthur," Suzanne responded. Gazing into the café, she saw that another table had come available. Springing into action, Suzanne rushed over and began clearing it off, vowing to one day hire a full-time busboy— one who didn't have to be in school during their busiest hours.

Then two more groups poured in, Petra hit the bell signaling for a pickup, and the phone rang. When it rains, it pours!

CHAPTER 4

"YOU grab the phone," said Toni, "I'll take care of the rest."

"Bless you," Suzanne murmured, speeding into the Book Nook and grabbing the phone. "Cackleberry Club," she answered brightly.

"It's Gene," said a raspy, male voice.

Rats. Gene Gandle, the annoying reporter-slash-sales guy from the Bugle.

"Is this for take-out?" Suzanne asked in her most professional-sounding voice, hoping Gene would take the hint that she was too busy to talk.

"No, it's for print, Suzanne. I'm not interested in placing an order. Inquiring minds want to know what happened at your place last night."

"Gene, we're swamped. I don't have time . . ."

Gene plowed ahead anyway. "Give me a few minutes," he wheedled. "Talking over the phone is a lot easier than my coming over and interviewing you in person. Think about it, do you really want a reporter asking questions about last night's *murder* in front of your customers?"

"Who says I'd give an interview?" Suzanne's demeanor dropped a few degrees colder than frozen. "I have nothing to say to the press, so stop badgering me."

"You want me to put that in the newspaper?" Gene

asked. "Sounds awfully suspicious, like you've got something to hide. How do you think readers will react? Or your customers?"

Suzanne gritted her teeth and stared at a needlepoint on the wall that said, *My disposition is subject to change without notice.* "Are you trying to blackmail me?"

Gene's voice was silky smooth now. "Not in the least, Suzanne. Just trying to cobble together a plausible story. I already talked with a few of your customers from last night. Your read dating folks." He gave a sort of snort. "Now I'd like to get your view of things."

Suzanne hesitated. Truly, Gene Gandle was a boorish clown.

"I'm on deadline," Gene said, pressing.

"Today's Monday. The *Bugle* doesn't come out until Thursday."

"I like to get a jump on things," said Gene. "Just play fair with me, okay?"

Suzanne's eyes darted around, looking for some sort of excuse or escape. Anything to get her out of this conversation. It came in the suddenly blessed form of Sheriff Roy Doogie, walking into the café and plopping himself down heavily at the counter.

"Can't talk now, Gene," Suzanne told him. "The sheriff just arrived."

Speeding into the café, Suzanne grabbed a pot of coffee out of Toni's hand and slipped behind the counter. She put a large white ceramic coffee mug in front of Doogie and poured out a steamy cup of coffee. Then she placed a knife and fork on top of a blue gingham napkin and set a glass of fresh ice water beside it. Doogie reached for the glass and gulped the water down immediately.

As he wiped his lips with his sleeve, Suzanne said, "Find any evidence out there, Sheriff?" She had to know, she couldn't wait!

Doogie gave a surreptitious glance around, then nodded.

"Really?" Suzanne was suddenly heartened. Maybe there was a plausible explanation for last night. Maybe Doogie would actually solve the case!

Then the pass-through door slammed open and Petra called out, "You want something, Sheriff? I saw you grubbing around out back and figured you might have worked up an appetite."

"Anything you got is good," said Doogie.

"Anything?" Suzanne asked, lifting an eyebrow. Usually Doogie was picky beyond belief.

"Eggs Mornay is good," spoke up Doogie. "Taters if you got 'em." Doogie hadn't earned the moniker "bottomless pit" for nothing.

"Pumpkin pancakes?" Petra asked.

"Sure," enthused Doogie.

"Coming right up," said Petra.

Doogie scratched the back of his neck. "Why the heck you got a cornfield growing directly out back? I stumbled through it and almost got myself lost!" He didn't look happy. "Lots of bugs in there, too."

"It's a corn maze," Suzanne told him. "For Halloween." Then she leaned across the counter and spoke in a low voice with very deliberate inflection, "What . . . did . . . you . . . find?"

Doogie dug a hand into his pants pocket, jingling around what sounded like keys and coins. Finally he pulled out a blue plastic key card and slid it across the counter to Suzanne.

Suzanne stared at it. "A key card?"

"Looks like," said Doogie.

"You think it's from the motel up the road?" she asked.

"Wrong color," said Doogie.

Suzanne's brow furrowed slightly, but she didn't ask the sheriff how he knew what color the Super 8 key cards were. Doogie was a widower and what he did on his own time was his private business.

"Besides," Doogie added, "it looks a little high tech for a motel. See that little magnetic strip?" He scratched at it with a stubby fingertip.

Suzanne nodded.

"It's got a miniature hologram. The kind you see on high-limit credit cards."

"Maybe the card's from your own law enforcement center," said Suzanne. "The jail must have high-tech security."

"We do, and nope, it isn't," said Doogie. "Wrong kind and color."

"What about the hospital?" Suzanne proposed. "It's got that depressing hospital-blue look."

Doogie slid the key card back into his pocket and took a noisy slurp of coffee. "Don't know. But at least it's something to check into." His flat, gray eyes drilled into Suzanne. "But that's it. I didn't find another darn thing out back."

"How far was the key card from our building?" Suzanne asked. She figured it was a good way of determining how close the killer had actually come to her and Toni last night. How close they'd been to the fine edge of disaster.

"Maybe twenty feet or so," said Doogie. "It was just lying in a little patch of dry grass. Not stepped on or anything. Like it had been dropped fresh."

"Hmm," said Suzanne, as Petra bustled out and placed a humongous platter of food in front of Doogie.

"Okay?" Petra asked.

"Better than okay," said Doogie, already grabbing for his fork, blue napkin forgotten.

Suzanne thought for a few moments as Doogie tucked into his breakfast. "Anyone could have dropped it," she reasoned. "There were lots of people here last night. Parked all around the place."

"Yeah?" said Doogie, between bites. "But I bet no one called here and asked if you guys found a key card, did they? So it's a clue. A good clue."

"I see your point," said Suzanne, as Toni edged up to the counter and dropped down on the stool next to Doogie. For some reason, it didn't sag and creak under her weight as it did his.

"You find out anything about crossbows?" Toni asked.

"Did a little research," Doogie told her. "They're not as common as you might think. And I already checked with the DNR on how many bow hunting licenses were issued last year as well as this year in the three county area."

"How many?" asked Suzanne.

"Five," said Doogie.

Suzanne nodded. That could narrow it down.

"Anybody we know?" pried Toni.

"Nobody that stands out," said Doogie, stabbing at a pancake. "A couple of brothers named Miller who live over in Deer County. A Jeb Brill who lives out by Borchard's Corner. And another guy by the name of O'Dell."

"O'Dell," said Suzanne. "He's been in here a few times. Strange duck."

"How so?" asked Doogie.

"Kind of quiet in a weird way," said Suzanne. "I can never get him to look me in the eye."

"Lots of men are like that," said Toni. "Shy guys." She giggled, then added, "Not everyone's a confident stud muffin like our sheriff here."

Suzanne pursed her lips to avoid an outburst of hysterical laughter, while Doogie pointedly ignored Toni's remark.

"You ticked off four names," said Suzanne. "Who's the other bow hunter?"

"Can't recall at the moment," said Doogie, shifting his bulk on the stool. "But it's in my notebook."

"I don't think I know much about any of them," said Toni, wiping her hands on her apron, looking suddenly apprehensive.

"On the other hand," said Doogie, "it could be somebody who owns a crossbow primarily for target practice. Never applied for a hunting license." He hesitated. "But he's moved on to . . . something else."

Suzanne looked pained. "If it's *something else*, we've got a real sicko on our hands. Someone quite determined."

"I agree," said Doogie. "Because Peebler couldn't have been much of a target. Skinny, string bean guy like that."

"Actually," said Suzanne, "he made a fairly good target. The kitchen light was on behind him and the door was open. He was probably silhouetted perfectly."

Doogie thought for a moment. "Ergo your clean shot."

"Ergo?" said Toni, sliding off the stool. "Now you're spouting Latin? Well, thank you, Aristotle."

Aristotle was Greek, Suzanne thought.

Then Suzanne stared intently into Doogie's eyes. "The shooter had to know what he was doing," she theorized. "Because a crossbow isn't a weapon for amateurs. You'd expect an amateur to use a gun, or a knife, or even the occasional cast-iron skillet. But a crossbow? That's got to be premeditated."

"Unless," Doogie said, waffling slightly, "it really *was* an accident. Even the most skilled hunter can make a mistake."

"Six times?" Suzanne asked, tallying up the number of arrows that had whooshed around the backyard last night. Two stuck in the wall, three on the ground, a fatal arrow in Peebler's skull.

"Point taken," said Doogie.

Petra emerged from the kitchen where she'd obviously been listening. "I just wish this whole thing would go away," she told Doogie.

He gazed at her placidly. "It's not going to. And besides, whoever shot Peebler was pussyfooting around in your woods. There's no telling what they want or if they'll come back."

"Don't say that," said Petra, waving an index finger. "I don't want to hear it. I don't want anything tarnishing the Cackleberry Club's reputation." Petra shook her head and retreated to the kitchen, where she planned to alleviate her anxiety by punching out an innocent batch of sourdough.

"Where does someone even buy a crossbow?" Suzanne asked.

"Anywhere they sell hunting gear," said Doogie. "Sporting goods stores, big-box stores, even on the Internet."

"The Internet?" said Suzanne. "You can just order up a crossbow?"

"Cripes, Suzanne," said Doogie, "where you been the last few years? Mars? You can buy a thermonuclear bomb on the World Wide Web if you search long enough."

"Even I know how to use Google," said Toni, strolling by again. Then her head whipped around and she added, "Or I should say ogle. Considering what just walked in."

Four of Kindred's volunteer firemen strolled to a vacant table, dressed in their navy blue uniforms. Young and hunky, each of the guys looked good enough to pose for a *Playgirl* magazine calendar.

"You look awfully busy, Suzanne," said Toni, unbuttoning the top button of her fitted yellow cowgirl shirt. "I'll take care of these beefcakes . . . uh, breakfast customers." Toni scrambled toward the front door, her hips twitching, her stride morphing into a strut.

Suzanne turned her attention back to the sheriff. He'd managed to drip only a few splotches of syrup on his shirt. A good record for Doogie. "So what else can you tell me about crossbows?" she asked.

Doogie chewed, then swallowed. "They're fairly easy to use. You don't need a lot of expertise or skill like with a regular bow and arrow."

"How so?" Suzanne questioned.

"You aim the crossbow pretty much like a rifle," said Doogie. "The smaller draw and cocking mechanism doesn't require a terrific amount of arm strength." He held up his hands, one near his chest, the other outstretched in front of him, as if he was actually brandishing the age-old weapon. "You just cock the device and shoot." He let out a swooshing sound and rocked back on his stool for emphasis.

"Interesting," said Suzanne.

"So even a woman could have used one last night to kill Peebler," said Doogie. He bolted his last slurp of coffee and swung his bulk around. "Gotta go make the rounds of the area sporting goods stores now. Then I'm going to drop by Darlington College and have a talk with Jane Buckley."

"You think Jane snuck back here and shot Peebler?" Suzanne snorted. "That's just plain ludicrous. While you're out chasing down a middle-aged museum registrar, the real killer is probably laughing at you."

"Gotta start somewhere."

"Not there," said Suzanne.

Doogie hesitated. "Then where, smarty-pants?"

Suzanne thought for a minute. "That key card you found? Maybe you should take a drive out to the prison and talk to Lester Drummond." Drummond was the warden of the newly established, for-profit Jasper Creek Prison that hunkered like an evil empire on the outskirts of town. With its gray concrete and miles of razor wire, Suzanne considered the place an architectural eyesore of unredeeming proportion. She'd lobbied hard against it, but Mayor Mobley had gotten his way, as he usually did.

"You want me to talk to the warden?" Doogie asked, frowning at her. "Be serious."

"It's a start," said Suzanne.

"You know what your problem is?" said Doogie. "You just don't like Drummond."

"You got that right," Suzanne answered, feeling no need to explain her dislike.

"Besides," Doogie continued, "they probably got better security out there than just key cards."

Let's hope so, was Suzanne's final thought.

CHAPTER 5

THE breakfast rush at the Cackleberry Club ended at 10:42 A.M. on the dot, leaving Suzanne, Toni, and Petra less than twenty minutes to regroup and get the café ready for the next wave of famished townsfolk.

"At other cafés," said Toni, as she wrapped knives, forks, and spoons in blue-and-white-checked napkins, "lunchtime begins at noon. Our customers come galumphing in at eleven."

Suzanne placed the silverware rolls on the tables as she aligned chairs and checked sugar bowls. "They line up early for breakfast, too. Especially *this* morning."

Toni nodded her head in agreement as she pushed her Fleetwood Mac T-shirt into the waistband of her jeans. For some reason, she'd changed shirts. Maybe because the day was getting warmer, maybe because Toni considered herself a Stevie Nicks sort of gal.

"I'm not surprised at our early eaters," said Petra, carrying a tray of pumpkin oatmeal cookies into the café. "We're midwesterners. Almost a farm community." She slid open the door to the glass pastry case and placed the cookies, almost as big as Frisbees, inside. "People just have more get-up-and-go."

Suzanne responded with a twinkle in her eyes. "If the

Cackleberry Club was located in New York City, folks would still be banging on the door early in anticipation of your cooking."

"But I wouldn't be there." Petra chuckled. "I like a small town with small-town values."

"With the exception of last night," Suzanne murmured, as Petra retreated to the kitchen with her empty tray.

Bang, bang went the front door.

"Here come noisy customers," complained Toni, jabbing her broom at a bit of crinkle-cut fried potato that was stubbornly hiding beneath a chair.

"I think not," said Suzanne, just as the door burst open and Ralph Reston stepped tentatively inside. Clad in olive drab overalls, he carried a familiar large, square cardboard box. "Hey, Ralph," she called.

The gentle giant of a man ducked his head in embarrassment. "Sorry, Suzanne," he murmured, glancing down at his worn overalls and scruffy work boots. "I'm really not dressed good enough to come in your front door, but there was this yellow-and-black tape strung all around . . ."

"Not to worry, Ralph," said Suzanne. "You look just fine. Half of our male customers dress the same way you do. Besides, a working man's uniform never goes out of style." She was chattering a bit, nervous that Ralph might inquire about the crime scene tape. Bless his soul, he didn't.

Ralph blushed and said, "I've got the eggs you gals ordered. This box and one more out in the truck." Ralph started for the kitchen, carrying the box filled with twelve trays of jumbo brown eggs as if they weighed no more than a monarch butterfly.

Ralph and his wife, Matty, ran Calico Farm, the largest organic, cage-free poultry farm in Logan County. Their eggs were nest-laid in comfy straw, not on an awful wire grid of an industrial farm. The hen's treasures were gathered by hand as well, and the chickens were free to roam their yard or stay put in their sparkling clean henhouse.

Suzanne had evolved into a real stickler when it came to using the freshest, locally sourced produce whenever possible. Eggs from Ralph's Calico Farm, cheeses from Mullen's Dairy, fruits and vegetables from various local organic farmers. She and Petra even hoped to get an organic farmer's market going in Founder's Park next summer.

"Right this way," said Toni, holding open the swinging door for Ralph.

"Thank you, ma'am," said Ralph.

Toni clapped a hand to her chest. "Yikes, Ralph. You just ma'amed me. A hit-and-run ma'aming. Please try to remember I'm still young enough to be your girlfriend." When Ralph's face turned beet red, she added, "Well, *somebody's* girlfriend." Ralph looked greatly relieved when the door swung shut.

"You ride that man something awful," said Suzanne, glancing around.

"All in fun," said Toni.

"Plus you're still married to Junior," Suzanne pointed out. Although she wished that Toni would finally make up her mind and file for divorce.

"Please don't remind me," said Toni. Then she glanced at her watch and said, "Jeez, I better refill ketchup bottles."

In a mumble meant more for herself than Toni, Suzanne said, "You could just forget about—"

Toni interrupted. "Not on your life, Julia Child. And I'm not having this discussion one more time. If it were up to you, ketchup would be banned from the entire universe.

But most of our old-timers adore it. They squirt it on their eggs, hash browns, even their muffins. The same way ex-navy guys use Tabasco sauce.

"Agh," said Suzanne, making a face.

"Not everybody lives by your standards, Suzanne."

"Sorry," said Suzanne. "Didn't mean to foist my preferences on anyone."

"Sure you did." Toni grinned.

Fact is, that was exactly the case when the Cackleberry Club first opened and customers had been confused by the lack of deep-fried dishes.

"They'd eat fried butter if they could," Suzanne had lamented.

"At the Texas State Fair I hear they do," Toni declared.

But their customers had nibbled, experimented, and in the end, had been pretty much won over by Suzanne's commitment to wholesome, fresh, good-for-you foods.

"You gonna do the blackboard?" Toni asked. Every day they listed their specials on the blackboard in colored chalk. It was another Cackleberry Club tradition.

"Yup," said Suzanne, grabbing a piece of yellow chalk.

"Petra gave you the menu?"

But Suzanne was already printing chicken and peapod stir-fry at the top of the board.

"All right!" enthused Toni.

Suzanne added three more entrées: chicken chili, chicken divine, and a Tom T sandwich. Then she drew a cartoon slice of pie on a plate, added a starburst next to it, and wrote in sour cream apple pie, two-ninety-five a slice.

"Gonna have me a slice of that," said Toni.

Just as Suzanne was dusting chalk dust from her hands, Dr. Sam Hazelet came rushing in. He was tall, in his early forties, and awfully good-looking with tousled brown hair and devastating blue eyes.

Suzanne saw Sam, grinned, then grabbed his hand and led him into the Book Nook where they could enjoy a small amount of privacy amid the narrow aisles of romance novels, mystery novels, and cookbooks. For the past two months Suzanne and the good doctor had been quietly seeing each other. Dinners, an occasional movie, walks in Bluff Creek Park. Nothing terribly serious, but Suzanne felt it certainly *could* turn into something serious. An altogether surprising turn of events, she'd decided one night, when she'd caught herself humming away, to once again find someone that she cared for. Heartening, too. Proved that life does indeed go on.

"I just heard about last night," Sam said, his voice and face filled with concern. "Why didn't you call me?" He placed a hand on her shoulder and kneaded it gently.

"Because by the time Peebler's body was zipped into a body bag it was almost midnight?" she said, deadpan. "Or how about this. You're a terrific doctor, but it never occurred to me you could actually raise the dead?"

"No," he said, "I thought maybe you'd have called me because you were scared." He paused. "Weren't you scared?"

"For a couple of minutes, sure. Until all the shootin' was over and Sheriff Doogie showed up."

"And then?" asked Sam.

Suzanne gazed at him, her heart warmed by his caring and sincerity. No wonder people thought so highly of him as the town doctor. No wonder her heart skipped a beat every time she saw him. Probably screwed up her EKG reading, but it surely *felt* wonderful.

"You mean," she asked, "did I think the killer would trail me home and try to pop me?"

Sam nodded.

"Not really," Suzanne answered, then decided if she'd been a tad wiser, maybe she *should* have been worried.

"You weren't scared all by yourself in that great big house?"

"No," said Suzanne. Then, "What are you getting at?"

"What do you think?" Sam winked.

She led him back into the café and sat him down at the table.

"Just lunch?" he asked, grabbing for her hand.

"Just lunch. And no need to peruse our blackboard, because I intend to order for you," Suzanne told him.

"Who doesn't love a surprise?" Sam replied, a lazy smile creasing his handsome face.

Scooting across the floor, dodging tables, Suzanne had to check her stride. *My hips are swinging just like Toni's,* she told herself, feeling a little startled. *Gotta watch that.* Then. *Oh heck. But it feels good to be happy.* Then she checked herself again. *As happy as one can be the morning after a murder.*

Petra glanced up from the stove where she was sprinkling fresh ground pepper into a big pot of roasted corn chowder. "You're looking awfully chipper," she remarked.

"Sam's here," said Suzanne, trying to sound nonchalant but not having much success.

"Aren't you the lucky lady," said Toni, who was standing at the butcher block table, tossing a salad. Carrots, florets of broccoli, and bits of red pepper clunked against the sides of the large industrial-sized metal bowl.

"Let me guess," said Petra, as she added judicious

amounts of garlic paste, jalapeño peppers, green chilies, and fresh cilantro to her soup, tasting and sniffing, as if she was concocting a magic potion. "You want me to whip up an order of breakfast egg pizza, even though it's not on the menu today." It was a statement, not a question.

"Could you?" answered Suzanne. It was one of Petra's specials. A whizbang of a dish. Not completely heart healthy, but surely heartwarming.

"And you're requesting this, let's call it what it is, *special order*, even though I have a dozen other orders to get out?"

"Um . . . yes?" said Suzanne. She bounced lightly on the balls of her feet in anticipation of Petra's answer.

Petra looked up and gave Suzanne a cool, appraising look. "Lord, that man better be the best kisser in Kindred."

Toni stopped tossing the salad and moved closer, the better to overhear.

"He is," Suzanne said in a small voice.

"Okay then," said Petra. "Far be it from me to stand in the way of love."

"Love?" said Toni, looking supremely interested now. "Really? I never heard the L word mentioned before."

Suzanne slipped an arm around Petra's shoulders and gave her a quick squeeze, then keeping her lips pressed together in a smile, slipped back out into the café. Toni's remark could be addressed at a more appropriate time. Like . . . later. Once she figured out where she and Sam were really heading.

Much to Suzanne's surprise, the café was suddenly buzzing with customers. Which meant she had to hurry up and seat four parties, dole out emergency cups of coffee to two tired truckers, and explain the concept of afternoon tea to two farmers who'd apparently studied every word printed on the little table tent that advertised the Cackleberry Club's afternoon tea.

"So the sandwiches are small?" asked the first farmer.

Suzanne held out her thumb and forefinger to show him. "So-so."

"And what kind?" asked the second farmer.

"Chicken salad, cream cheese with cucumber, smoked salmon roll-ups, and sometimes we do creamy goat cheese with crushed pineapple," she explained.

"Can men come?" asked the first farmer.

"Of course," said Suzanne, stifling a giggle. "There's no gender requirement for enjoying tea. And we won't even make you wear white gloves or a fancy hat."

Then she and Toni started taking orders and the fun began in earnest.

"Two bowls of chicken chili and a Tom T," Toni yelled through the pass-through to Petra. A Tom T was a Cackleberry Club concoction, a sandwich of sliced turkey breast spread with homemade apple butter, sprinkled with blue cheese, and grilled on two slices of artisan wheat bread. Sometimes it was served with sweet potato crisps, today it came with a salad.

A few minutes later Petra slid the chilies through the pass-through. "Suzanne," she called. "Your special's up."

Suzanne grabbed the dish and hustled it over to Sam. "Here you go," she said, setting it down in front of him. "Enjoy."

"My goodness," he exclaimed. Then he took a bite. "Oh joy," he mumbled as he chewed. "This is fantastic." Only it came out *fantashtic*. "This is . . . *what* is this?"

"Our special breakfast egg pizza," said Suzanne. "With pork sausage, red pepper, and cheddar cheese."

"So much better than hospital cafeteria food," Sam enthused.

"Don't swoon over it too much," Suzanne advised. "Because we've also got pie for dessert."

OF course, Sam didn't get away completely free. A parade of townsfolk stopped by to bid him hello.

"Hey, Doc, how ya doing?" Clyde Hunsicker asked, edging his large, jiggly frame close to the table.

"Fine, Clyde, and you?" Sam responded.

"I got this little crick in my back and my right knee is . . ."

Overhearing this little exchange, Suzanne shook her head. She knew the drill. Her husband Walter had been constantly pressed for free medical advice, too. Like he'd always said, a small-town doctor was never off the clock.

"We're jammin'," sang out Toni, as she slid by Suzanne with a tray full of soup bowls and a fresh pot of coffee. "Gettin' it done."

"Has anybody asked about the murder last night?" Suzanne asked Toni in a low voice.

Toni did a hasty double-take and scrunched up her face in amazement. "Are you kidding? That's *all* they've been asking about."

Suzanne pulled her mouth into a lopsided frown. "Maybe they've just been too polite to say anything to me."

"Maybe," said Toni, but she said it like she didn't believe it. Then she saw the look on Suzanne's face and said, "Cheer up, hon, they've also been asking when Petra's gonna make her pumpkin crème brûlée."

And just when things couldn't get any crazier, Mazy

Goddard strolled in with a basket stacked with loaves of homemade cranberry nut bread.

"Is this a bad time to make a delivery?" Mazy asked. She was a wiry sixty-something lady with a feathery cap of white hair who still managed to run the occasional half marathon. She was also a baker par excellence.

"Not a problem," Suzanne told her. "Just stack your bread in the cooler, as usual."

Just outside the Knitting Nest, Suzanne had installed a sputtering old cooler whose shelves were continually stocked with an array of homemade banana and cranberry breads, jars of dill pickles, canned jellies and jams, vegetables, and organic blue and cheddar cheeses. These were items that local producers brought in for the Cackleberry Club to sell. It was really a win-win situation for everyone. Suzanne took a small percentage of retail sales and the growers and producers got the lion's share. She knew one woman who'd helped finance her daughter's cosmetology classes on what she made from selling her line of organic baby foods.

"In fact," said Suzanne, grabbing one of Mazy's loaves, "I'll take one of these myself." She made her way to Sam's table, set the bread down, and said, "This is for you. A take-home goodie."

His eyes crinkled. "That's it? There isn't any more?"

"Sour cream apple pie?" she asked.

"Mmm, I had something else in mind."

Suzanne walked Sam to the door, didn't kiss him though she wanted to, and proceeded to clear a few tables. This was the time she enjoyed most at the Cackleberry Club. Lunch practically over, sliding gracefully into an afternoon of coffee, tea, and desserts. Much easier to manage, nobody in an all-fired rush.

She carried the gray plastic bins to the counter and stuck them in back. Then Suzanne waved through the pass-through at Petra, and said, "Thanks for the special."

Petra gave her a quick grin, then her eyes shifted and her smile froze on her face.

"What?" said Suzanne. Then she realized Petra was focused on something behind her. Spinning on her heels, Suzanne caught sight of Jane Buckley standing at the front door. The woman's shoulders were slumped; her face seemed in turmoil.

Oh no, thought Suzanne. *Doggone Doogie.*

Then Jane was speeding across the café, wiping tears from her eyes as Petra came careening out of the kitchen to meet her.

Jane collapsed in Petra's strong arms, her tears spilling freely now. "Last night's murder . . ." she sobbed.

"What? What?" Petra murmured in sympathetic tones.

Jane sniffled, rubbed at her nose, then wailed, "Sheriff Doogie says I'm the number one suspect!"

CHAPTER 6

"Do you need a glass of water?" Suzanne asked. "Or maybe a cup of tea?" Jane was slumped in a big, comfy chair in the Book Nook, her demeanor a fragile mix of rage and woe. Petra sat on a lumpy footstool, holding Jane's hand and making soft cooing sounds.

"Only if it has a dram of gin in it," Jane managed to answer. Then added, "Sorry, I didn't mean to sound snippy. It's just one of those museum-world clichés. The old maid who sits at home nipping Bombay gin or drinking dry sherry while tending a herd of cats."

Suzanne made a noise in the back of her throat. "You have cats?"

"Just two," said Jane. "Which is actually well within the normal range." She coughed, then added, "And truth be told, I don't drink much at all, except for a single glass of wine last night to help me relax in case I actually *met* someone." She pulled a hanky from her handbag and blew her nose loudly. "And now look at me, a messy little lump of sadness."

"You're not, either," said Petra.

"What exactly did Doogie say to you?" asked Suzanne.

Jane let out a breath of despair. "He said I was at the top of his suspect list."

"He has a list?" Petra asked, skeptically.

"What were his exact words?" asked Suzanne. "Did Doogie say you were on his list because of your fight with Peebler?"

Jane edged herself farther back into the comfort of the upholstered chair and nodded. "I didn't realize every single person in the Cackleberry Club overheard us."

"I doubt they did," said Petra, always the staunch ally.

"But the whole town's talking," said Jane. "Sheriff Doogie told me so himself."

"The whole town's *not* talking," said Petra.

"Yes, they are," said Toni, suddenly appearing in the doorway. She held a tray that contained an ornate red teapot and three small Chinese-style cups. "Everybody's been buzzing about the murder all morning and I don't think it's going to stop anytime soon."

"They'll stop," said Petra, as if her strength and iron will could make it so.

"I'm not so sure about that," said Suzanne, accepting the tea tray from Toni. "Thank you."

"You bet," said Toni, backing away.

"Everything okay out there?" Suzanne asked. She didn't want to leave Toni in the lurch for afternoon tea.

"Nothing I can't handle," said Toni.

Petra poured a stream of jasmine tea into a teacup and handed it to Jane. "Straight tea, no cream or sugar."

"You always remember how I like my tea," Jane murmured. "You never forget anything."

"Or anyone," said Petra smiling warmly at Jane. "Now, tell us what we can do to help."

Jane took a quick, appreciative sip of tea and said, "Since you brought it up . . ."

"Because if you want me to speak to Doogie . . ." began Petra. "Really let him have it . . ."

Jane plucked nervously at the sleeve of her blouse. "Actually, I came here to . . . um . . . ask Suzanne for help."

"I see," said Petra, in a quiet voice.

"What?" Suzanne yelped.

"The thing is," said Jane, turning an imploring look on Suzanne, "you were so smart about straightening out that terrible mess when Ozzie was killed."

"Oh, not so much," said Suzanne. She waved a hand, trying to make light of it, make it seem like a minor little incident.

Jane continued in a rush. "And, of course, you're awfully close to Doogie."

Suzanne grimaced. "Not really."

Petra gave Suzanne a level gaze. "Sure, you are. You two went to school together."

"He was a few years ahead of me," said Suzanne, as her brain whirred into overdrive. *How to get out of this?* she wondered. *Just beg off nicely? Sure, that's the ticket. Petra will probably even back me up. She knows I really don't want to get involved in chasing down suspects in Peebler's murder.*

"Obviously," said Petra, furrowing her brow and staring directly at Suzanne, "Jane really needs our help. And by that I mean *your* help."

So much for backing me up, thought Suzanne. "I could probably recommend a good attorney."

"No!" cried Petra. "We're not at that point yet!"

"Listen," said Suzanne, crossing her arms in front of her, trying to look as uninvolved as possible. "Doogie already knows how I feel about Jane as a suspect. I told him he was wasting his time."

"Thank you," said Jane. "I think."

"Then what's the harm in your speaking with Doogie *again*?" asked Petra. "Surely you could make him understand that Jane wouldn't hurt a fly!"

Suzanne was feeling frustrated. "There's always a risk I could make things worse! When you defend something once too often, Doogie has a tendency to use the 'doth protest too much' argument."

"It's probably the only line from Shakespeare he can quote," stewed Petra.

"Please," Jane implored Suzanne. Tears sparkled in her eyes then spilled down her pale cheeks. "Couldn't you just *try* to talk to him?"

In the end, of course, Suzanne relented. Agreed to speak with the duly elected Sheriff Doogie and make an impassioned plea regarding Jane's innocence.

With one small codicil.

"I have to ask this," said Suzanne. "What were you and Chuck Peebler arguing about last night?"

"Oh, it's really stupid," said Jane, waving a hand.

Suzanne stood firm. "You still need to tell me."

"The thing is," said Jane, "I used to be friends with Peebler's aunt."

"The one who died last month?" asked Petra.

Jane gave a thoughtful nod. "That's right, Evelyn Novak. A very nice lady. Caring and socially committed. She even donated a couple of nice paintings to the Darlington College art museum. Anyway, Peebler was asking me about some antiquities his aunt owned that were missing from her house."

"What's *that* got to do with anything?" huffed Petra.

Suzanne peered at Jane. "Excuse me, but Peebler thought you *stole* them?"

"That was the basic gist of the conversation," said Jane, giving Suzanne a baleful look. "Chuck Peebler seemed absolutely convinced that I strong-armed his aunt into donating them to the museum."

"Why would he think that?" asked Petra. "Why would he jump to that conclusion?"

"I suppose because the items are missing?" theorized Jane. "Because she'd donated items before?"

"And you are the registrar," Suzanne murmured. She thought for a minute. "What exactly are these items that are missing?"

Jane shrugged. "No idea. Peebler wouldn't tell me, just kept haranguing me, saying, 'You know what they are!' and treating me like I was some kind of criminal." Jane stared worriedly at Suzanne, then at Petra. "But you know I wouldn't . . . I couldn't . . ."

"We know you wouldn't, dear," said Petra, patting Jane's hand.

Suzanne placed an index finger between her brows and massaged her frown lines. Decided this was all very strange.

A half hour before closing, Arthur Bunch strolled into the Cackleberry Club. As he quickly scanned the café, his stack of Quilt Trail brochures shifted in his hands and began to spill.

Suzanne dashed forward and made a quick save before the colorful brochures hit the floor. "Slippery buggers," she said, grabbing for them.

"Thanks, Suzanne," said Bunch. "Guess my mind is elsewhere."

Suzanne noticed Bunch's oversized black galoshes with

his tweed trousers stuffed inside. "It's wet enough for rain gear?" she asked.

Arthur gave a quick smile. "No, but it's about to start spritzing any minute, so I got all suited up." He offered a lopsided grin. "I plan to drive the entire Quilt Trail tonight and make each and every stop. I want to make sure everything is perfect!"

"Have you eaten yet?" Suzanne asked, feeling sorry for this quaint middle-aged man in his tweeds and boots. She'd seen Bunch at garage sales and tag sales, rummaging through piles of clothing, and figured that's where he found his slightly out-of-date tweedy wardrobe. On the other hand, a civil servant, especially one who worked at a small county historical society, didn't exactly pull down a hefty income.

Arthur shook his head as his eyes lit up. "No lunch yet. Been awfully busy."

"We've still got scones and chicken chili," she told him. "Have a chair and we'll get you fortified."

Bunch stumbled to a table, sat down heavily, then gazed up at her, a worried look shadowing his face. "I heard what happened here last night," he murmured. And now he looked slightly unnerved. "Mr. Peebler was shot with an arrow?"

"A special kind of arrow," said Suzanne. "From a crossbow."

"That a fact?" Now Bunch looked even more worried. "A ghastly way to go. Just like in the days of King Arthur or Cromwell. Do you know, does the sheriff have any idea who . . . ?"

"No idea," said Suzanne. "Sheriff Doogie's really just begun his investigation." *And I guess so will I.*

The mild-mannered Bunch was still unsettled. "Because the idea of a random killer . . . you know, like that crazy sniper who stalked the Washington, D.C., area some years back?"

Suzanne nodded.

"A random killer would be utterly terrifying," said Bunch. "I hope it's nothing like that," he added hastily.

"The sheriff's thinking it was probably an isolated incident," said Suzanne.

"If even a hint of worry gets out," said Bunch, "it could affect the Quilt Trail. A lot of people have worked extremely hard to make this happen." He bobbed his head for emphasis. "We've got historical sites all over the county that are scrubbed and polished and staffed with hardworking volunteers. Plus we've been promoting it like crazy for the last three months."

"I know you have," said Suzanne.

"Plus the smaller merchants, like antique shops and cafés, are counting on an influx of tourists for this event," said Bunch. "Business has been tough for them these last couple of years."

"I hear you," said Suzanne, as she counted her blessings once again. For some reason the Cackleberry Club had weathered the vicissitudes of a bad economy. Whether it was the cozy café, the Book Nook, or the Knitting Nest that attracted people, there had been a steady uptick in their bottom line. They hadn't scored a huge profit, mind you, but they were making a decent living.

Suzanne plated a scone for Bunch and added a huge dollop of Devonshire cream. Two seconds later, Toni brought out a large bowl of chili and placed it in front of him.

"A veritable feast," declared Bunch.

Suzanne slid into the chair across from him, while Toni finished setting up tables for tomorrow. "Mr. Bunch . . ." she began.

"Arthur," he said, spooning up chili at a rapid rate.

"Arthur," said Suzanne. "Do you, by any chance, know a woman by the name of Evelyn Novak?"

He shook his head without breaking pace. "I don't think so."

"It's possible she could have donated some items to the historical society."

Now he paused. "Novak? And you say she donated items?" He looked thoughtful. "Doesn't ring a bell."

"I said she *might* have," explained Suzanne. Then she quickly summarized her reason for asking. Told him about Peebler's quarrel with Jane Buckley concerning the missing items.

"Oh my goodness," said Bunch, finally seeing the connection. "I see what you're driving at. So you want me to check our records, in case the pieces are with us? I can surely do that for you."

"Would you?" said Suzanne, feeling better already. "That would be great."

"And these were paintings?" asked Bunch.

"That's what Evelyn Novak donated to the Darlington College museum, but I don't know what items were missing from her house."

Bunch sat back and pursed his lips, looking suddenly academic, as if he was about to deliver a lecture. "You realize, the Logan County Historical Society specializes in American pieces only. Artifacts that have to do with early settlers."

Suzanne smiled as Bunch went on with his little speech.

He really was a man dedicated to his job. Plus he had kindly agreed to deliver a short lecture at their Quilt Trail Tea on Wednesday. Probably, Suzanne decided, he'd be the perfect counterpoint to all their tea and frills.

THIRTY minutes after Arthur Bunch left, with an extra scone tucked in his baggy jacket pocket and a take-out cup filled with Darjeeling, Suzanne, Toni, and Petra were ready to throw in the towel. Busy days were welcomed, stressful days were not.

"Whew," breathed Petra as she plopped down in a frayed velvet armchair in the Knitting Nest. She shucked off her Crocs and gave her feet a much-deserved rest on the opposing ottoman.

Toni joined her in a swoopy orange swivel chair that looked like it had once belonged to the Jetsons. "Glad I cancelled book club tonight." She sighed. "I just don't have it in me."

Suzanne was right on their heels, also ready to call it a day. "The coffeepot's turned off and the front door is locked," she told them.

"What about the back door?" Toni asked, in an ominous tone.

"Checked that, too," said Suzanne. "Unless we have customers storming the parapets, we're done for the day." She eased herself into a slightly frayed blue club chair. When four thirty rolled around, this was where the three of them usually convened. To talk things out, giggle about the day, or just de-program. Petra usually grabbed a pair of knitting needles and worked on one of her many projects, the clacking of the needles lending a decidedly soothing sound. Petra was crazy over knitting and quilting—they were her favorite forms of relaxation. Although to Suzanne both needlecrafts looked like awfully tricky business.

"I just love that quilt," said Toni, gazing at the wall where a striking blue-and-red-star pattern quilt hung.

"Still time to bid on it," said Petra. The Knitting Nest was holding a silent auction on a number of handmade items, with all the money earned earmarked for Alzheimer's research. "Come Wednesday, I'm going to hang it outside."

"Then the bids will really skyrocket," said Toni, morosely.

"You know," said Petra, kindness in her voice, "I'd make you a quilt anytime you want."

"Really?" said Toni, thrilled.

"Of course," said Petra, gazing happily at the wooden walls that were festooned with knitted mittens and caps, felted bags, and quilted throws and coverlets. Antique highboys held skeins of cotton and wool yarns in all colors of the rainbow. Large ceramic crocks were filled with knitting needles, baskets held blocks of six-by-six-inch fabric pieces. These square motifs came in different colors and designs including baby motif, calico, Christmas, floral, and batik. Petra also made sure they were well stocked with jelly rolls—pre-cut strips, forty to the count, and just perfect for quilting.

Toni hauled herself out of her chair, wandered over to the knitting needles, and picked up a pair of bamboo needles. Pretending to use them like chopsticks, she said, "Considering what happened last night, today went fairly well."

"Agreed," said Petra. "I was so busy most of the time I didn't have a chance to think about poor Chuck Peebler."

"Me neither," said Toni. "Except when I hauled out the

trash. The arrow holes in the back wall are still an ugly reminder."

"Stick a little putty in them," said Suzanne, letting her eyes flutter closed. "Be good as new."

"Too bad they couldn't do that to Peebler," mused Toni.

The smile dropped off Petra's face and she focused on Suzanne with a steady gaze. "Suzanne? You think you can help Jane?"

Suzanne opened her eyes and squinted at Petra. "I promised I'd try. Although, I'm not exactly sure what I promised. I don't really know what to do or where to start."

"But you told Doogie where to start," said Toni. "Just this morning. I heard you."

"I'd like to tell him where to get off." Suzanne sighed.

"Doogie listens to you," said Petra. "He many be an obstinate man, but he's savvy, too."

"And Suzanne's a smarty," Toni enthused, as she pulled out a pocket mirror and fluffed her hair. "A perfect blend of Nancy Drew and Xena the Warrior Princess!"

Suzanne smiled, but all she could think was, *Oh dear*.

"Man, I wish I could do something about these wrinkles," said Toni, still peering in her mirror. "It ain't easy being over forty."

"Don't think of them as wrinkles," counseled Petra, "just consider your face as being gravitationally challenged."

BY the time Suzanne loaded up Baxter and arrived home, she didn't know which of them was hungrier. So she dumped a cup of kibble into Baxter's aluminum dog dish, then, while he crunched and noshed, explored her well-stocked refrigerator for something quick.

The something quick turned out to be a little leftover beef Stroganoff. Forgoing the noodles tonight, Suzanne heated the beef mixture on top of her stove, stirred in a dollop of sour cream at the last minute, then poured it all onto a slice of toasted baguette. She loaded her plate onto a wicker tray, then went back to the refrigerator and poured out a half glass of Barolo Riserva.

Baxter was finished by then, so he accompanied Suzanne into the living room for a casual dinner on the leather couch.

As Suzanne ate and watched TV, Baxter watched Suzanne eat.

"Not this," she told him. "Not tonight."

Baxter edged his muzzle onto the couch and tried to convey a sad, appealing look, but no dice. Suzanne ate her own dinner, cleaned up, then found herself back in front of the TV. When nothing seemed all that interesting, she turned down the sound and reached for Kostova's novel, *The Historian*, which she'd promised herself she'd start reading.

Suzanne was deep into chapter six when the doorbell rang. One loud, long *briiiing* that startled both she and Baxter.

Leaping up from where he'd been twitching and snoozing, Baxter raced to the door, head held stiffly down, hackles bristling.

Tiptoeing after him, Suzanne was also wary, recalling last night's bizarre incident and, at the last second, stepping to one side before she asked, "Who is it?"

CHAPTER 7

"It's me," came Toni's muffled voice.

Suzanne pulled open the door. "Toni, what are you . . . ?" Suzanne stopped abruptly when she recognized the stunning young woman who was standing next to Toni. "Kit?" she said, her voice rising in surprise.

A smile lit Kit Kaslik's clean, scrubbed oval face. "You remember me," she said in a soft voice. Then she shrugged back her long blond hair, looking supremely pleased.

"Of course, I do," said Suzanne.

"From when I pinch-hitted at your cake show," said Kit.

"Sure," said Suzanne, still slightly blown away by Kit's appearance on her doorstep. Kit normally worked evenings, churning out a living as an exotic dancer at Hoobly's roadhouse, a big, ugly Quonset hut of a place out on County Road 18. Though Kit wasn't a stripper per se, because technically she didn't remove her clothes, Suzanne had still urged her to pursue more suitable work, since exotic dancing wasn't the most promising career move. But Kit, for whatever reason, by personal choice or by dint of simple economics, was still prancing about in black go-go boots and red lace undies on Hoobly's postage stamp–sized stage.

"We gotta talk," said Toni. "It's real important. Besides . . ." She did a quick little dance and shrug. "It's starting to rain like crazy."

"Come on in," said Suzanne, opening the door wider.

Toni shrugged off her brown leather bomber jacket and hung it on the antique walnut coatrack that stood in the entry. Kit, dressed in denim jacket, baggy sweater, and cargo pants—clothes that certainly didn't scream, *Look at me, I'm a wild and crazy dancer!*—opted to keep her jacket on.

"Hey, Baxter," said Kit, bending down to pet Baxter, who pretended not to eat up the attention, but immediately stuck his muzzle in Kit's hand when she tried to pull it away.

"Don't mind him," said Suzanne. "He'll bug you for hugs and pets and treats all night."

"Sweet guy," murmured Toni, smiling at Baxter. Then her eyes seemed to shift into serious mode and they all trooped into the living room, settling into chairs somewhat self-consciously.

"We interrupted your dinner," said Kit, spying a tray on the coffee table.

"Not really," said Suzanne. "I was just having tea and banana bread. There's plenty of banana bread left if anybody wants some. And a little bit of beef Stroganoff if anybody's real hungry."

Both women shook their heads. "Pass," said Toni.

"How about something to drink?" Suzanne asked.

Toni shifted nervously. "You got any wine?"

"Sure," said Suzanne. "I've got open bottles of Chardonnay and Barolo Riserva, although there may only be a couple of fingers left of the Barolo. What's your choice?"

"The white stuff," said Toni. "Whichever one that is."

"Sure," said Suzanne. She looked at Kit. "Kit?"

"Nothing for me," said Kit, holding up a hand. "I don't really drink."

Toni seemed surprised. "Seriously? You work at Hoobly's and never tip back a brewski now and then?"

"Trust me," said Kit, "if you worked out there, you wouldn't drink, either."

Suzanne brought back a glass of Chardonnay for Toni and the almost-empty bottle of Barolo for herself, then settled cross-legged on the floor. Baxter slunk over and lay down next to her, pressing his warmth against her body.

"Okay," said Suzanne, trying to keep the conversation light, even though a nervous buzz had started pulsing in her brain. A warning blip that said, *Something's about to happen here.* "You darkened my doorway and said you had important news for me."

Toni cleared her throat, then said, "Here's the thing. I know it's gonna sound weird, but we've got some information that relates to Chuck Peebler's murder."

"What?" said Suzanne.

Toni held up a finger. "Strangely enough, it also dovetails with your looking into things as a special favor to Jane . . ."

"Okay," said Suzanne, wishing Toni would get to the point.

"The thing is," said Toni, "it's something that could sort of . . ." She searched for the right word. ". . . *impact* the investigation."

"I'm listening," said Suzanne, wiggling a foot nervously, wondering where all this was going.

Toni took a quick sip of wine, set her glass down, and said, "Junior took me out to Hoobly's earlier tonight for a beer and burger."

Suzanne wanted to say, *Big mistake*, but didn't. Instead she said, "Uh-huh."

"After we were done eating, I ducked into the ladies' room," said Toni. "And that's when I ran into Kit."

Kit looked slightly embarrassed. "The dancers don't have their own bathroom like they do at big clubs," she explained.

"We were standing at the mirror," said Toni, "minding our own business and refreshing our lip gloss. And somehow we started talking about Chuck Peebler's murder. Which is on *everybody's* radar right now."

Suzanne gave an acknowledging nod.

"Anyway," said Toni, looking decidedly nervous and taking another sip of wine, "we jabbered about the murder and . . . well, you tell her, Kit. Tell Suzanne exactly what you told me."

Kit stared at Suzanne with big, guileless eyes. "Chuck Peebler, the guy who was killed last night . . . ?" She hesitated, her courage seeming to falter.

"Yes," said Suzanne, tiredness seeping into her voice now. "Toni and I were there when it happened, and I'm sure she gave you all the gruesome details."

"True crime, up close and personal," muttered Toni.

"And what about Peebler?" Suzanne asked Kit.

"Well," said Kit, "Chuck Peebler used to . . . how shall I phrase this? He used to frequent Hoobly's."

"You mean he was campaigning there?" asked Suzanne. "Asking for votes? Glad-handing the customers, such as they are?"

"Actually, it was more like manhandling," said Kit, in a disgusted voice.

"What!" said Suzanne. Now they really had her attention.

"Peebler used to hang around Hoobly's and pester all

the girls who worked there," explained Kit. "But, most of all, he had a thing for dancers."

"Lot of that going around," muttered Toni. "Pestering, I mean."

"Wait a minute," said Suzanne, holding up an index finger. "Peebler was old enough to be . . ." Her mouth snapped shut. This information was not only weird, it put a whole new spin on things. "I had no idea," Suzanne murmured, still digesting Kit's words. "But, but . . ." She knew she was sputtering now. "Peebler was running for office! He was on the ballot to be mayor of Kindred!"

"Interesting, huh?" said Toni.

"And if you can believe the straw poll that the *Bugle* conducted," said Suzanne, "Peebler was even showing a slight lead over Mayor Mobley." She inclined her head toward Kit. "You sure about this?"

Kit nodded. "Oh yeah."

"Kit's not making this up," said Toni. "She wouldn't do that."

"You'd think Peebler would have been a whole lot more careful," said Suzanne, "considering Hoobly's is a fairly public place. That he would have toed the line and conducted himself with a little more dignity."

"It sure isn't dignified to chase girls half your age," agreed Toni.

"You got that right," said Kit, "but the thing is, Peebler went beyond that. He was . . . creepy. Always sitting at the edge of the stage, flashing a wad of cash, trying to, you know, tantalize the girls with what he thought was his power and magnetism. Then he'd hang out by the dressing rooms, trying to grab a look-see, always talking a steady stream of patter. A little nasty, a whole lot aggressive."

"You could knock me over with a feather right now," said Suzanne. Peebler had been a card-carrying member of the Methodist church. He'd served on the school board. True, he was a single man, but he'd always acted conservative. *Looked* conservative in his JCPenney suits. Had probably voted Republican, too.

"Tell her the rest," Toni urged, polishing off the last of her wine.

"There's more?" said Suzanne.

Kit glanced about nervously. Baxter, seeming to sense her unease, pulled himself up and padded over to her. Kit draped an arm around Baxter's furry neck and continued, as if heartened by his display of doggy solidarity. "And the really weird thing," continued Kit, "is that Peebler had pretty much singled out one girl as his . . . favorite."

"You?" Suzanne asked, fearing the worst.

Kit gave a vehement shake of her head. "No, not me, thank goodness."

Suzanne pursed her lips together. "So what exactly are you saying? That Chuck Peebler had been stalking one girl in particular? Harassing her?"

"Harassing," said Kit. "Yes, I'd say that pretty much hits the nail on the head. Peebler would tail her to her car, trying to put his hands all over her. Made overt suggestions that they hook up." Kit let loose a deep and heavy sigh.

With her fortysomething years of experience behind her, Suzanne wanted to say, *What did you expect would happen out there? You gals are dancing under red lights in your Victoria's Secret underwear?* But she didn't. This wasn't the time or the place to deliver a lecture.

"So what's the bottom line on this?" Suzanne asked. "Are you saying that this girl might have despaired of Peebler's unwanted attention and taken matters into her own hands? That she *killed* Peebler?" Just verbalizing the notion sounded awfully crazy to her.

"Or maybe her jealous husband did," Toni muttered.

"What particular dancer are we talking about?" asked Suzanne. So far, no names had been mentioned, but she knew there had to be at least a dozen different girls who performed on Hoobly's red-lit stage. All of whom must have acquired a certain patina of toughness by now.

Toni and Kit glanced nervously at each other. Silence hung heavy between them.

"You guys drove all the way over here just to drink wine and clam up?" Suzanne asked, putting a little extra oomph in her voice.

Kit dropped her head forward, her fine blond hair draping across her face. "Okay," she said. "It was Sasha."

"Sasha," said Suzanne, not recognizing the name. "I don't think I know her."

"That's 'cause you don't go to Hoobly's," said Toni.

"That's right," Suzanne agreed. "And neither should either of you . . ." She caught herself. "However, that's a discussion better left for another day. So . . . Kit, tell me exactly why you think Sasha might be involved in Chuck Peebler's murder?"

"Because Sasha wasn't afraid to stand up to Peebler," said Kit. "She was tough and tenacious and even threatened to kill him if he ever laid a hand on her."

"You actually heard her say this?" asked Suzanne.

Kit nodded vehemently. "So did some of the other girls. And Frankie, the owner."

"Huh," said Suzanne thinking. She picked up the bottle of Barolo, poured the last half inch into her wineglass, picked up the glass, and swirled it around, contemplating what Kit had told her.

"What's Sasha's last name?" Suzanne finally asked.

"O'Dell," said Kit.

"Oh crap," said Suzanne. She was pretty sure O'Dell had been one of the names on the deer-hunting licenses that Doogie had tracked down via the DNR.

"What's wrong?" asked Toni, suddenly on the alert.

"Nothing, I hope," replied Suzanne. "But we have to tell Doogie." She made a slight grimace. Better to get it all out in the open. "The thing is, Doogie's already talked to the DNR officials about bow-hunting licenses and O'Dell was one of the names they gave him."

"Holy moley," said Toni, giving a low whistle, "I think you're right."

"I really didn't come here to get Sasha and Mike in trouble," said Kit, a touch of defiance creeping into her voice.

"You know," said Suzanne, "I think it might be a little late for that."

CHAPTER 8

"YOU think Kit's friend is in trouble?" asked Petra, standing at her butcher-block table, chopping onions. "What was her name again? Sasha?"

"Yes, I do," said Suzanne, watching Petra's knife flash back and forth. "Or maybe Sasha's husband is." She'd brought Petra up to speed on the conversation from the night before because she wanted to get her take on the situation.

"I guess you can't go around threatening to kill a guy," said Petra, "even if he is a no-good jerk." She chopped furiously for a few moments, then looked up and blinked. "Do you think anybody else in Kindred knows Peebler was a no-good jerk?"

"Only if they patronized Hoobly's," said Toni, as she bumped open the swinging door and made her way into the kitchen. "If they hung around to shoot a little eight ball or check out the dancers."

"And all the while Peebler put up a carefully cultivated front," said Petra. "Passed himself off as a trusted pillar of the community, managed to get himself on the ballot for mayor. He was even vice president of the Downtown Booster Club, for gosh sakes."

"Now they'll just have to boost without him," said Toni.

Petra dumped a heaping pile of chopped onions into an aluminum bowl already filled with chopped red peppers. Today was Hot Mama Frittata day at the Cackleberry Club and Petra was prepping like crazy. "What irks me is that I would have voted for Peebler! If he hadn't been killed, that is."

"A lot of people would have," said Suzanne.

"Want to know what's really sad?" Toni asked, pouring herself a glass of freshly squeezed orange juice. "Peebler's secret life practically makes our incumbent Mayor Mobley the moral choice for mayor. That and his untimely death."

"Don't kid yourself," said Suzanne. "Mobley's just as bad. Maybe worse." She'd heard constant rumors about Mobley's improprieties regarding zoning committees and planning boards. Grease his chubby little palms with greenbacks and your building or zoning plans, no matter how unfavorable to Kindred, would get rubber-stamped and shoot right through city hall, like grain through a goose.

"Oh no!" Petra screamed. Then lost her focus and dropped her knife on the floor.

"Toes up!" shouted Toni.

"What's wrong?" asked Suzanne. Petra was generally unflappable, but this Peebler thing really had her going.

Twin spots of color bloomed on Petra's cheeks. "I just remembered that I donated twenty dollars to Peebler's mayoral campaign." Now she looked really worried. "Do you think the money ended up as tips at that strip club?"

"Strippers have to make a living, too," reasoned Toni. "Although Kit and the gals prefer to be called exotic dancers."

"Same thing," snorted Petra, as she ferried her bowl to the stove.

Toni moved in closer to Suzanne. "When do you think Doogie's gonna pay Mike O'Dell a visit?"

"I'd be surprised if he hasn't already," said Suzanne. She'd called Doogie first thing this morning and related all the information pretty much the way Kit had presented it. Doogie had listened carefully, thanked her, and promised to follow up.

"You spilled the beans to him, didn't you?" said Toni. "About Sasha."

"You knew I would," said Suzanne. "Besides, Doogie's not a complete idiot. He'd have gotten around to Mike O'Dell sooner or later, and then he'd talk to Sasha and probably even that manager . . ."

"Frankie," supplied Toni.

Pans rattled on the stove. "At least Doogie's not sniffing after Jane anymore," Petra reasoned. "So thank goodness for that. Now we can get on with our busy lives."

"I suppose," said Suzanne. But somehow, she didn't think solving Peebler's murder was going to be that cut-and-dried.

"We're supposed to open in twenty minutes," said Petra, "and I'm not nearly ready for the breakfast rush." As she grabbed for a mixing spoon, the sleeve of her white chef's jacket caught a glass measuring cup filled with dry oatmeal and sent it tumbling to the floor.

"Incoming!" said Suzanne.

"Oh doodlebug!" yelped Petra, doing a quick two-step away from the flying glass. "Now look what I did."

"Don't anybody move," said Toni. She grabbed a broom and dustpan and began sweeping up broken pieces of glass. "Besides, you can't cry over spilled . . ."

"Oatmeal," finished Petra, shaking her head and making a growling sound. "You know what? I feel like all the nervous tension I have about Jane and Peebler is going to shoot straight out my fingertips and end up in my cooking."

Toni stopped sweeping and peered at her. "Um . . . seriously? Because that sounds decidedly paranormal to me."

But Petra wasn't about to be deterred. "Yes, seriously. When my heart and mind are filled with loving thoughts, the food is lovely, too. But anger and fear will only . . ."

"Stick in your throat," said Toni. "Okay, I'm getting your message loud and clear." She paused. "You're not going to start speaking in tongues or anything, are you?"

"Well hardly," said Petra, looking a little annoyed.

"I know what," said Suzanne, grabbing a cream-colored Red Wing crock from where it sat on a top shelf. "Let's take a couple of moments for an affirmation." Whenever the ladies needed to lift their mood or feed their spirits, they reached for the crock instead of the cookie jar. Well, almost every time.

"Yeah, let's," Toni enthused. The crock was filled with inspirational thoughts and quotes they'd jotted down and tossed in. The only exception being the note Toni had taped on the outside, which read, "Open in case of spiritual emergency!"

"You first," said Suzanne, pushing the jar toward Toni.

Toni reached in and pulled out a yellow Post-it note. Unfolding it, she read, "Your talent is God's gift to you. What you do with it is your gift back to God." She smiled. "I'm feeling better already."

"I knew you would," said Suzanne. She pushed the crock toward Petra. "Now you, Petra."

Taking a deep breath, Petra drew out a little scrap of paper, then read it aloud. "I know God won't give me anything I can't handle. I just wish He didn't trust me so much." Her face was lit with a smile now. "Mother Teresa said that."

"Sounds more like you," Toni told Petra.

"Maybe we're kindred spirits," Petra murmured.

"I know you are," said Suzanne, pulling out her own note and unfolding it.

"I hope you drew a doozy," said Toni.

Suzanne read it, then gave an acknowledging nod. "I think I did."

"What's it say, honey?" asked Petra.

Suzanne cleared her throat then read, "Choose a job you love, and you will never have to work a day in your life."

"That's you, Suzie Q!" Toni declared. "CEO, CFO, PR lady extraordinaire, tea connoisseur . . ."

"And chief bottle washer and dog trainer," finished Petra. "Group hug?"

"Group hug," agreed Toni, the three of them huddling together, arms flung across each other's shoulders, heads bowed as they contemplated their affirmations as well as the coming day.

Finally, Suzanne glanced at the clock. "Okay," she announced, "time to roll."

"Don't forget the love!" Toni called after her.

FIVE customers were already lined up outside the Cackleberry Club by the time Suzanne unlocked the door. By the time they were seated, another twenty had arrived.

"Oh my gosh," said Toni, as she raced around the café, "we're getting slammed."

"Slammed equals business," Suzanne told her when she

caught up to her at the pastry case. "Which translates into revenue."

Toni suddenly looked interested. "Maybe I can buy those new baby blue cowboy boots I've had my eye on."

"Hey, you two," Petra called from the pass-through, "stop fooling around and take some orders!"

Suzanne dashed into the kitchen. "I've got orders." She glanced at her order pad. "Two Hot Mama Frittatas, a short stack of cakes, and a Cackleberry scrambler."

"Now you're talking," said Petra, as she grabbed a brown egg from a bowl of eggs and cracked it one-handed.

"You still want to drive the Quilt Trail this afternoon?" Suzanne asked. She was fanning out strawberry slices on top of a wedge of pineapple. Garnishes, in her opinion were meant to be eaten. And if they were healthy, so much the better.

"Absolutely," said Petra. "And I can't wait to get a gander at the oversized squares that my quilting friends created to mark the historic points."

"It's a nifty idea, all right," Suzanne agreed.

"Oh hey," said Petra, dishing out scrambled eggs and sausage. "Toni's orders are up. Will you take them out to her?"

"Gladly," said Suzanne. But when she ran out into the café, handed the orders off to Toni, a new problem suddenly presented itself.

Mayor Mobley stood poised in the front door of the Cackleberry Club, his chest so puffed with pride he looked like a balloon from Macy's Thanksgiving Day Parade. He was dressed in his finest, which, as always, looked discount-store tacky. His bright lime green golf shirt stretched tight across his prominent stomach, his khaki slacks were a muddy pinky beige. Three of his own oversized campaign buttons, featuring a slightly smudged image of his piggy, pudgy face, were pinned to his shirt. Atop his head, a fluorescent golf cap sported a button, too. Still, his outfit did exactly what the mayor had hoped to accomplish. Everyone in the restaurant turned to stare.

Ever the campaigning politico, Mayor Mobley grinned and waved at those folks seated near him. Most nodded and waved back. Allan Sharp, his flunky campaign manager, stood a step behind him.

Suzanne sped over to greet the mayor. "Good morning, Mayor," she said pleasantly. "Can I get you a table?" Since she seemed to be stuck with Mobley for the moment, she was bound and determined that he was going to sit down at a table and eat, not just wander around at will, annoying her customers as he tried to solicit votes.

Allan Sharp answered instead. "Sure, we'll take a table." Sharp was tall and angular, with greasy black hair slicked back from his receding hairline. His movements were jerky and odd and, for all his apparent thinness, his stomach pouched out like he'd just digested an entire rump roast. Sharp wore a gold golf shirt and khaki pants, but took his persona one step further with a heavy gold ID bracelet, gold neck chain, and double rings on his thin, spidery fingers.

Mayor Mobley held up a hand. "Give me a minute. I want to greet my constituents."

"You mean my customers?" Suzanne shot back, as Mobley dove for the nearest table.

"With the election just a week or so away, you can't blame the mayor for shifting into full campaign mode," Sharp explained to her in a dreary monotone.

Suzanne pulled out a chair and instructed Sharp to "sit!" Just as if she was training Baxter.

Sharp complied, but said, "We've only got time for a cup of coffee. Lots of hard-charging on our agenda today." His thin shoulders hunched forward and he managed a dry chuckle. "We're running this pretty much like an old-fashioned whistle-stop campaign."

"That so?" said Suzanne, failing to see any apparent humor in his words.

Sharp's long face turned sober. "Just because his opponent's dead, Ms. Dietz, doesn't mean we can afford to sit back and twiddle our thumbs."

"Strike while the iron is hot, huh?" said Suzanne.

Sharp frowned. "When you put it that way . . ."

Suzanne had never cared for Allan Sharp and now she decided her dislike ran even deeper. Sharp was a snake-in-the-grass lawyer who'd made money in real estate by buying large homes from elderly townsfolk and flipping them to yuppie types who thought they wanted to live in a small town without all the problems of a big city. Then, of course, they moved to Kindred and discovered that, even with its picturesque old Chicago brick buildings and Catawba Creek running through, it still had all the problems of a big city. Burglaries still occurred, cars were vandalized, the infrastructure of bridges and roads continued to crumble as time marched on. Drug dealers and a few unsavory types stalked the tree-lined streets where craftsman cottages and stately American Gothic homes sat side by side, seemingly unaware of the myriad changes taking place.

Suzanne grabbed a tray, placed coffee cups, napkins, and spoons on it, then pulled a fresh pot of French roast off the burner. She carried it all to Sharp's table.

"So kind of you," oozed Sharp, watching her pour out coffee and arrange the cream and sugar.

Suzanne tallied up a check and slapped it down on the table, lest he think the coffee was gratis. "Always happy to oblige a paying customer," she said, flashing a brusque smile. Dodging away, Suzanne skirted around the mayor, who was going great guns now.

"The election's only ten days away!" Mobley sputtered to a couple of farmers, who appeared colossally bored.

Suzanne sidled up to the counter where Toni was garnishing a toasted bagel with sliced strawberries and a pat of cream cheese.

"The mayor's acting like Peebler is still among the living and gaining momentum," said Toni. "Instead of lying in a pine box over at Driesden and Draper Funeral Home."

"We're just not used to a candidate with a professional campaign manager," Suzanne replied in a sardonic tone.

"No kidding," sniggered Toni. "Most candidates just put up a couple of signs, pass out a few flyers, and hope for the best."

"Mobley must have been seriously worried about having Peebler as his opponent," observed Suzanne. "Since he hired Allan Sharp to be his flunky."

Toni lifted her chin and indicated Mobley. "He's not nervous anymore," she said in a cryptic tone.

Suzanne stared across the café at Mobley. He was smiling, swaggering, and gobbling up any and all attention he could garner. *No, he's not worried anymore*, she thought. And a nasty ping echoed in the back recess of her brain. *Not one bit nervous about the competition, because there is no competition.*

As Toni went back to her bagel and Suzanne measured

out spoonfuls of English breakfast tea into a cheery paisley teapot, Mayor Mobley steamrolled his way to the counter.

"Hmhmhm," he coughed, in an effort to attract their attention.

"Mayor?" said Suzanne, turning. "Something we can do for you?"

"Ladies," he said, spreading his legs apart and posturing like Yosemite Sam, "I wanted to extend my sincere sympathy concerning the terrible events here the other night."

Suzanne almost believed him, until she realized that Mobley's voice was booming across the café and he was checking the crowd's reaction via his peripheral vision, making sure they were all aware of his Academy Award–worthy performance.

"Sure thing, Mayor," said Suzanne. She'd had an earful of his false sympathy and was hoping he'd go away.

"Chuck Peebler was a darn good man," Mobley continued. "A worthy opponent."

"*Was* being the operative word," murmured Suzanne. "Wouldn't you say so?"

Mobley's eyes suddenly flashed with rage, then narrowed into piggy little slits. "You implying something, Suzanne?" His words were an angry hiss.

"If the shoe fits," said Toni, adding her own two cents' worth.

Expelling a raspy sound, Mobley spun on his penny loafers and headed back to the table where Allan Sharp waited patiently. Mobley sat down, sipped at his coffee, and a whispered conversation ensued. Then they both rose from their chairs and headed for the door.

"Will you look at that?" exclaimed Toni, sticking her pencil behind her ear and clamping her hands on her hips in defiance. "They left the check sitting on the table. They're skipping out on the tab!"

"Let it go, Toni," urged Suzanne. "It's not worth a confrontation."

Toni, not always one to listen to reason, took a step out from behind the counter and called after them. "Hey, Mobley!"

Mobley stopped, turned, and glanced back at her. If looks could kill, Toni would be laid out stone-cold on the floor.

"Too bad the Rogaine's not working!" Toni shouted at him.

That brought an onslaught of loud laughter and guffaws from the two dozen or so customers.

Mayor Mobley turned bright red and glowered at Toni, even as Sharp grabbed his elbow and tried to usher him along.

Toni flapped a hand and let loose her best Three Stooges impression. "Nyuk, nyuk, nyuk."

CHAPTER 9

AFTER erasing the breakfast menu, Suzanne doodled a border of hearts and flowers around the edge of the blackboard, then set about listing the luncheon menu. Petra had seemingly outdone herself today with her featured deep-dish chicken pot pie. Made with chicken, fresh carrots and peas, and her own creamy gravy, the dish was baked in its own ramekin and arrived golden and bubbly at your table.

The sandwich today was rosemary grilled chicken. Home-baked rosemary-infused focaccia bread was slathered with mayonnaise, Dijon mustard, and chopped fresh rosemary. Then a skinless chicken breast, sautéed in garlic, pepper, and olive oil, was snugged between the two thick slabs of bread.

Vegetarian autumn stew rounded out their trio of entrees. A savory dish that combined diced sweet onions, butternut squash, sweet potatoes, carrots, celery, lentils, tomatoes, and set off with a tangy splash of apple cider vinegar.

Suzanne was getting hungry just printing out the specials, let alone inhaling the smells that wafted from Petra's kitchen.

And just as she was scribbling at the bottom of the board, rounding out the menu with raspberry chocolate tart and honey walnut cake, Sheriff Doogie came strutting into the restaurant. He nodded as he brushed past her, heading straight for the counter. His wide bottom eased onto the end stool; his elbows hit the counter.

"Coffee?" Suzanne asked him, sliding behind the counter. He was just the man she wanted to see.

"Much as you can fit in one cup," Doogie told her in a weary tone. Then he reached for the sugar bowl, dropped in one lump followed by numero two and three.

Picking up on Doogie's need for a sugar fix, Suzanne grabbed one of the apple turnovers from the pastry case, slid it onto a plate, and held it in front of Doogie. "Apple turnover?" she asked.

"You bet," said Doogie, gazing at it hungrily.

Suzanne set it in front of him, like she was awarding first prize for a correct answer.

Doogie managed a quick bite, then asked, "Is everybody still talking about it?"

Suzanne knew the *it* Doogie was referring to wasn't the special of the day.

"I'm pretty sure the entire town is still gossiping about Peebler's murder," she told him. "And will be until the killer is apprehended." Of course they'd jaw and speculate. People were on edge. Weird, freaky assaults by crossbows didn't happen every day.

"Until *I* apprehend him, you mean."

"You're the duly elected sheriff," Suzanne told him, but not unkindly.

Doogie took a slurp of coffee. "Lucky me."

"Excuse me," said Suzanne, looking askance, "but aren't you a candidate in this upcoming election, too? Didn't you toss your modified Smokey Bear hat into the ring some months back?"

"That I did," murmured Doogie. "Though things could change, you never know."

"Don't talk like that," she warned him. "You're a good sheriff; people here trust you."

He cocked a rheumy eye at her. "Do they?"

"Yes," she said. "Of course, they do." *At least I think they do. But you don't need me planting any seeds of doubt. You've managed to accomplish that all by yourself.*

"Not all killers get caught, Suzanne," said Doogie, looking both detached and philosophical as he said it. As though he'd taken a step back from the case.

"Not in this instance," said Suzanne. "Not when *you're* on the case."

Doogie managed a half smile as he took another bite of turnover.

Leaning forward, Suzanne asked in a low voice, "So did you talk to Mike O'Dell?"

"I did," said Doogie, chewing. "As well as his amusing spouse, Sasha."

"And?"

"O'Dell's a taciturn guy. Then again, you might be in a perpetually cranky mood if your wife was a stripper and brought home more money than you did."

"Gives new meaning to the phrase, 'bringing home the bacon,'" said Suzanne.

Doogie shrugged. "I guess strippers earn big bucks."

"I think Sasha's more of an exotic dancer," said Suzanne.

Doogie raised an eyebrow, looking askance. "There's a difference?"

"A slight technicality," said Suzanne, wondering why she was even offering an explanation. "I don't think the women at Hoobly's actually remove their clothing."

"So a lingerie show," said Doogie. He sounded just this side of interested.

But Suzanne wasn't buying it. "Don't tell me you've never been out there!" She snorted.

"Only on official business," said Doogie.

"Which just proves that Hoobly's *is* a shady place. All kinds of things probably go on out there."

"It's not exactly the Knitting Nest." Doogie sighed.

"Getting back to Peebler's murder," said Suzanne. "I'm assuming you're ready to cross Jane Buckley off your list?"

Doogie pursed his lips and shook his head. "Nobody's completely in the clear yet."

"Surely Jane told you about the argument she had with Peebler," said Suzanne, frustration evident in her voice. "A fairly nonsensical accusation on Peebler's part about stealing antiques from his aunt's house?"

Doogie chewed slowly and stared at her.

Suzanne continued. "Peebler accused Jane of trying to convince his aunt to donate a few items to the Darlington College art museum."

"So she says."

"Jane wouldn't lie," said Suzanne. "She's not like that. Peebler's rant was just that—a rant. He didn't even know what items were missing."

"And now Peebler's gone, so we can't ask him," said Doogie.

Suzanne stared at him. "Dead men tell no tales?"

Doogie's brow furrowed. "They do, it's just a little tougher to pry it out of them."

* * *

LUNCH at the Cackleberry Club was a roaring success. Suzanne and Toni worked the café like a professional tag team, understanding each other's needs before they were even articulated. Coffee was poured, plates delivered then whisked away, checks magically appeared. Petra, meanwhile, was basically on lockdown in the kitchen, preparing order after order and shoving them out the pass-through with breathtaking speed.

When everyone had a sandwich, soup, or dessert in front of them, Suzanne took a well-deserved breather. But Toni spotted a potential problem. Or maybe a business opportunity, depending on the way you looked at it.

"We've got a ton of people wandering around in the Book Nook," she told Suzanne.

"Then that's where I'm headed," said Suzanne, pulling her long, black Parisian waiter's apron over her head and stashing it behind the counter.

"Call me if you need help," said Toni.

"Call me if *you* need help," replied Suzanne.

Secretly, of course, Suzanne was always thrilled to spend time in the Book Nook. Reading was her passion, and she loved nothing more than unpacking a new box of books, fingering their uncracked spines, and arranging them on the narrow wooden shelves. There was something satisfying about the fact that so many lovely thoughts and spellbinding plots were contained between those covers. How, she wondered, could anyone ever abandon a lovely, highly tactile paper book for a mechanical e-book?

At one-fifteen, Petra emerged from the kitchen carrying a steaming cup of tea. She gazed about the café with satisfaction, then delivered the tea to Suzanne.

"Thought you could use this," said Petra.

"Bless you," said Suzanne, taking a quick sip.

"To me taking a break means escaping into the far-off flavors of tea from around the world," said Petra. "Thailand, India, Ceylon, or good old China."

"Where are we flying off to today?" asked Suzanne, playing along.

"Nepal," said Petra. "By way of organic Kenchajanga green tea."

"Perfect," murmured Suzanne.

But perfection is often short-lived. Because just as Suzanne was taking a second dreamy sip, Junior Garrett stumped his way into the Cackleberry Club.

With his chin stuck out, his stride clipped and determined, Junior looked like a bandy rooster who'd just invaded the henhouse. His dark hair was swooshed into a pompadour that would have made James Dean proud, and he'd slathered on enough grease to start a forest fire. Junior's tight, straight-legged jeans and black bowling shirt with the name "Junior" stitched in white thread polished off his look.

If it had been the mid-1950s instead of 2011, Junior Garrett would have been considered a cool cat. Now he was just considered a quirky anachronism by most, a juvenile delinquent by Suzanne.

"Too bad the community theater's not having a casting call for *West Side Story*," Petra remarked. "Junior would be a shoe-in for one of the Sharks."

"You gals talking about me again?" asked Junior. A sardonic grin was plastered across his face; a toothpick was clamped firmly between his teeth.

"Just small talk," replied Suzanne.

"Aww," said Junior, clearly hurt.

"What are *you* doing here?" Toni asked, as she came hurtling out of the kitchen. "You know I told you never to drop by without calling first!"

Theirs was a marriage in crisis. An abrupt union that had been fueled by overactive hormones, too much Jack Daniel's, and a lack of functioning brain cells. Although Toni had tried valiantly to make the marriage work, it was apparent the relationship had cooled even before their plane touched down on its return trip from their Las Vegas nuptials.

A few months later, the cake was iced when Toni discovered a piece of purple net lingerie in the backseat of Junior's car. Confident it wasn't hers—since she wore red and a size smaller—she promptly tossed Junior, his toolbox, and various rebuilt motors, out of their apartment. Now they lived apart, in a kind of netherworld of bickering and making up. Not completely in love, but not quite ready to file for divorce, either.

"Did you get fired?" Toni demanded of Junior. Grabbing the back of his collar she steered him to a table and forced him into a wooden chair.

Junior gazed up at her with round, innocent eyes. "No! Cross my heart! I'm still workin' diligently at Shelby's Body Shop."

Suzanne and Petra shuffled in to watch the show. If you were in the right frame of mind, Junior could be pretty darned amusing. Fodder, almost, for a TV sitcom. Think Fonzie meets Homer Simpson.

"You sure you're still working?" Toni asked, bunching her right hand into a fist. "Because I'll clock you if . . ."

"Whoa, whoa!" said Junior, putting up an arm in mock defense. "Whatever happened to innocent until proven guilty? Seriously, babe, I just dropped by to get a bite."

Toni glanced up at Suzanne. "What do you think?"

Suzanne gave a shrug. "If the man's hungry, I say go ahead and feed him."

"Just do it quick," said Petra, making her escape. Then she called back over her shoulder, "Thank goodness we're not real busy."

Toni brought Junior a leftover chicken sandwich and a bowl of vegetable soup. "Watch out," she warned him, "that soup is so hot it could boil your eyeballs."

Junior nodded. "Okay."

"And you're going to have to pay for this," Toni nattered. "We've catered to enough freeloaders for one day."

"Jeez," said Junior, "will you chill out? I got money. I can pay."

"Still raking it in at Shelby's, huh?" said Suzanne. Honestly, how much could a guy make repairing fenders and ironing out dents? On the other hand, maybe quite a lot.

"I got something going on the side, too," Junior told Suzanne. He gave a cocky, knowing look as he took a big bite of sandwich.

Toni looked unhappy. "What are you talking about?" To the best of everyone's knowledge, none of Junior's hare-brained, get-rich-quick schemes had ever panned out. Not the Cuban tax haven, plastic antenna balls, or bait business.

"I'm going into the scrap metal business," Junior boasted.

"Excuse me?" said Toni.

"There's money in that?" Suzanne asked.

"Oh yeah," said Junior, suddenly looking more confident. "Me and Marsh Freedman are gonna be partners."

"Isn't Freedman the guy who used to wander through town with a plastic sack, picking up pop cans?" Suzanne asked, trying to stifle a grin.

"Ancient history," said Junior, waving a hand. "Now we're partners, fifty-fifty."

"And what does this partnership entail?" asked Suzanne. She was a tiny bit fascinated by Junior. It was probably the same fascination a mongoose felt for a cobra. A bit of danger, but still that hypnotic lure.

"We're going to scour the countryside in our truck," Junior told her, delighted to have an audience. "Picking up discarded car parts, old farm equipment, appliances, milk cans, bedsprings, tire rims, pretty much anything we can get our hands on. Then we'll sell it at the scrap yard over in Jessup."

"No kidding," said Suzanne. The whole idea sounded sort of old-timey, like something from the forties, when people supposedly donated tin cans and scrap metal to the war effort.

"Of course, the really primo stuff is copper," Junior said, knowingly. "You can pull in three bucks a pound for scrap copper, did you know that?

"Where exactly are you going to find this scrap copper?" Suzanne asked.

Junior looked suddenly evasive. "Around."

"Hmm," said Toni, in a suspicious tone.

Petra leaned out of the kitchen, rubbing flour from her hands onto her red calico apron. "Suzanne? I just remembered, we still need to order pumpkins for Saturday night. With all we've got going this week, we could easily overlook it." Saturday night, Halloween night, they'd planned a huge outdoor Halloween party at the Cackleberry Club. Complete with decorations, costume contest, live music, bobbing for apples, fire pit for roasting hot dogs, cider and doughnuts, and a major theatrical surprise.

"Hey!" exclaimed Junior, "I know a guy who's got a bumper crop of pumpkins."

"No, thanks, Junior," said Suzanne, "I'm going to . . ."

But Junior persisted. "No, seriously. This guy owes me a *huge* favor, so I can get you guys a whole truckload of pumpkins for free."

"How's that?" asked Suzanne. Maybe Junior really could help.

"This guy had a car accident but didn't want to tell his wife," Junior explained. "It was her car, a Toyota Celica, and he was just this side of tipsy when he had a close encounter with a bridge abutment."

"Why am I not surprised?" said Toni, rolling her eyes.

"Anyway," continued Junior, "I ironed out the dent and touched up the paint. Made it look good as new, all on the QT. And now he owes me big-time."

"Really," said Suzanne. What with a Quilt Trail Tea, Mystery Tea, book signing, and Halloween party going on this week, maybe Junior really could lend a helping hand.

Junior hooked a thumb and touched his chest, trying to look important. "You need pumpkins? I'm the guy who can hook you up."

"We're talking pumpkins," said Suzanne. "Vegetables. Members of the squash family. You're acting like we're dealing in human body parts."

Junior was undeterred. "Still," said Junior, "I'm your connection."

An hour later, Suzanne and Petra sped through downtown Kindred, heading for the Westvale Medical Clinic. They'd taken off an hour early, determined to drive as much of the

Quilt Trail as possible. Toni had agreed to hold down the fort until closing, then drive Baxter to Suzanne's house and feed him his cup of kibble. Doggy day care at its finest.

"What's in your care package?" Petra asked, as Suzanne pulled into the clinic's parking lot.

"Soup and scones for Sam, scones and sticky rolls for everyone else."

"Good for you," said Petra. "I hate to see anything go to waste."

"Believe me, it won't," said Suzanne, climbing out of the car. "You gonna wait here?"

Petra pulled her nubby sweater around her and nodded. "I think so."

Suzanne dashed into the clinic, exchanged hugs with Esther, the clinic manager, then handed over all her loot.

"Wow!" exclaimed Esther, peering in the larger bag. "Thanks loads. And it's all low cal, right?"

"And low carb," said Suzanne. "Especially the sticky rolls."

You want me to give Sam a buzz?" Esther asked. She was cheery and upbeat, dressed in pale blue scrubs. "I can see if he's free."

"No," said Suzanne, "Petra and I are driving the Quilt Trail today. Gotta run."

"Oh fun," chirped Esther. "I'm hoping to do it this weekend."

"You're still coming to our Halloween party on Saturday night, aren't you?" asked Suzanne.

"Wouldn't miss it," Esther called, as Suzanne skipped out the door.

"That was quick," said Petra, as Suzanne climbed in and turned the key in the ignition.

"We've got a . . . what?" said Suzanne. "Thirty-five-mile drive ahead of us?"

"Something like that," said Petra, studying the map. "Maybe more. First the log cabin, then the round barn, then . . ."

"Seat belt," Suzanne reminded her, as she backed out, noting Sam's BMW parked three stalls down. She smiled, glanced in the mirror, and happened to catch a quick reflection of Lester Drummond, the prison warden, emerging from the Hard Body Gym next door. He was a big man with shaved head, craggy face, and a forehead full of worry lines. Suzanne always thought Drummond had the kind of hard face and hard muscles that came from serving hard time. Except, of course, Drummond *ran* the prison.

Drummond had just tossed his Nike gym bag into his black SUV, as Suzanne swung around in a turn. He nodded at both of them and gave a perfunctory wave.

Smiling and waggling her fingers back at him, Petra murmured, "Drummond creeps me out."

As Suzanne sped away, she happened to glance in her rearview mirror. "I see what you mean."

"Hmm?" said Petra.

"Because he's still watching us."

CHAPTER 10

"I really adore the idea of the oversized quilt squares," said Petra. "They're just so perfect."

"A new kind of X marks the spot," agreed Suzanne.

Twenty-eight hand-painted blocks, six by six feet in size and mimicking a quilt square pattern, now dotted the landscape of Logan County. Each marking a designated historical site on the Quilt Trail map.

"The first one's easy to find," said Suzanne, as she goosed her Taurus across a narrow bridge that rattled beneath her tires. "I've been by it a hundred times."

"But have you been *in* it?" asked Petra.

"No," said Suzanne.

Number one on the Quilt Trail was an old log cabin built by Christian Schmitt, one of the first settlers in the area. Over one hundred years since its inception, the cabin fit so naturally into its woodsy surroundings it appeared to have grown directly out of the pine and hardwood forest.

"Look at this," Petra exclaimed, as they ducked through the doorway and surveyed the tidy little cabin. "Can you imagine living here?"

The log cabin, constructed of hand-hewn logs and shake shingles, was small and cheery, with a fire hissing and crackling in its small stone fireplace.

"Welcome," said the guide. She was dressed in long denim prairie skirt, blouse, and bonnet. "Make yourself at home."

"Tiny," murmured Suzanne. The home was only ten logs high and the ceiling seemed to press down on her.

"Oh, but there's a sleeping loft," the guide told her. "Climb up there if you want."

"I'm sure it's very cozy," said Suzanne.

The second quilt square marked a round, red barn that had been constructed in 1912. Old-timers believed that a round barn was more efficient for housing cattle, though it was also rumored that many round barns were built out of superstition. Apparently, an old wives' tale claimed that the circular shape provided no corners for evil spirits to lurk!

"Logan County is just rich in history, isn't it?" Petra exclaimed, as they pulled away from the third site, the slightly down-at-its-heels Pine Grove Spiritualist Church.

"The history is amazing," Suzanne agreed. "But I'd take this drive just for the scenery." The black asphalt road they were speeding down was winding and narrow. Red and gold trees lined both sides as they traversed wooden bridges and wound their way deep into gullies.

A barrage of red and gold leaves streamed down and fluttered against Suzanne's windshield. When she flipped on her wipers, they flew away.

"It's raining leaves!" Suzanne exclaimed.

"The weatherman's predicting three inches," Petra joked back.

The wind continued to swirl and whistle and more foliage fell on the car in a colorful kaleidoscope of red, orange, yellow, and rust.

Rolling down the passenger side window, Petra stuck

out her head and let the wind restyle her mop of salt-and-pepper hair.

"Enough." Suzanne laughed, as a couple of red leaves sailed in. "We're getting blown to bits!"

"But isn't it fun?" said Petra.

Twenty minutes later, Petra had checked off eight sites on her Quilt Trail map and the sun was sinking rapidly, barely an orange glow on the horizon.

Still they kept going. The ribbon of road was hypnotic and the dark trees and fields of dry cornstalks seemed to hold wonderful secrets.

"Hungry yet?" Suzanne asked.

"Starving," Petra admitted.

"What's the next place?"

"Cappy's General Store," Petra announced, with some delight in her voice. "So . . . perfect timing."

Cappy's was a family-run grocery and deli that could have been a stage set out of a 1930s movie. Much of the inventory was still rooted in the past and included canning supplies, penny candy, beeswax candles, and barrels of pickles. Of course, Cappy's also stocked today's basic essentials: milk, bread, eggs, coffee, deli foods, chips, beer, and lottery tickets.

Suzanne and Petra headed directly for the deli, which was basically an old-fashioned meat-and-cheese counter with three small marble tables hunkered nearby. Massive country hams hung from the ceiling, while blocks of cheddar cheese, rings of bologna, and home-smoked meats were stacked high in the cooler. Black-and-white tiles covered the floor in a checkerboard pattern, and ceiling fans (the *original* fans) circled lazily above them.

"Love this old-time feel," remarked Petra.

"Love their food," sang Suzanne, as they pulled out high-backed kitchen chairs and sat down at one of the tables.

Petra squinted at the soup-splotched menu. "What are you going to have?"

"I'm thinking soup and sandwich," said Suzanne. She and Walter had stopped here two years ago, on one of their antique scavenging trips, and she could still taste the thick-sliced, brown sugar–cured ham on crusty rye bread topped with homemade Thousand Island dressing. Very tasty. So maybe time for a redux of that fine sandwich?

"I think I'm a Cappy's Classic Club kind of gal," said Petra.

"And soup," said Suzanne. "See?" She touched a fingertip to the parchment paper menu. "They've got roasted butternut squash soup."

"Think it's as good as mine?" Petra asked with a playful grin.

"No," said Suzanne, "but just on the off chance it's tasty, I'm going to give it a try."

"Nicely put," said Petra. "And oh so politically correct."

Which suddenly reminded Suzanne of politics and Mayor Mobley.

"How much do you trust Mayor Mobley?" Suzanne asked.

"About as far as I could pick him up and throw him," said Petra. "Which for me is nada." Then she squinted at Suzanne. "Why? What are you getting at?"

"Just that Peebler's death pretty much paved the way for Mobley to stay in office," said Suzanne. "It was just so . . . convenient."

"Too convenient?"

"I don't know," said Suzanne. "That's really the sixty-four-thousand-dollar question, isn't it?"

They pushed that upsetting notion away for the time being while they ordered, took a quick wander through the store, and were finally served their sandwiches.

"Look," said Petra. "Creamy cole slaw in little paper containers. I love that." She paused. "Why do I love that?"

"Not sure," said Suzanne. "But I think there's something reassuring about it. Maybe some deep-seated memory from childhood? Of going to an old-fashioned drive-in?"

"Versus a drive-through," said Petra. "Yes, I think you may be right."

Twenty minutes later they were stuffed, satiated, and ready to get back on the trail.

"If we take County Road 9 back," said Petra, studying her map, "I think we can still see the Atherton School House and the Cole house."

"Let me see that," said Suzanne, reaching for the map. She scanned it, said, "Oh."

"Too far out of the way?" asked Petra.

"Up in the Highland Hills area," said Suzanne. She glanced at her watch, said, "I'm not sure those two sites will even be open."

"Maybe not," said Petra, "but I'd still get to see the quilt squares that Toby Baines painted."

"Okay," Suzanne agreed, "then let's get going."

They paid their check, grabbed a loaf of pumpkin bread in the bargain, and climbed into the car.

"And away we go again," said Petra.

"You really had a great idea," said Suzanne, complimenting her on the whole concept of the Quilt Trail.

"Scoping out historic spots, then highlighting them with the oversized quilt squares. Very inventive."

"Well, thank you," said Petra. "It was a labor of love. Of course, I had lots of help from quilters and all the volunteers at the historical society."

Putting her car in gear, Suzanne backed up slowly. And then, because she was boxed in and rain had started to patter down, Suzanne rolled her driver's side window down so she could stick out her head for a better view.

And that's when a noisy, beat-up clunker of a pickup truck suddenly tore in front of her.

"Whoa!" Suzanne exclaimed, braking hard as she was suddenly enveloped in a headache-inducing cloud of exhaust fumes.

"How rude!" cried Petra. The clunker shuddered to a stop, then a man in olive drab slacks and a camo jacket jumped out. He slammed the truck's door, then paused to stare at them through the streaming windshield. As his eyes bored into Suzanne, he bared his teeth and flashed her a look of pure, unadulterated hatred.

"Oh rats," muttered Suzanne.

Petra's head whipped toward Suzanne. "You know who that is?"

Suzanne's fingers drummed nervously against the steering wheel. "I'm pretty sure that's Mike O'Dell."

"The guy with the deer-hunting license?" asked Petra. "The stripper's husband!"

"Yeah, I'm pretty sure it's him."

"He looks positively unhinged," said Petra, watching as O'Dell ducked into Cappy's. "And furious."

Suzanne gunned her engine and shot out of the parking lot, fishtailing onto the narrow blacktop road. "If looks could kill," she murmured.

To soothe their nerves, Suzanne slid in a CD and pushed Play. The relaxing strains of Mozart's Piano Sonata no. 11 immediately filled the car.

"This is nice," said Petra.

"It's actually a CD of afternoon tea music," said Suzanne. "All different classical artists, but conducive to tea and very soothing."

"Soothing is good," Petra acknowledged.

As Suzanne felt the music flow around her, her breathing quieted and she relaxed her grip on the steering wheel. Humming down the dark road, she took stock of the area. They were out in the most distant part of Logan County now, an area rife with steep hills, dark valleys, and rushing creeks.

This was a favorite spot for hikers and all manner of outdoorsman. There were woodsy ridges and rocky gullies where a hunter could hide. Gurgling streams teeming with brown trout and rainbow trout. And even a few paths where hardy hikers or mountain bikers could test their skills over rocks and rills. It was beautiful, it was indeed God's country, and it was very remote.

Petra turned on a small overhead light to study her map. "I'm pretty sure the schoolhouse is out this way." She nodded to herself. "Yup, this has to be the right road." She folded up the map. "We're on course."

"Hope so," said Suzanne. The strange encounter with Mike O'Dell had left her nerves feeling raw and jangled.

"I'm just dying to see one last quilt square," Petra chattered. "It's the wedding-ring pattern that Toby Baines designed."

"Toby still writes the advice column at the *Bugle*?" Suzanne asked.

"She does, but she's trying to get out of it." Petra chuckled. "Are you interested?"

Suzanne shook her head. "Not on your life; I have enough trouble writing my once-a-month tea column."

Petra popped her head up like a gopher, peering ahead as the road unfolded. "You see anything yet?"

"Not a thing," said Suzanne. "Maybe we took a wrong turn? It's awfully dark."

"The rain stopped," Petra said with a hopeful lilt in her voice. "Maybe we could give it a couple more miles?"

"Okay," said Suzanne, but she'd already decided to backtrack if something didn't turn up soon. It was getting awfully late.

Suzanne kept an eye on her odometer as she drove. One mile. One and a half. Two miles. Still nothing. Decision time looming. "I think we took a wrong turn."

"Ohhh," said Petra, sounding disappointed.

"Just too dark, I guess," said Suzanne, easing off the accelerator and edging toward the shoulder so she could negotiate a U-turn on the narrow road.

That's when her headlights picked up the outline of a car, dead ahead of them. "Who's that?" Suzanne murmured. The car was pulled way off to the side of the road, tilting crazily.

"Someone had car trouble?" speculated Petra. "Ran out of gas?"

"Holy smokes!" said Suzanne, as she bumped forward and her headlights finally revealed the true outline and markings on the vehicle. Because there was no mistaking the whip antenna, reinforced bumpers, light bar on top, and official emblem on the door.

"That's one of Doogie's cruisers," Petra exclaimed.

Suzanne tapped her brakes and eased over onto the shoulder directly behind the cruiser. "It sure is. And it looks unoccupied." She wondered what Doogie or one of his deputies could be doing way out here. Maybe an emergency call? Or call of nature.

Putting her car in park, Suzanne said, "Sit tight, I'm gonna take a quick look." She hopped from her car, engine still running.

A low vibe had started to prickle up and down Suzanne's spine. A car parked in the middle of nowhere? Seemingly unoccupied? The woods on both sides of the road felt dark, dense, and slightly ominous. If—and this was a wild thought that suddenly cascaded through Suzanne's brain—if an archer was waiting with a bow and arrow cocked, she'd never see him. Doogie wouldn't have seen him, either.

Stepping silently over to the cruiser, Suzanne peered cautiously inside. And saw . . . nothing. No body slumped in the driver's seat or crumpled in a heap on the floor.

Doggone it, she thought. *If I had any common sense, I'd hightail it out of here.* But Suzanne stood firm, her curiosity burning like a signal flare.

Cupping her hands to her mouth, Suzanne called out, "Doogie! Are you out there?" She hesitated. "Is anybody out there?"

There was no answer, save the low hiss and rattle of wind through the forest.

Suzanne backtracked a few steps toward her car, her nerves jacked up high.

Petra rolled down her window, looking worried. "What do you think happened?" she called out. "Would Doogie or one of his deputies just leave their cruiser like that?"

Suzanne shook her head, puzzled. "I don't know. Maybe, if they had car trouble. But I'm going to take a quick look around, just in case."

"You want me to come with you?" Petra asked. But her quavering tone implied she'd much rather stay in the warmth and safety of the car.

"No, that's okay," Suzanne called, already heading toward a sort of opening in the woods. "I'm just going to take a quick peek."

"Be careful," Petra called.

Careful is my middle name, Suzanne thought, all the while knowing she was dead wrong. *Just my way of whistling in the dark, that's all.*

Putting her hands in front of her, Suzanne parted a stand of tall reeds. And stepped into darkness.

The woods were dark and dreary now, and the words *Sleepy Hollow* pinged in Suzanne's brain. The sunset's encouraging glow had long since vanished and blackness loomed in front of her in the form of twisted oaks and scruffy buckthorn. The mournful hoot of an owl echoed off dead and wind-stripped trees, and off in the distance she heard a high-pitched yip. Probably a coyote, she decided. Lots of those little pests thronging the woods these days.

Turning up the collar of her jacket to keep the chill wind at bay, Suzanne called out, "Doogie?" Then, because the only other deputy whose name she could remember was Wilbur Halpern, she cupped her hands and called out, "Wilbur?"

No response.

She tried again. "Deputy Halpern?"

As Suzanne ventured a few more steps into the woods, her eyes slowly became accustomed to the dark. Now she could see what might be a faint trail—a deer trail?—and a couple of places where cattail stalks looked freshly broken. As though someone or something had blundered hastily through the woods.

So maybe . . . a person?

She pushed her way into the tangle of woods, mindful of wind rustling dead leaves and making them sound suspiciously like stealthy footfalls. Her nose caught the putrid, rotten egg scent of brackish swamp water nearby.

Two more steps brought her to the edge of a small pond and more broken cattails.

"Doogie?" she called again.

Pushing her way into a small clearing, Suzanne felt a sharp prickle, then bent forward to pick a cluster of brown burrs off her slacks. Her heart pounded a timpani drum solo of nervousness in her chest and she felt dampness seep into her loafers. *Probably shouldn't be . . .*

Overhead, the gray veil of clouds suddenly parted and a not-quite-full moon shone down its faint waterfall of silvery light.

And that's when she saw Deputy Wilbur Halpern.

He was kneeling in a sort of clearing, head bowed, as if in prayer. His arms were pulled around a skinny poplar tree, a pair of standard issue handcuffs locked tight about his wrists. The young man's eyes were open wide, his pupils fixed and dilated, mouth drawn back in a feral rictus of pain.

And he was dead. Shot execution style in the back of the head.

CHAPTER 11

STANDING transfixed, Suzanne stared at the dark slickness at the back of Deputy Halpern's head, the deep, purple grooves where handcuffs had dug into his wrists. Probably, she decided, Wilbur had struggled terribly. The poor guy hadn't gone down without a fight.

She felt curiously solemn, like she should say a prayer or something. Until she heard a faint rustle nearby, maybe the wind, maybe not, and decided the smart thing, the sane thing, was to get the heck out of there!

Sprinting to her car in record time, Suzanne clambered in and punched the locks.

"What's wrong?" asked Petra.

Suzanne struggled to catch her breath. "Call Doogie," she said, frantically. "Hurry up and call Doogie!"

Realizing something bad had just gone down, Petra yanked her phone from her quilted tote bag and hit 911. Then she quickly passed the phone to Suzanne.

Suzanne gave a hasty, abbreviated, shrill explanation to the dispatcher, fearing it might even be the same one from the other night, then listened for a few moments. "Yes, this time I'll stay on the line." She handed the phone back to Petra, looking nervous as well as distracted. "We're supposed to keep an open line."

Petra, who'd listened, wide-eyed and shaking, to Suzanne's blow-by-blow report, put a hand to her mouth and moaned, "Oh no. That poor boy."

Suzanne, meanwhile, put her gearshift into reverse and jammed her foot firmly on the brake. "If we see or hear anything out of the ordinary," Suzanne instructed Petra, "be prepared to fly backward. I'll goose this buggy up to a hundred miles an hour if I have to."

PETRA was the first to spot the flashing light bars. "He's here. Doogie," she said, as multiple red-and-blue pulsing lights careened toward them. One car swerved to a halt, followed by two more.

Doogie emerged from his vehicle, ashen-faced and stiff-legged. And for the first time in decades, Suzanne saw him out of uniform. In his baggy gray sweatpants and coordinating hoodie sweatshirt, Doogie could have easily passed for a sloppy, aging jogger. Except for the fact that he held a gun.

"Where is he?" Doogie asked in a terse, tension-filled voice, as his remaining three deputies crowded around him. He looked more anxious and upset than Suzanne had ever seen him.

"Over here," said Suzanne. "Follow me."

She led them back to the path, then they all crashed through buckthorn and scrub willow, branches swatting their faces and tearing at their clothes. Thirty seconds later Suzanne, Doogie, and deputies arrived at the clearing.

"There," said Suzanne, pointing.

Four flashlights were suddenly focused directly on Deputy Halpern, bleaching his face white and revealing the terrible circumstances of his death.

Doogie stood for a few moments, taking in the scene. Then he stepped softly over to Deputy Halpern and put a hand on the boy's shoulder, in an almost fatherly gesture.

"Dang. Wilbur," Doogie murmured, softly. He sounded beyond sad, he sounded almost defeated.

For the first time in her life, Suzanne watched Doogie wipe away tears. Then he stepped back and bowed his head. "What am I gonna tell that poor boy's mama?"

Nobody answered, because nobody had the answer.

Doogie pulled it together then, his lawman's instincts overriding his emotions. "Check the woods," he barked to the other deputies. "But go easy, this is all one big crime scene." The men scurried away, weapons drawn, flashlights probing, as Doogie clicked on his cell phone and called the state crime lab. Muttering softly for a few minutes, he concluded with, "He's one of ours."

"What can I do?" Suzanne asked in the silence that spun out.

Doogie opened his mouth, hesitated, then said, "Let's hike back to the road."

They tromped back and met up with Petra.

"I'm so sorry," Petra told Doogie. "Wilbur's mom is one of our volunteers at church. She'll be . . . she'll be devastated."

Doogie nodded.

"You have questions?" Suzanne asked. Doogie looked so forlorn and out of it, she felt she ought to prod him a bit.

"What the heck are you two doing out here?" he finally asked. "Driving through these woods at night?"

"The Quilt Trail," said Petra.

Doogie shook his head. "Kind of late to be taking in historic sites, don't you think?"

"We were lost," said Petra.

"We were trying to find the old schoolhouse and got turned around," Suzanne added.

"Lost?" said Doogie. "The old schoolhouse is right up this road, about a quarter of a mile." He gave a half wave, as if it didn't matter anymore.

"Oh," was all Suzanne said.

"So let me get this straight," said Doogie, rubbing the back of his hand against his stubbly cheek. "You were out here driving the Quilt Trail."

"Correct," said Petra.

"Okay," said Doogie, "but what the heck was Wilbur doing out here in the boonies?"

"No idea," said Suzanne. "We pulled over when we saw his empty car. Maybe he'd been . . . responding to a call?"

"Might have," said Doogie. He shook his head again in disbelief. "The thing is, Wilbur was a real friendly type. Talking with everyone, always making with the PR. He even gave out his private cell phone number. In case, you know, like the law enforcement center line was busy."

"Busy?" said Suzanne.

Doogie shrugged. "Cutbacks. Only got three lines now and one's to the jail."

"Wait a minute," said Suzanne, "so you're saying that if Wilbur got a call, it wouldn't necessarily have been routed through the switchboard at the law enforcement center?"

"That's right," said Doogie.

"So no way to trace it," said Petra.

"Oh, we can trace Wilbur's cell phone," said Doogie. "It just might take a couple of days."

The three deputies came shuffling back, looking angry and a little defeated.

"Anything?" asked Doogie. They all shook their heads.

"Dang," said Doogie.

"Double dang," echoed one of the deputies.

They all stood around and looked at each other then, shuffling feet, feeling bad, trying to keep warm.

"We should be getting back," Petra said, tugging gently at Suzanne's sleeve.

"Sheriff," said Suzanne, "do you think one of your deputies could give Petra a ride back to town? I've got something I . . ."

"I have to head back, ma'am," said one of the deputies, a blond surfer type whose nametag read Smalley.

"Go ahead, Petra," Suzanne told her. "I'm going to hang around here for a little while longer." She gazed at the sheriff. "You're going to bring in an ambulance and tow truck, right?"

Doogie nodded as Petra, somewhat reluctantly, followed along with Smalley.

"What's up?" asked Doogie, once they'd pulled away.

"I ran into Mike O'Dell some thirty minutes ago."

Doogie set his jaw and gave Suzanne a hard stare. "Where?"

"At that little general store," said Suzanne. "Cappy's. He looked . . ." She was going to say angry, but instead she said, "He looked purposeful."

"What do you mean?" asked Doogie. "Like maybe he was up to something?"

"I don't know. Maybe."

"You see anything interesting in his car?" asked Doogie.

"Truck," said Suzanne. "And if you're asking about guns or crossbows, the answer is no. But that doesn't mean they weren't there." She hesitated, then plunged ahead. "Do you think Wilbur might have had a run-in with O'Dell? Maybe Wilbur was trying to work the Peebler case and asked one too many questions?"

"Don't know," said Doogie. "It's possible." He hitched at his sweatpants, then walked over to Wilbur's cruiser. Suzanne followed.

Doogie opened the driver's side door, reached in gingerly, and grabbed a spiral-bound notebook off the front seat. He paged through it and said, "Nothing's written in Wilbur's patrol activity log. Not a darned thing."

"Too bad."

"But I doubt if Wilbur was way out here on a joyride. So he must have had something going," mused Doogie.

"You think O'Dell somehow got the drop on him?" asked Suzanne.

"I don't know," said Doogie. "Maybe."

"Or he was lured out here," said Suzanne. "Face it, you yourself said Wilbur was a nice guy, but investigating wasn't his strong suit."

Doogie scuffed the toe of his shoe in the soft dirt. "Two murders in three days?" he said. "Looks like it might not be my strong suit, either."

FIVE minutes later, an ambulance screeched to a halt and the same men Suzanne had encountered Sunday night, Dick Sparrow and Sid Pauley, jumped out. They grabbed a gurney and rattled it anxiously across the bumpy asphalt road.

"Is it true?" asked Sparrow, looking grim. "Was Wilbur shot?"

"Afraid so, boys," said Doogie. "And there's no need to hurry. We gotta wait for the state crime lab to show up. We're going to handle this one strictly by the book."

"Can we see him?" asked Pauley.

Doogie hesitated. "As long as everything is kept in complete confidence."

"We've got battery-operated tripod lights in the truck," offered Sparrow. "We could set them up out there."

Doogie nodded. "Maybe we can get a jump on the investigation, after all."

SUZANNE took off just as the crime scene unit arrived in their shiny, black, state-of-the-art van. No sense hanging around because, chances are, the state guys wouldn't *let* her hang around. And she'd already traded theories with Doogie . . .

Blasting down the road, Suzanne continued to shiver even though the heater was cranked up full blast.

Nerves, she told herself. *Just nerves and some unwelcome adrenaline trying to get the best of me.*

Punching on the radio, she got the night DJ at KLGN and listened halfheartedly to a Muzak version of "Do You Know the Way to San José."

Not very good. Awful, in fact.

She took her eyes off the road, momentarily, to switch stations, and when she glanced back, her headlights revealed a dog hobbling right down the center line!

CHAPTER 12

PUMPING her brakes hard, Suzanne swerved wildly, missing the poor creature by a matter of inches. Then she rocked to a stop on the narrow berm and drew a shaky breath.

Deep in Suzanne's heart was a pity and concern for any injured animal, domestic or wild. So, of course, she shut off her engine and hopped out.

The dog was standing still as a statue now, staring at her. Watching. Waiting.

"Here, boy." Kneeling down on the pavement, Suzanne held out both arms to welcome him. "Come," she said, thinking maybe the dog might respond to a familiar command.

Instead, the little dog just lay down and cowered.

Oh no. Poor thing. Did I hit him?

It was a mongrel type, but cute in a long-haired Disney dog kind of way. Maybe a collie-shepherd mix.

Suzanne decided to try again. "Come on, boy." She let loose a low, cajoling whistle. "Come on, you can do it."

The dog lifted his head. It watched nervously for a long couple of seconds, then it slowly stood up and began limping toward her. When Suzanne extended her hand again, she felt warm breath and a soft, wet tongue.

"You want to be friends? Let's be friends." Suzanne reached out and touched the dog's neck. The dog trembled but didn't pull away. "You okay? Sure you are." She ca-ressed his shaggy brown-and-white pelt, moving her hand in slow, repetitive circles from his neck down to his chest and sides. When her fingers touched something sticky and moist, she knew he must be injured.

Uh-oh.

"You want to come home with me, fella? Maybe get something good to eat?" From the looks of him, he could use a good meal. And a safe place to sleep.

"C'mon." Suzanne tapped her hand against her leg and slowly walked around the car to the passenger side. Mi-raculously, the dog followed. When she pulled open the passenger side door, the dog put his front paws on the front seat and let her gently boost him in.

"Atta boy."

Suzanne dialed her cell phone one-handed as she drove, knowing she was probably a traffic hazard, but not really caring.

When Sam Hazelet picked up on the second ring, she said, without preamble, "Can you come over to my house? Right away?"

"What's wrong?" Worry permeated Sam's voice. He could obviously tell from Suzanne's tone that something was seriously out of whack.

Where to start?

"Deputy Halpern was shot."

"At your place!"

"No, no," said Suzanne, realizing she had some serious 'splaining to do. "Out in the country. Along the Quilt Trail. Anyway, he's dead. Murdered. Sheriff Doogie's there with him now. It's kind of a long, involved story. But the thing is, I found a dog, too. And I think he might be hurt pretty bad."

"Are *you* okay?" Sam asked, quickly.

"I'm fine," Suzanne told him, then paused, her voice catching. "I could take the dog to the vet, but . . . I'd like to talk to you. In fact, I'd like to see you tonight." She let out a shaky sigh. "Sorry if I'm not making a whole lot of sense."

"I'll be there in five minutes," said Sam. "You can tell me the whole story then."

"Better make it ten, I'm still on the road."

But when Suzanne pulled into her driveway, Sam was standing there, bouncing up and down on the balls of his feet, waiting expectantly.

Jumping from her car, Suzanne launched herself into his arms. She didn't quite burst into tears, but the thought did cross her mind. And the hug was oh so warm and comforting. But of course, there was the injured dog to take care of first.

Sam thrust a black medical bag into Suzanne's arms. "Take this, I'll get the dog."

"Just carry him into the kitchen," she said, "then we can work on him there."

"Baxter?" said Sam, gathering up the injured dog.

"He'll be cool."

And Baxter *was* cool. Like a good canine nurse, Bax stood by the kitchen table, looking somber yet interested as Sam examined the dog with practiced hands.

"Cuts," said Sam. "Lots of cuts and puncture wounds with some being fairly deep. Tell me about Wilbur Halpern."

"I'm getting to that," said Suzanne. "You think somebody was deliberately cruel to this dog?" The thought struck dread in her heart.

"It's certainly possible. Do you have any hydrogen peroxide or Betadine?"

"Peroxide," said Suzanne. She ran to the first-floor bathroom and grabbed the bottle from beneath the sink. Grabbed a couple of old towels, too. Then she ran back and handed everything to Sam.

"First I'm going to clean up these wounds," said Sam.

"What should I do?" asked Suzanne. She nibbled nervously at her fingertips.

"Maybe . . . make a pot of coffee?"

"Sure." Suzanne busied herself, measuring out Jamaican Blue Mountain coffee, keeping one eye on Sam as he worked on the dog. "You need any help?"

Sam reached into his bag and pulled out a small vial along with a syringe. "I'm going to give him a shot of lidocaine to numb things up. Then I'm going to close this larger wound."

"So a few stitches," Suzanne murmured. She glanced sideways and grimaced as Sam administered the injection. "Ouch."

"I think this is bothering you more than the dog," observed Sam.

"I think you may be right."

By the time the dog was numbed up, the coffee was perked and ready to serve.

"You're going to use that?" Suzanne asked, looking at the contraption in Sam's hand. It looked like an industrial staple gun from the Home Depot.

"Staple gun," said Sam. "Easier than stitches. Quicker."

"I've always wondered, don't those little thingies hurt when they dig in?"

"Not with lidocaine. Seriously, we use staples on patients who've had open-heart surgery. On kids with head lacs."

"Okay," said Suzanne. "You're the doctor."

"And a lucky thing that is," said Sam, wiggling his eyebrows and doing a sort of Groucho Marx impression. "Okay, *now* please tell me about the deputy."

"Petra and I were driving the Quilt Trail . . ." Suzanne began.

"On a dark and stormy night?" Sam pulled the trigger and planted a staple.

"It didn't start out that way," said Suzanne. "But, granted, we dawdled a bit. Then Petra wanted to catch one more quilt square . . ."

"Okay," said Sam. Another staple went in.

"And we ended up driving this backcountry road, searching for an old schoolhouse, and figured we'd taken a wrong turn . . ." She filled him in on the rest of their strange encounter and finished with, "And that's how I discovered poor Wilbur Halpern. Dead."

"Was he shot with an arrow?" asked Sam.

"No, I think maybe with his own gun. I didn't exactly get a chance to *analyze* the crime scene. By the time my mind processed what had happened out there in that swamp, I got scared and just sort of . . . ran away."

"Smart lady," said Sam, putting an arm around her and pulling her close.

"And then I called Doogie. And then after that I found the dog and called you."

"Doogie's bringing in the state crime lab?" asked Sam. Suzanne nodded.

"Only thing to do at this point," said Sam.

"THERE you go, Scruff." Suzanne set an aluminum bowl on the floor, filled with kibble and topped with a handful of warm, chopped-up chicken. "Bon appétit, you brave little patient."

"You've really taken a liking to that mutt, haven't you?" asked Sam, gazing at the collie-shepherd mix as he gulped his food, looking like he'd just won the doggy lottery.

"Baxter won't mind having a buddy around," Suzanne told him. "Dogs being pack animals and all."

"Man's best friend," said Sam. Then he smiled at Suzanne. "And women's, too, I guess."

"No, sir," Suzanne said with a laugh, "diamonds are a girl's best friend."

Sam chuckled as he snaked an arm around her waist. "This has been a tough couple of days for you. All this criminal activity, ripped from the headlines as they say."

Suzanne laughed, hiccupped, and oozed a few tears. "That's the same thing I told Toni. Maybe I should fictionalize my story, self-publish, and sell it in the Book Nook."

"I'd buy it," he told her, "but only if you promise to autograph it." He kissed the top of her head.

"Oh my gosh," Suzanne said suddenly, "I never offered you anything to eat!"

Sam's eyes crinkled with warmth as he gazed at her. "I got coffee."

"How about a nice glass of wine and some actual food?" Sam shook his head.

Suzanne gave him a long look. "Me?"

"I thought you'd never ask."

THEY took their time. Suzanne lit scented vanilla candles and put on soft music. Then, like a couple of innocent college kids on their first date, they held hands and kissed. A prelude to their first night together.

Afterward, just hovering on the edge of sleep, Suzanne and Sam cuddled like spoons.

A soft snore, from Baxter, not Sam, caused Suzanne to glance over at the doggy beds where the two dogs slumbered and twitched.

"Do you think Scruff might have been attacked by wild pigs?" Suzanne murmured.

Sam wrapped an arm around her and pulled her closer. "Looked more like he was roughed up by another dog."

CHAPTER 13

WEDNESDAY was Crabby Omelet day at the Cackleberry Club, but this morning the usual fun and frivolity was somewhat diminished. Pans still rattled, plump sausages sizzled on the grill, coffee cups thunked on the marble counter, but talk among the three women was tense and terse.

"The thing is," said Toni, as she busily shredded a chunk of cheddar cheese, "I can't help wonder who's next?"

"Don't say that," said Petra. Hunched over her stove, she cracked eggs into a large ceramic bowl. "Please don't talk like that." Grabbing a wire whisk, she went to work on the eggs, swirling and whipping them into a froth.

"I say that because we now have *two* murders on our hands," said Toni, throwing a cautionary glance at Suzanne. A warning look that clearly said, *Petra's in a mood.*

"Not on *our* hands," snapped Petra, liberally sprinkling salt and pepper into her beaten eggs.

"They kind of are," Suzanne said, finally. "Since the first murder happened right here and the second one . . . well, I don't have to explain that to *you.*"

"Man," said Toni, shaking her head and looking both distracted and sad. "It must have been something, discovering poor old Wilbur Halpern like that."

"Something awful," agreed Suzanne.

"People are really going to chatter now," said Petra, peeling open a package of fresh crabmeat.

"You mean talk about us?" said Suzanne.

Petra nodded silently.

"There are always a few people who'll gossip and spread rumors," said Suzanne. "We just need to keep a level head on our shoulders and our answers to the bare minimum." *And hope Doogie comes up with some answers fast,* she wanted to add.

"But what," asked Toni, "is *really* going on? Ouch!" she yelped, almost grating her own finger.

"Doogie's probably going to blame Jane again," Petra snapped.

"No, he won't," said Suzanne. "Doogie's not going to do that. Not now. Not after last night."

"It's possible the two murders are unrelated," said Toni. "But, somehow, it doesn't feel that way." She stabbed at the last bit of cheese. "You probably won't be surprised to hear that Mike O'Dell has moved up to suspect number one on my list."

"Mine, too," said Petra. "If you could have seen him last night . . ."

"A very scary guy," agreed Suzanne. "You could feel a definite threat level."

"You think Wilbur Halpern might have been trying to impress Doogie?" asked Toni. "I mean, obviously Doogie told him about O'Dell having a bow-hunting license, so maybe Halpern decided to follow up on his own. Only he somehow . . . blew it."

"Blew his brains out," muttered Petra.

"Petra!" said Suzanne. "Of all of us you're the one who's always the most positive."

"Not today," said Petra. "Not when I have to face Winnie Halpern at church."

"Got it," said Suzanne. She grabbed a loaf of zucchini bread, started cutting it into chunks.

"Time to change the subject?" Toni asked. "Maybe go over the specials?"

"Petra?" Suzanne glanced over at her friend and chef.

"Crabby Omelets," said Petra, without her usual preamble. "With hollandaise sauce. A breakfast parfait of vanilla yogurt, cubed zucchini bread, sliced almonds, and cranberry topping."

"Tasty," said Toni.

"And Jumpin' Jack scrambled eggs," said Petra. "Plus we have our full complement of ham, spicy sausage patties, and turkey bacon."

"People always roll their eyes when I tell them it's turkey bacon," said Toni.

"Then don't tell them," said Petra. "Just say bacon."

"Is that kosher?" asked Toni. "I don't mean the bacon, I mean to deceive our customers?"

Petra just shook her head and frowned. "Lord knows, *I* don't want to be the one responsible for half of Kindred dropping dead from coronary infarctions."

"Okaaaay," Toni murmured.

"On a happier note," said Suzanne, "Petra's quilt looks beautiful hanging over our front door."

"Doesn't it?" said Petra, brightening a notch. "I had one of the fellows who's helping rebuild the church next door drag his ladder over and put it up."

"So are we going to be able to pull ourselves out of our blue funk and have a successful Quilt Trail Tea this afternoon?" asked Toni. They were cohosting the tea with the historical society and were expecting around thirty customers.

"I was so looking forward to the tea," said Petra, "but Wilbur's murder puts a terrible damper on things."

"I just hope it doesn't scare people off," said Toni.

"Arthur Bunch already called, worried about that exact same thing," said Suzanne.

"He's still coming, isn't he?" asked Petra. Bunch was scheduled to deliver his little talk midway through the tea.

"He'll be here," said Suzanne. "I told him the tea was still on. That it was possible Wilbur's murder would bring in even more people." She glanced out the pass-through toward the front door, where a half dozen people were already lined up.

"You can bet Gene Gandle will have a big, splashy article in the *Bugle* tomorrow," said Toni.

"Gene does adore his bylines," Suzanne tossed back over her shoulder, as she went to unlock the door.

"Isn't this Waffle Wednesday?" a bearded man in overalls asked Suzanne, as she stood at his table, pen poised above her order book.

"That was last week," she pointed out. "Today's different. Crabby Wednesday. Crab omelets with hollandaise sauce are our special today."

"You should have seen the waffles!" Mr. Overalls exclaimed to his companion. "They had waffles with apple and raisin sauce, even Belgian waffles stacked a mile high with caramelized bananas and whipped cream." He grinned at Suzanne. "If you have a sweet tooth like I do, it was one fantastic breakfast."

"So," Suzanne said with a smile, trying to move the ordering process along. "Two Crabby Omelets with hash browns?"

"Done," said the man in the overalls, though he looked a little wistful.

As more customers poured in, the mood seemed to lighten. Petra, who usually hid out with her eggs, even stepped out of the kitchen to deliver an order of French toast to a friend seated at the counter.

"You're looking decidedly more upbeat," Toni remarked, as they both hastened back into the kitchen. Then Suzanne came running in with another order for a Crabby Omelet.

"I'm feeling better," said Petra. "But we're perilously low on crabmeat."

"Which means your omelets are a big hit," said Suzanne.

Petra looked thoughtful. "Think I could substitute shrimp?"

"Shrimpy omelets?" said Toni. "Sounds weird to me."

"Sounds delicious," said Suzanne. "But let me check with a couple of customers."

She came back forty seconds later and nodded at Petra. "Shrimp it is. Only with baby Swiss cheese instead of cheddar."

"I agree," said Petra.

Toni plunked her bottom on a wooden stool and said, "You know what? I was watching *The Bachelor* last night and all those women were *soooo* competitive. They were, like, scratching each other's eyes out to get a rose from that poor goombah and try to win his heart."

"What would you have done?" asked Suzanne. "I mean, in their place?"

"I dunno," said Toni. "Be nicer than *they* were." She glanced at Petra. "How about you, Petra?"

"Lay around and read a book," said Petra. "Hope he picked somebody else."

"Hah," said Toni, poking an index finger at her. "Good one."

Five minutes later, the wall phone in the kitchen jingled.

"I'm up to my armpits in egg yolks and flour," said Petra. "Suzanne?"

Suzanne grabbed for the phone, then was glad that she had. Sam.

"How you doing today?" he asked.

"Good."

"Just good?" He was toying with her now. "You can't talk?"

"Not exactly."

"Okay, on a score of one to ten . . ."

"Twelve," she told him.

"Wow. And I was just warming up."

"I don't know," said Suzanne, her cheeks a little flushed now. "I thought it was all amazingly hot."

"Excellent. So how's the dog?"

"Scruff's doing great," Suzanne told him.

"You've named him," said Sam. "That's a dangerous sign. You can give away a nameless dog, but never a dog with a cute name."

They chatted for another couple of minutes, then Suzanne hung up, hoping she didn't look as excited and tingly as she felt way deep down inside.

"What was *that* about?" Toni asked, eyeing her suspiciously.

Suzanne tried to muster a look of supreme innocence. "Nothing."

"Didn't sound like nothing," said Toni. "More like . . . oh, I don't know, hot stuff?"

Suzanne put an index finger up to her mouth and pulled Toni into their small walk-in cooler. "If you must know, Sam stayed over last night."

"Finally!" cheered Toni. She pumped an arm and said, "You go, girl!"

MIDMORNING found Suzanne in the Book Nook, experiencing an emotional roller coaster that alternated between nervous giggles and a seriously manic high. She knew she wasn't in love with Sam, but she sure was in like.

Humming to herself, a slowed-down version of Beyoncé's *Single Ladies*, Suzanne grabbed the new John Sandford novel and stuck it on the shelf. Found a copy of *Winnie-the-Pooh* that sure didn't belong in the Mystery/Thriller section. But when she checked the Children's section, she found that was the last copy. So time to order.

Suzanne stepped behind the desk and jotted a note. When she looked up, Carmen Copeland was standing there staring at her.

"Jeez!" Suzanne clapped a hand to her chest, startled.

"Scared you?" Carmen sounded pleased, in an evil kind of way.

"Kind of," said Suzanne. Carmen Copeland was a prominent romance author who lived in the neighboring town of Jessup. She was snooty, snotty, exotic-looking, and the *New York Times* bestsellers she consistently churned out had made her rich. Which meant she could indulge her taste in clothes and jewelry and always wrap herself in the latest couture. Today her red silk jacket and black pencil skirt were pure Dolce and Gabbana, paired with four-inch-high, Dior red alligator pumps.

Because Carmen considered herself a fashionista and far superior to everyone else in matters of taste and style, she'd recently opened Alchemy Boutique in downtown Kindred. Suzanne figured it was Carmen's twisted, fiendish scheme to bring fashion and flair to what she perceived as the dowdy women of Kindred. But to Suzanne's surprise and—dare we say it, disappointment?—Carmen's plan was working. Women were actually buying J Brand jeans, bright-colored faux furs, and oversized cocktail rings at Alchemy. Surprise, surprise.

"How can I help you, Carmen?" Suzanne asked.

Carmen stared at her with glittering green eyes. "Did you forget?"

"Um . . . no, of course not." Carmen's upcoming event *had* slipped her mind, like a pat of butter off a stack of griddle cakes.

"I'd like to briefly review the menu for Friday's Cashmere and Cabernet event which you, ahem, agreed to cater?"

"Absolutely," said Suzanne, gritting her teeth. Carmen was staging a trunk show at Alchemy, a first ever for Kindred. Vendors for Rock & Republic jeans, Marc Jacobs boots, and Donegal cashmere sweaters were coming in to set up shop and woo customers.

"You do have the menu prepared?" Carmen asked, in a challenging tone.

"Let me run into my office and grab it," said Suzanne. "Take a seat if you'd like."

Carmen looked askance at the two rump-sprung floral upholstered chairs that squatted invitingly in the Book Nook. "Thanks anyway," she said in a nasal, peer-down-your-nose tone of voice.

Suzanne dashed into her office, took forty seconds to scratch out a menu, then was back in a flash.

"Carrot and ginger tea sandwiches and miniature crustless quiche, just like we discussed. Plus I was thinking of adding lobster salad and cucumber cream cheese sandwiches."

"Mmm," said Carmen. "And madeleines and chocolate mousse bars?"

"Absolutely," said Suzanne, though she knew she'd have to conjure up a few good recipes.

"Fine," said Carmen. Reaching into a tan Birkin bag, she pulled out a leather notebook and pen.

"How's Missy doing?" asked Suzanne. Missy was Melissa Langston, a friend of Suzanne's and now Carmen's overworked boutique manager.

"She's fine," said Carmen. She clicked her pen and with a friendly barracuda smile, said, "Now tell me about the murders, Suzanne."

"Oh, Carmen," said Suzanne, trying to muster a look of disappointment, "I really can't do that."

"Of course you can, dear."

Suzanne shook her head. "I'm under strict orders from Sheriff Doogie."

Carmen toyed with a strand of her long, dark hair. "I understand you were witness to both murders."

"Not exactly," said Suzanne.

"The first one was here at the Cackleberry Club," said Carmen, doodling on her pad. "The arrow."

Suzanne managed a tight nod.

"And the one last night . . ." Carmen's eyes danced with eagerness. "The hapless deputy shot with his own service weapon. That *you* once again discovered."

"Are you by any chance planning to write a book about this?" asked Suzanne. "Move beyond the romance genre into police procedural?"

Carmen dimpled prettily. "You never know."

"I certainly admire your creative bent, Carmen," said Suzanne, "but I really can't spill any details."

"Very well," said Carmen, looking cool and calm, "then I'll get them somewhere else. And make no mistake, I *will* get them."

"I believe you," said Suzanne. And she really did.

As Carmen made a big fuss of tucking her notebook back into her bag, she bumped a small sign on the counter, causing it to topple over. She frowned, picked up the sign and read it, then frowned again. "You're having a book signing here on Thursday?"

"A local author is joining us for our Mystery Tea," explained Suzanne. "Julie Crane."

"Never heard of her," said Carmen, her voice going frosty. "And what exactly has she written?"

"A nonfiction book," said Suzanne. "*Ghostly Lore and Legends*. Really a compilation of area haunted house legends, published by Palette Press at Darlington College. Kind of fun, but in a slightly academic way."

Carmen's ruby red lips pursed together to form a perfect oval. "Oh. A small, local publisher. So this woman isn't an actual author. Not an author anyone would have heard of."

"Julie's not been on the *New York Times* Bestseller List, no," said Suzanne.

Carmen, who'd enjoyed her fair share of trips to that much-coveted list, gave a self-satisfied smile. "Mmm. Pity."

TEN minutes later, Sheriff Doogie walked into the Cackleberry Club. Not with his usual cocky saunter, but with a deliberate slowness, as though his joints ached and he was toting the weight of the world on his broad khaki-clad back. He maneuvered to the counter and sat down heavily, his shoulders drooping, his bloodshot eyes cast downward.

Suzanne and Toni exchanged worried glances. Toni grabbed a coffeepot and headed straight for him, while Suzanne's tactical weapon of choice was a sticky bun drizzled with caramel and covered in pecans.

"How ya doing, Sheriff?" asked Toni, plunking the coffee in front of him.

Doogie gave a vague nod.

Suzanne slid the sticky bun, always a surefire cure for what ails you, in front of Doogie.

"No, thanks," said Doogie. He shrugged and pushed the plate away.

Suzanne's eyes grew wide with shock. This was serious business. She'd never—repeat, *never*—seen Doogie turn down food.

Doogie sighed deeply, twined his fingers around the coffee mug, and took a sip. No fussing with multiple cubes of sugar, no tsunami of heavy, artery-clogging cream. Suzanne knew Doogie hadn't suddenly gone on a Dr. Oz–type wellness kick and put himself on a Spartan diet. Rather, he was punishing himself, probably overwhelmed by guilt and frustration about last night.

"What's wrong, Sheriff?" Suzanne asked him. She knew what was wrong but wanted to hear Doogie articulate it. Maybe, if she could get him talking, she could get him fired up again.

Doogie looked up, focused rheumy eyes on her, and said, "I shouldn't have been so hard on Wilbur. Shouldn't have pushed him."

"You were teaching him," said Suzanne. "Toughening him up so he'd be a better deputy."

"Didn't work," said Doogie.

"You don't know that," responded Suzanne.

Doogie took another sip of coffee and grimaced. "And I shouldn't have cussed at him."

"Well, no, you really shouldn't have," Suzanne said in a soft voice. "But that's . . ." She paused to think. Was the phrase "water over the dam"? Or under the bridge? Or both?

"The thing is," continued Doogie, "Wilbur was a pretty good kid."

"He always tried very hard," said Suzanne, reaching across the counter to pat Doogie's burly hand, "and he was a very kind boy."

Doogie looked up, as in a daze. "Was he?"

"Sheriff," said Suzanne, trying to offer some comfort, "you had no way of knowing what would happen to Wilbur."

Doogie stared at her. "I'm a law enforcement officer. Wilbur was a law enforcement officer. Every second we're at work we run the risk of putting ourselves in a dangerous situation. We should always be . . . vigilant." He was barely able to choke out this last word.

"I understand that."

"But Wilbur's mama won't," said Doogie.

"No," said Suzanne, "I don't suppose she will." Her fingers toyed with the plate that held the sticky roll, then she slid it across the counter. "Have a roll. It'll make you feel better."

"No, it won't," said Doogie, reaching out a big finger to tow the plate in. "But I'll have it anyway. Sugar will do me good."

"Probably will," said Suzanne, deciding it was definitely time to change the subject. Doogie seemed poised on the verge of a self-pity jag. "Have you, uh, found out anything more about the key card you discovered out back?"

"I did," said Doogie, chewing, "and it's no big deal. Belongs to the courthouse. So anybody who works there could have dropped it." He gave a nonchalant shrug. "Heck, you yourself said lots of different folks were here Sunday night for that reading thing." He continued to munch.

The courthouse? Mayor Mobley's fleshy face suddenly swam before Suzanne's eyes. The courthouse was where the mayor worked, where he manipulated his shady little deals.

So . . . maybe Mayor Mobley was involved in Peebler's murder after all. But . . . and this was a big but . . . had Mobley been that greedy and nervous about winning a small-town election to protect his self-interests? Could Mobley have shot Peebler because the handwriting on the wall predicted he was going to get booted out of office?

Of course he could have shot Peebler, Suzanne decided. *Mobley is a conniving weasel capable of almost anything.*

Okay, hold everything. What about Deputy Halpern? Had the deputy been about to get on top of the mayor about something, but Mobley struck a preemptive blow? Had Mobley lured Halpern out into the middle of nowhere and shot him? Or simply followed Halpern when he was on patrol?

Maybe. Possibly. Though that theory was predicated on the fact that Wilbur had figured something out.

Suzanne glanced at Doogie, wondering if she should voice her suspicions. On the other hand, she knew she was conjuring up some fairly wild notions that she really couldn't prove. And she surely didn't want to burden Doogie any more than he already was. So . . . what to do? Maybe, like industrial-strength coffee grounds, she should just let this mess percolate for a while longer?

For now, yes. Yes, I will.

Doogie was mumbling something as he gathered up his hat and slid off his stool.

"What?" Suzanne shook her head. "Sorry."

"Talk to you later," said Doogie, giving her a kind of half salute.

"Count on it," responded Suzanne. She tracked him to the door, watched Doogie through the front window as he hefted himself into his cruiser. "Well, that's just ducky," she muttered out loud, irony tingeing her voice.

Then the front door banged open and a tall man caromed in. Head bobbing atop his stalklike neck, Gene Gandle, the *Bugle*'s persistent and insanely intrepid reporter, made a beeline for her.

"Suzanne, we gotta talk," he gasped. "A double murder!" Gene's eyes danced crazily. "This is big time stuff!"

CHAPTER 14

"KINDRED has its very own serial killer!" exclaimed Gene, practically bursting with warped civic pride.

Suzanne wasted no time in lambasting the reporter who sat at her counter. "Shush, Gene, you don't know that for a fact!"

"But we might," Gene taunted back.

"No way," said Suzanne. "Highly doubtful."

"Then a double murder," said Gene, gleefully.

Suzanne shook her head like a disapproving schoolteacher. "A double murder is when they're related."

"Who says they're not?" asked Gene.

He had her there. Obviously, she wasn't the only person in Kindred who'd made a leap to that conclusion. Probably, weird old Freddy, the bartender down at Schmitt's Bar, had come up with the same idea.

Suzanne grabbed an order pad and a pencil. "You here for lunch?" she asked.

"Sure," responded Gene, "I'll take anything on the menu as long as you're willing to open up to the press."

"You're not press, Gene," said Suzanne. "You write human interest stories on church suppers, bingo nights, and the occasional frost warning. And you peddle advertising on the side."

"It's still press." Now Gene's voice carried a petulant tone.

"Whatever," said Suzanne, "I'm still not going to blab any details to you."

Gene gave her a sly look. "You will if you want customers to keep coming back to the Cackleberry Club."

"Excuse me," said Suzanne, leaning toward him, "but do I detect a threat in your words? Or, worse yet, would you be trying to *blackmail* me with some sort of wild exposé?"

"Draw your own conclusions," said Gene.

Suzanne let loose on him. "If you *dare* to implicate the Cackleberry Club in any way, I'll call up Laura Benchley and have her deep-six your story in a heartbeat." Laura Benchley was the editor of the *Bugle* and a friend of Suzanne's. "And maybe even get your precious press card pulled."

"What about freedom of the press?" whined Gene.

"What about placing an order?" snapped Suzanne.

"ARE you ignoring Gene?" asked Toni. She stood at the counter, her back to the café, assembling a sandwich for a take-out order. Roast beef, cheddar cheese, slices of Vidalia onion, and mustard. With a fat, juicy slice of heirloom tomato for good measure.

"You got that right," said Suzanne. "I figure if we don't take Gene's order he'll eventually slither away."

"Sounds like a plan," said Toni.

"Gene threatened to write some fearmongering story about the Cackleberry Club," said Suzanne.

"That so?" said Toni. "No wonder he was trying to interview a couple of customers."

"Rats. Did they talk to him?"

Toni snorted. "Are you kidding? They were too busy snarfing up omelets. I kind of hate to admit it, but Petra's shrimp omelets have been a big hit."

"Glad to hear it," said Suzanne. She glanced at the clock above a shelf cluttered with ceramic chickens. Big red-and-black roosters, little yellow chicks, and white chickens were all gathered together, watching over the place like a kind of Greek chorus of poultry. Except they never, ha-ha, made a peep.

Toni followed Suzanne's eyes. "Getting toward lunch-time."

"Yeah," said Suzanne, digging in her apron pocket for the menu Petra had scrawled for her.

"You gonna put up the menu or you want me to?"

"I'll do it," said Suzanne.

"I'll finish this sandwich, then go insult Gene," said Toni.

"Bash him good," said Suzanne.

Toni grinned. "He'll feel like a piñata by the time I'm done with him."

"CHICKEN a la king," Suzanne murmured to herself. She listed that at the top of the blackboard menu, then added a grilled sandwich of smoked turkey, brie cheese, green apple, and watercress. She grabbed a piece of green chalk, drew a big soup bowl with steam rising off it, then scrawled creamy broccoli soup. At the bottom of the chalkboard she used orange chalk to draw a pumpkin and printed pumpkin roll cake. Suzanne wrote $2.99, then wiped it off with her hand and changed the price to $3.99. The difference between making a living and making a profit was a fine line indeed, she decided.

Suzanne stepped back, pleased. The Cackleberry Club wasn't offering an extensive menu today. Then again, they were hosting the Quilt Trail Tea at two o'clock. So their kitchen could only prep and serve so much in any given day. Petra did have her limits.

"Gene took off," said Toni, whipping by with a tray that held two bowls of molten hot broccoli soup.

"Excellent," said Suzanne. "Nice work."

They did their tag-team thing then, taking orders, hustling them out to customers, fending off any probing questions about the two murders. By one o'clock, things had slowed down to a dull roar and Suzanne was able to dash into the Book Nook.

In honor of today's Quilt Trail Tea, Suzanne laid out one of Petra's basket pattern quilts on a round wooden table, then arranged a display of teapots, books about tea, and books about quilting. When she was finished, she studied her arrangement, then ran into her office and grabbed a white ceramic crock filled with stems of bright red bittersweet. She added that to the table along with a stack of Quilt Trail brochures. There, now everything looked cozy and cute, a real tribute to the Quilt Trail and a lovely autumn in Logan County.

Except, of course, for the fact that her Quilt Trail experience had been fraught with terror.

Hopefully, Doogie was keeping a lid on things and too many details weren't being revealed. Then the Quilt Trail could go on as planned and hopefully draw hundreds of visitors who'd be charmed by both the landmarks and the picturesque drive.

Suzanne put a hand to her cheek, thinking. Maybe . . . check the Knitting Nest, too?

She rushed in, found two women sitting in chairs, working away. That was cool. In fact, it was the whole philosophy behind the Cackleberry Club. Create a warm, welcoming environment where women could spend an hour or two. Or three or four.

Suzanne bustled around the Knitting Nest and arranged baskets of knitting needles, tossed a few more skeins of organic wool yarn into a giant wooden bowl, stacked pre-cut quilt squares as well as the ubiquitous jelly rolls.

Okay, good, she decided, then dashed back out into the café.

Where she ran smack-dab into Joey Ewald, their skateboarding busboy. Who, today of all days, was dressed like a gangbanger!

"Joey," said Suzanne, in an almost but not quite accusatory voice, "I almost didn't recognize you!"

Joey, a skinny sixteen-year-old with a mop of dark hair and dark, almond shaped eyes, grinned fiendishly. He pointed an index finger and scanned down his baggy, outlandish outfit. "Cool, huh?" he asked.

"Oh my gosh," breathed Suzanne, taking a real look at him. Joey's pants were so big and baggy they sagged halfway down his hips, revealing not one but two expanses of colorful underwear. A belt cinched tightly around Joey's hips kept his faded denim pants from slipping down around his Air Jordan–clad feet. His orange shirt was oversized as well and embroidered with the words *L.A. County Jail*. His Chicago Bulls cap was turned backward.

Petra chose that moment to stroll out of the kitchen, bearing a large wicker basket. She opened her mouth, closed it, then opened it again. Finally she managed to ask, "Is that your Halloween outfit?"

"Yo, Miz P., it's my gang outfit," Joey answered in a serious tone.

"There's a gang in Kindred?" Suzanne asked with a fair amount of skepticism.

Joey shook his head, mournfully. "Naw, but the mall over in Jessup carries this stuff. With the money I earn today I'm gonna buy a gold chain to wear around my neck." He looked far more pleased than if he'd said he was going to plunk it in a savings account.

"A necklace?" asked Petra.

"Necklaces are for girls," said Joey. "You wouldn't catch Fitty Cent wearing a necklace. Man goes for the bling."

"Fitty Cent?" asked Petra, like she thought it might be a newly minted coin. A cousin to the Sacagaweas.

"Young man," said Suzanne, "you're not going to earn anything, Fifty Cent or fifty bucks, unless you change your clothes."

"Oh man," said Joey, disappointed. "Do I have to?"

"There's a health code regulation," said Suzanne, making it up as she went along, "that prohibits restaurant workers from showing their underwear." She glanced at Toni, who was spreading white linen tablecloths across all the tables. Her pink bra peeped out from her tight-fitting red cowboy shirt. "Toni," Suzanne hissed.

Toni glanced up.

Suzanne made rapid buttoning motions and Toni complied. Thank goodness, case closed. Blouse, too.

"So I gotta put on regular clothes?" Joey whined.

"Sorry," said Suzanne. "But rules are rules. And health

code regulations in particular are almost inviolable." *Although maybe not so much at Hoobly's,* she decided.

"Okay," said a reluctant Joey. He swung his backpack off his shoulder and picked up his skateboard all in one motion.

"You run in back and change," Suzanne instructed.

"Nice rags," Toni called, as Joey scooted by her.

Suzanne shook her head. "Don't encourage him."

"Ah, he's just a kid," said Toni. "A couple of years from now he'll be wearing golf shirts and khaki slacks, looking like a cookie-cutter used car salesman." Toni got a wild gleam in her eyes. "Besides, remember how we used to dress in the eighties?"

"Don't remind me." Suzanne grimaced.

"How'd you used to dress?" asked Petra, interested now.

"I was the Cyndi Lauper of Kindred," Toni bragged, "and our dear Suzanne here was a mini Madonna."

"No!" said Petra.

"Complete with crinolines and ripped fishnet stockings!" Toni finished.

"Seriously?" asked Petra.

"Not really," said Suzanne.

"Oh yeah," said Toni. "With mall rat hair." She glanced at Petra's basket. "What's in there, honey?" She reached out and flipped up the corner of a red gingham napkin. "Ah, scones."

Petra nodded. "I baked an extra two dozen. I'm going to take them over to Reverend Yoder and the other men who are helping rebuild the Journey's End Church."

"It's really coming along," said Suzanne. "Might be ready for Christmas yet."

"The bell tower went up last week, so that's a positive sign," said Petra.

Toni gave a shrug. "And Reverend Yoder's been there every day, rain or shine, trying to help out even though he's surely not much of a carpenter."

"Just mentions them in his sermons," said Petra, a sly smile on her face.

"Amen," said Toni.

"OKAY," said Suzanne, glancing at her clipboard. "As soon as Petra gets back we need to do a final heads-up. Make sure we're all on the same page."

"How many reservations today?" asked Toni.

"Twenty-two," said Suzanne. "But I won't be surprised if we get another dozen or so walk-ins."

"You think?" asked Toni. "Because if word is out about last night . . ."

"Hopefully it's not *too* out there," said Suzanne.

"What if people stay away in droves?"

"I don't think they're going to perceive the Quilt Trail as being dangerous," said Suzanne. "They're going to believe that Deputy Halpern got himself into a situation he couldn't handle."

"No kidding."

"But you're right," said Suzanne. "People will talk. Even Carmen Copeland was asking questions like crazy."

"Carmen drives me crazy," said Toni. "She's a Type A—annoying."

"I just hope she doesn't go bugging Doogie," said Suzanne. "Seems like he's barely hanging on."

"Doogie's a tough guy," said Toni, "he'll pull it together."

"It's hard for him, though," said Suzanne. "Doogie's alone and probably doesn't have a lot of close friends to lean on. No sounding board, nobody to bounce ideas off."

"Like we do," said Toni. "Even if we are a little off the chain."

Suzanne nodded. "You can say that again."

CHAPTER 15

As if by magic, merry old England seemed to drop from the skies and land smack-dab in the middle of the Cackleberry Club. Or, at the very least, a charming little tea shop from a village in the Cotswolds.

Because an amazing transformation had taken place at the Cackleberry Club. White linen tablecloths now draped the normally battered tables. Red and gold chrysanthemums bobbed their shaggy heads from crystal vases that graced each table. Creamy white tapers flickered and reflected off polished silverware. The best china had been laid out and soft music—a nocturne by Chopin—played in the background.

"Fantastic," said Suzanne, as she surveyed the room.

"It's like a fairy godmother waved her magic wand," agreed Toni. "Bippity-boppity-boo."

"Perfect for a proper English tea," chimed in Petra.

"Oh hey," said Toni, glancing out the front window. "Here's Arthur already."

The front door flew open and Arthur Bunch, dressed in his trademark tweeds and bow tie, stepped inside. His scruffy brown leather messenger bag hung from one shoulder; he held another stack of Quilt Trail brochures in his hands.

"Aren't you the optimistic one," said Toni.

"Don't be negative," said Petra, scolding. She scurried toward Arthur and dragged him into the middle of what had become a showplace tearoom. "Pay no attention to Toni," Petra instructed with a laugh. "She's our problem child."

"If only," Suzanne murmured.

"We're just delighted you can join us today," Petra continued, hanging on Arthur's arm. "Thrilled you agreed to give a little talk."

Arthur Bunch smiled, blinked, and gazed about the tea shop. "Oh my goodness," he rasped. "This is absolutely lovely! You ladies have brought about a spectacular transformation."

"Watch it," drawled Toni, "you make it sound like we were all running around in gingham dresses and smoking corncob pipes."

"I didn't mean . . ." said Bunch, in a rush.

"Joke," said Toni. "Joke. Take it easy and chill out, okay?"

Suzanne stepped in to address Bunch. "Maybe you'd like to hang out in the Book Nook until things get under way? Our guests should . . ." She glanced at her watch, a Timex that seemed to be running late. "Should be arriving within the next ten minutes or so." She gave her stubborn watch a little tap.

"That sounds fine," said Bunch, eager to escape Toni and her sharp tongue. He dogged Suzanne's footsteps into the Book Nook, dropped his messenger bag on the counter and said, "I checked my records about those donations you mentioned."

"Hmm?" said Suzanne, turning back to him with two more quilting books she'd decided to add to her table display.

"You asked about Evelyn Novak making a donation to the historical society?" Bunch prompted.

"Right," said Suzanne, focusing now.

"She didn't," said Bunch. "Not as far as I could see, anyway."

"You looked through your records," said Suzanne. "And found nothing for Novak."

"I went back three years," said Bunch. He looked at her expectantly. "You want me to go back further? I sure can, if you want me to. What was it you were looking for specifically?"

"Maybe . . . paintings?" said Suzanne. She knew that's what Novak had donated to the museum at Darlington College.

"Like I mentioned before," said Bunch, "we don't really accept anything that's of European origin. Our mission as set forth is quite clearly focused—nineteenth- and twentieth-century Americana. And we prefer items directly related to the settlement of this particular area." He gazed at her, saw she was still troubled. "But I could certainly search further back in our records . . ."

"No," said Suzanne, "it was just a wild hunch. Thanks anyway; you've done enough."

"Glad to be of assistance," said Bunch, as a chorus of eager female voices suddenly shrilled from the other room.

"And we're off and running!" said Suzanne.

LOLLY Herron's grand entrance would have made Agatha Christie proud. Although she lived on a farm out on Highway 22, Lolly could have easily passed for an aging BBC star. Her sensible Miss Marple attire, classic tweed skirt, carpetbag tote, and shoes with heels sturdy enough to construct a skyscraper on, screamed God Save the Queen! She'd wisely chosen to top off her outfit with a brown felt beret, held on with a jeweled hatpin that could probably double as a rapier.

"Am I too early?" Lolly breathed breathlessly, then saw that one table was already filled. "Oh perfect," she said.

"I am loving that outfit!" Suzanne exclaimed.

"Got it all at Goodwill," said Lolly. "Which accounts for the mingled aroma of Estée Lauder and mothballs."

"Even the shoes?" asked Suzanne.

Lolly grinned. "Actually, these were mine to begin with." A few laugh lines appeared on her pleasantly plump face.

"Well, you're perfectly dressed for a proper English tea," said Suzanne, leading her to a table. Then she headed back to the front door to welcome yet another arriving group of women.

These women had taken what Suzanne always thought of as the fifties matriarch approach. That is, demure suits, veiled hats, rhinestone cluster pins, and white gloves. And was one woman even wearing nylons with seams? Oh yes, she was!

As Suzanne continued to seat guests, Toni rushed to greet Minerva Bishop, also known as Mrs. Min. The tiny octogenarian was barely counter height, yet she was dressed fashionably in a brown suit with beige piping.

"Over here." Suzanne waved as Toni lead the elderly lady to a chair that had been set up with a booster pillow. "There you go," said Suzanne, pushing Mrs. Min in snug to the table.

"She's so old she should be *displayed* in the historical society," Toni whispered in Suzanne's ear.

"Wait a few years," Suzanne whispered back, "and that will be us!"

A tap on Suzanne's shoulder caused her to turn, a broad smile still lighting her face. Her smile dimmed a bit when she found herself staring into Jane Buckley's tear-filled eyes.

"I just heard about Wilbur," Jane moaned, holding her arms across her stomach, as if she was in pain. "It's so awful."

Suzanne didn't pull any punches.

"Doogie's going to ask more questions, you know."

Jane bristled. "Like what?"

"Like where you were last night?"

"Home," said Jane, looking both wary and a little defensive.

"Home alone?" Suzanne asked.

Jane nodded, then she looked worried. "Oh no. He can't think that I . . ."

"Doogie's not thinking too clearly about anything right now," Suzanne said as she led Jane to a table where two giggling tea regulars were seated. The duo was already chatting, laughing, and sipping tea and Suzanne figured they'd be the perfect tonic for Jane right now.

WITH every chair in the house occupied and an aromatherapy-like haze of Darjeeling, Assam, and Lapsang souchong drifting over the café, Suzanne pushed her way into the kitchen. And stopped short when she saw what Toni and Petra had created.

"My goodness, those are gorgeous!" Suzanne exclaimed, gazing at the three-tiered silver serving stands that were brimming with goodies.

"You like?" asked Petra. She was just adding brown-and-gold-frosted petit fours to the top tier, squidging them next to the hazelnut scones.

"Incredible," said Suzanne. Really, Petra had outdone herself once again. With the top tier holding the sugar goodies, the middle tier displayed a heroic assortment of tea sandwiches. There were chicken salad with toasted almonds, roast beef and cheddar cheese, and chopped pineapple with cream cheese. The bottom tier held more savories. Miniature mushroom quiches, toasted ham roll-ups, and tarragon and tuna on crostini.

"Plus we've got pear butter for the scones," said Toni, "as well as Devonshire cream."

"Good for a sugar buzz." Suzanne grinned. She hesitated. "So, should we take them out? I think our ladies are ready to begin."

"Wait, wait!" said Petra. She grabbed a small wooden tray filled with pink and purple edible flowers. "Can't forget these!" She pinched the buds between her fingers and poked them in wherever there was room.

"As if our guests won't have enough to eat already," said Toni.

When the trays were delivered to the tables they proved to be an enormous success. With Suzanne, Toni, and Petra receiving applause, as well as whispered thank-yous, and more than a few giggles, kisses, and solemn words of thanks.

Just as Suzanne was carrying a pot of Formosan oolong to a table, a sensuous, husky voice called out, "Suzanne."

Suzanne spun around and saw Paula Patterson from Radio WLGN calling to her. "Paula, great to see you." Suzanne moved quickly over to Paula's table.

"Suzanne," said Paula, "would you do me a favor?"

Suzanne began to reach for the teapot nearest Paula. "Of course, what can I . . . ?"

"You, darling," said Paula. "Would you consider filling in for me this Saturday morning?"

"Filling in for you," Suzanne repeated. Then her eyes widened and she squawked, "You mean on air?"

"Just for an hour," said Paula. She was a languid, long-haired blond who sounded as interesting as she looked. "My *Friends and Neighbors* show."

"Wha . . . why would I want to do that?" asked Suzanne.

Paula grabbed her hand. "Because you're so fun and spunky. And after reading all those tea columns you wrote for the *Bugle* I got supremely jealous. I thought to myself, I just have to invite Suzanne on to be a guest DJ."

"I can't be a DJ," Suzanne sputtered.

Paula gave another throaty laugh. "Sure you can, darling."

"For one thing, I don't know the first thing about how to run a control board," Suzanne protested. "There are buttons to push and headsets to wear and . . ."

"That's why we have a producer," said Paula. "A lovely and very helpful man by the name of Wiley VonBank. He can teach you everything you need to know in about five minutes flat."

Suzanne was far from convinced. "But what would I say? What would I talk about?"

"Just be yourself," said Paula. "Talk about recipes, talk about tea. Take call-ins from listeners. That's what the show is really about anyway." Paula gave Suzanne a sideways look. "Of course, there'd be plenty of opportunity to shamelessly plug the Cackleberry Club, too."

That caught Suzanne's attention. "Really? And the Quilt Trail?"

Paula nodded.

"And my big Halloween party this Sunday night?" *Or am I pushing it?*

Paula lifted her shoulders in a shrug. "Sure, why not."

"I suppose I could give it a shot." Just like imported dark chocolate, it was too tempting for Suzanne to turn down.

"Perfect," said Paula. "It's settled then."

Suzanne edged away, wondering how she'd ever be able to fill an entire hour with idle chitchat. On the other hand, she and Toni spent hours in idle chitchat. So maybe . . .

"Everyone!" said Petra, stepping to the center of the room and immediately commanding their guests' attention. "I'd like to introduce Arthur Bunch, the director of the Logan County Historical Society." There was polite applause, and then Petra continued. "Arthur has graciously agreed to tell us a little about the historical society, our exciting Quilt Trail event, and the society's collection of over one hundred antique quilts."

Then Arthur stepped to the center of the room, ducked his head, and began his talk.

"How long is he going to drone on, anyway?" Toni asked. She and Suzanne were sitting in the kitchen, picking away at a plate of leftover scones, slathering on altogether too many calories' worth of Devonshire cream.

"Probably twenty minutes or so," said Suzanne. "You're not interested in quilts?"

Toni shrugged. "Only when they're on my bed, keeping me all warm and snuggy."

"Such an old-fashioned gal," Suzanne chided. "Dedicated to the home arts."

"Hey," said Toni, "I'm into home arts. Don't I got a picture above my bed? In my home?"

"A photo of George Clooney cut from the pages of *In-Style* magazine doesn't count."

Toni gave a slow wink. "It counts for me, cookie."

WHEN the applause sounded that marked the end of Arthur Bunch's talk, Suzanne propelled herself back out to the café.

"I just want to remind everyone," she said, "we have Quilt Trail brochures in case you want to take the tour. Plus there are some gorgeous quilt squares for sale in the Knitting Nest and a nice selection of quilting books in the Book Nook."

Suzanne quickly made the rounds of each table, handing out Quilt Trail brochures, then retired to the Book Nook where she met up with Bunch, who was beaming.

"I think my talk went exceedingly well," said Bunch.

"Couldn't have gone better," Suzanne agreed. "Do you know . . . how is the Quilt Trail going?"

"So far so good," said Bunch, then grimaced. "As long as nobody dwells on last night's tragic incident."

"Have the sites reported a lot of visitors?" Suzanne asked, trying to skip over Bunch's mention of last night. The less said the better.

"The sites that have reported in are quite pleased," said Bunch. "Of course, the real test will be this weekend."

"For sure," said Suzanne, deciding this might be the perfect time to pass out a few of her specially designed recipe bookmarks. Except when she reached for them, the too-tall pile she had stacked on the counter suddenly collapsed and slid all over the place.

"Let me help," said Bunch, scrambling to pick up the fluttering cards, his knees popping from the effort of bending down.

"Got too much going on," Suzanne muttered.

"A busy time," agreed Bunch. "The Quilt Trail, your tea today . . ."

"Halloween on Sunday," said Suzanne.

"The upcoming election," Bunch added.

Now it was Suzanne's turn to make a face.

"I hate the idea that Mayor Mobley's running unopposed," she told Bunch. "And poor Sheriff Doogie has to contend with Bob Senander." She paused, tamping her cards into a neat stack. "I worry that if Doogie doesn't solve these two crimes, he might not get reelected."

Arthur Bunch looked suddenly serious. "Come November second, we're going to have a couple of hotly contested races on our hands. You realize, one group in town is scrambling to find another mayoral candidate."

"Seriously?" said Suzanne. "Who have they got in mind?"

Bunch narrowed his eyes, thinking. "I've heard Gene Gandle's name mentioned."

"Say what?" said Suzanne, shaking her head. "The reporter at the *Bugle*? Whoa. Couldn't he simply slant the media in his favor?"

"Maybe," said Bunch. "You know, I've been asked to be one of the election judges this year, so I'm watching this whole thing fairly closely. Judges are tasked with making sure everything's fair and square, that nobody gets into the voting booths to upset things, that everyone gets a chance to vote on election day, and that ballots are handled properly."

"Thank goodness for that," said Suzanne, thinking that Bunch would probably be diligent to a fault. Then she said, "So, are voting booths and ballots and things usually handled properly?"

Bunch gave a wry grin. "That's what I'm about to find out."

But Suzanne was only half listening to his answer. Because she was suddenly picturing the blue key card that Doogie had found in her backyard. The one he'd told her probably belonged to the courthouse.

Could the key card somehow be related to the election? After all, the voting booths are stored in city hall.

It was an intriguing thought. And so Suzanne asked herself the next logical question.

Could someone have snuck in to tamper with the voting machines? And then something went wrong?

Maybe it wasn't possible to rig the machine so Mobley would come up as winner. So then . . . this person, the killer, presumably, had resorted to murder?

And could this someone be Allan Sharp—or even Mobley himself?

CHAPTER 16

"How are you guys doing tonight?" Suzanne asked.

Mocha Gent lifted his head and peered over the gate of his box stall. Next door to him, his neighbor Grommet the mule did the same thing. An even bigger guy, but awfully sweet natured.

"Who wants to go for a ride?" she asked.

Grommet swished his tail and gave a rough stomp. Then he turned his broad gray back on Suzanne and went back to sifting through tasty tendrils of alfalfa in his hayrack. Riding? A saddle on his back? Excuse me?

"Looks like it's just you and me," said Suzanne. She stood on her tiptoes to put Mocha's bridle on, then led him out of his stall. She adjusted the leather strap behind his ears, then slid her hand down the full length of the horse's neck. Slipping a red-and-black-striped saddle blanket on his wide back, Suzanne followed up with a well-worn mahogany brown saddle that seemed to gleam against his chestnut coat. The aged leather squeaked appealingly as Suzanne and Mocha played their little game of cinch-up. She pulling the cinch tight, while he rapidly sucked in air, trying to expand his stomach. Finally, when a happy state of detente had been achieved, Suzanne fastened the cinch and led him outside.

She stood for a few moments in the farmyard, gazing at the white clapboard farmhouse where the Ducovnys lived. Light spilled from its windows making it look cozy and inviting, a perfect little rural Kodak moment. Then Suzanne lifted her gaze to the blue black night sky where a lopsided white moon glowed on the horizon, looking like a ripe honeydew melon that was missing a slice. By Halloween that moon would be full. The hunter's moon. A portent of winter and freezing temps.

Placing her left foot in the stirrup, Suzanne sprang onto the horse's back and settled in comfortably. Mocha was a big sweetheart of a beast who loved chugging along a trail or cantering through an open field. Tonight there was just enough time for a quick ride around the perimeter of Suzanne's fields. After all, she still had places to go, people to see.

Giving a nudge with her heels and a quick flick of the reins, Suzanne urged Mocha into a fast trot. As they bounced along, Suzanne surveyed the farmland she owned. It had been an investment that Walter had proposed to her several years ago. When she'd put up a sort of pro forma resistance to the idea, worrying about purchase price, he'd teased her with the old adage, "They're not making any more land that I know of."

Now she was happy she owned it. Not just because the land had held its value, but because it gave her a genuine sense of pleasure, of being connected to the earth. She enjoyed looking over the undulating fields of soybeans, alfalfa, and corn as they sprouted, grew, and flourished, even if she wasn't the one doing the actual farming.

Even standing in the kitchen of the Cackleberry Club this morning, she had gazed out the back window and smiled at what was now an ocean of pale wheat and gold, stretching as far as the eye could see.

As Mocha pranced toward the stand of oak, sumac, cedars, and buckthorn that separated the farm fields from the backyard of the Cackleberry Club, an owl let loose his low, mournful hoot.

The sound momentarily startled Suzanne, then she decided it might be a perfect sound effect for their Halloween party this Sunday night. All the decorations were set, but she still needed something to tease the guests as they picked their way through the corn maze. Something a little more low-key and sophisticated than the cassette tape of bloodcurdling screams Toni had offered.

There was, of course, a lot more to be done for the upcoming party. Like putting up a giant tent, getting the fire pits in place, and pinning down a few games. Thankfully, she had her costume designed, as well as a neat little one-act play that should come as a terrific surprise to everyone!

As they clopped back toward the barn, in horsey cooldown mode, Suzanne glanced at her watch again. She had just enough time to brush Mocha, give him a fortifying cup of oats, then run home and take a quick shower.

Chuck Peebler's visitation was being held tonight at the Driesden and Draper Funeral Home. Which, sadly, was a place she was getting to know all too well.

"DON'T you just expect Emily Dickinson to step out onto that front porch?" Suzanne asked, nodding at the funeral home. "Wearing a velvet cape and gazing mournfully into the night?"

"I'm thinking more along the lines of Alfred Hitchcock," Toni replied.

They were standing on the sidewalk, gazing at Kindred's oldest and grandest clapboard structure. The muted gray funeral home was set well back from the street, guarded by a green moat of manicured lawn. Pointed-arch windows, like highly expressive eyebrows, stretched across the front of the building. The roofline was a visual joyride of turrets, finials, and balustrades. Though the architecture was a crazy combination of American Gothic and Victorian that shouldn't have worked, it did sort of work, conveying a sense of elegance and foreboding all at the same time.

"Ready to go in?" Suzanne asked.

"As ready as I'll ever be and still breathing," Toni replied. She'd changed into more formal attire for tonight: black cowboy shirt, slacks, and boots. Suzanne had selected her black funeral suit. It wasn't funereal per se, just an outfit she'd worn to several funerals in a row. Now it hung in the back of her closet, a respectful distance from her blue jeans, camisoles, and shift dresses.

Climbing the front steps, Suzanne and Toni pushed open the large oak door and were immediately assaulted by the mingled scent of florals and chemicals.

"Eeeyew," said Toni, wrinkling her nose and turning her head, as if searching for a whiff of fresh air. "Why do all funeral homes smell the same?"

"Because they . . ." began Suzanne. Then she stopped, bagged her terrible thoughts about chemicals and bodies, and amended her words to, "Because they just do."

Driesden and Draper's entryway was a depressing blend of dove gray carpet, drooping velvet draperies, and stuffy-stiff upholstered chairs. A guest book rested atop a heavy oak stand, a small, wobbly table held a lone box of Kleenex tissues. To the left, a large visitation room was thronged with Kindred residents who'd come to pay their last respects to Chuck Peebler. To the right, a second visitation room sat dark and unoccupied. Suzanne supposed that room had been reserved for Deputy Wilbur Halpern, who might even be at this very minute resting in repose in the back embalming room.

"This is awful," Toni breathed, as they peeped into the crowded visitation room and caught sight of the copper-colored casket that held Peebler's remains. "And it's an open coffin, too. I *hate* an open coffin. I don't even like to look at a dead bird, let alone a dead person."

"Just stroll around and keep your eyes down," Suzanne advised. "Look sad and nod at people."

"Are you serious?" said Toni. "That works?"

"Trust me," said Suzanne, who'd garnered more than enough experience at her husband Walter's funeral.

"Gosh, you're a good friend," said Toni, still sounding shaky.

"There's Doogie over there," said Suzanne, catching sight of the sheriff. "Looking as if he doesn't have a friend in the world."

"And he won't," whispered Toni, "if he doesn't solve these two murders!"

Suzanne headed directly for Sheriff Doogie while Toni eased her way around the room. "How are you doing, Sheriff?" she asked, placing her hand on his sleeve.

Doogie gave a perfunctory grimace. "Okay, considering I'm gonna have to attend another one of these darn things in a couple of days." He was referring, of course, to Wilbur Halpern.

"Sheriff," said Suzanne, "have you come up with any more clues on Peebler?" She understood that Peebler's murder must seem secondary to him now, while finding Deputy Halpern's killer was at the top of his list. Still, she had to ask.

"There's one or two things I'm looking into," said Doogie, "but I got so much piled on my plate . . ."

"And there's the election coming up," said Suzanne.

"There's that," allowed Doogie.

"Are you worried?" she asked. Then quickly added, "Because you shouldn't be."

Doogie shook his head in disagreement. "Bob Senander's running against me, and he's got credibility. The man's ex-highway patrol and I guess some women might even consider him a looker, what with all his silver hair. Though I don't think *that* should factor in."

Although it probably does, Suzanne thought.

Doogie looked thoughtful. And worried, too. "But I'll tell you this," he continued, "if I don't solve at least one of these cases, my goose is probably cooked."

"I doubt that," said Suzanne, kindly.

"No," said Doogie. "People want results. I don't give them results, I won't even get elected dogcatcher." He sighed heavily. "Besides, I should be further along on these two cases than I am. I should have figured something out by now. I should *know* who's committing murder in Kindred!"

"Stop it," said Suzanne, "you're obsessing now."

"I know," said Doogie.

"You're the duly elected sheriff," said Suzanne, "not an oracle from on high. You can't just *know* things out of the blue. All you can do is run the best investigation possible and glean clues and information along the way."

"I'm doing that," said Doogie. "Trying to anyway."

"Then I'm confident you'll unravel both of these cases."

"You're the only one," muttered Doogie, as he moved away.

Feeling frustrated, Suzanne watched Doogie melt into the crowd. She wished she could help him, wished she could . . .

"Hey there." A warm whisper was followed by hot breath in her ear.

Suzanne whirled, found Sam Hazelet smiling at her. He looked beyond adorable in his light blue scrubs top worn casually over blue jeans with a suede jacket topper.

"Don't you know you're not supposed to smile at these things?" she told him.

His gaze sobered. "I was smiling at you."

"Well . . . don't," she said, secretly pleased.

"Really?"

"Maybe smile on the inside," Suzanne joked.

"Believe me, I am," Sam told her, lifting one eyebrow.

"Now you're flirting."

"Not true! I'm looking serious, per your instruction."

"Now you're making me laugh," said Suzanne, biting her lower lip.

"How's the dog?" Sam asked. "Scruffy. Scruff."

"A terrific guy," said Suzanne. "Which is why I'm probably going to give him to you."

"Seriously?"

"Sure, I have great faith you'll be a wonderful pet parent. Besides, you could probably use the company, a single guy like you."

"What if I, um, meet someone?"

"You probably meet lots of women in your line of work."

"I mean someone I really care about?"

"I don't know," said Suzanne. "Maybe . . ." She was blushing now. "A blended family? Isn't that the term these days?"

"You two are looking way too cozy," said a throaty, female voice.

They both turned to find Carmen Copeland standing there, smiling at Sam.

"Hi, Carmen," said Suzanne.

"Hello," said Sam.

But Carmen was focused only on Sam. "Lovely to see you again, Dr. Hazelet." She was clad in a snug black dress that screamed evening rather than mourning. Her cleavage, which was prominently displayed, seemed to be edging its way toward Sam. A diamond the size of Mount Rushmore hung from a chunky gold chain.

"How goes the literary world?" asked Sam, being polite. "Must be awfully favorable, since I see your novels all over the place."

"Yes," said Carmen, with a predatory smile. "They are rather popular."

"I keep meaning to pick one up," said Sam.

"No need," said Carmen, moving a step closer to Sam. "I'd be delighted to drop a couple of books by the clinic."

"Kind of you," said Sam.

"Forward," said Suzanne.

"Excuse me?" said Carmen, her jaw going slack as she finally acknowledged Suzanne.

"We need to keep moving forward," said Suzanne. "Sam and I. We're, um, in line to offer condolences."

"Of course," said Carmen, with a disdainful curl of her lip.

* * *

"You two don't like each other much, do you?" asked Sam. "You were both acting like those weird frilled lizards, facing off against each other, hissing and spitting away."

"It's not so much dislike as . . ."

"Distaste?" filled in Sam.

"Maybe that," said Suzanne, "with a little mistrust thrown in for good measure."

"And you don't trust her with . . . me?"

"Oh please," said Suzanne. "You're your own independent adult person. You can do whatever you . . ." She hesitated, then said, "You can do whatever."

Sam gave her a searching look, his brows knit together. "Is that all we mean to each other? Whatever?"

Suzanne blushed. "Really," she said, "should we even be having this conversation? We're, like, ten feet from a dead body."

"Where should we continue this conversation?" Sam pressed.

"I don't know," said Suzanne. It was way too early for talk this serious, wasn't it?

"I can think of a nice place," said Sam.

Suzanne glanced around, then stepped closer and pressed her shoulder up against his. "I'll bet you can."

ONCE Sam took off for the hospital, Suzanne circled the room, looking to collect Toni. Instead, she noticed that the room seemed filled with electoral candidates, incumbents, and more than a few staff from city hall. And when Suzanne noticed Allan Sharp whispering in Mayor Mobley's ear, she sought out Sheriff Doogie again.

"What if those two clowns had been trying to fix the election?" she asked him. "And Peebler, as mayoral candidate, got wind of it?"

Doogie turned flat eyes on Sharp and Mobley. "It's not easy investigating a town's mayor."

"Then what about Sharp?" Suzanne asked. "What pies does he have his bony fingers in these days? Is there any sort of trail to follow?"

"Only thing I can think of," said Doogie, "is that Sharp was trying to get a parcel of land rezoned so he could build a pizza place and a sandwich shop."

"And he's doing it by the book?"

"Suppose so."

"Can you look at Allan Sharp a little closer?"

Doogie didn't look happy. "Maybe."

Still Suzanne persisted. "Then there's the small matter of Jane."

Doogie rolled his eyes. "I *knew* you were going to bring her up."

"You don't actually believe Jane's connected to any of this, do you?"

Doogie held his ground. "I gotta look at all the angles. Even if they're not pretty or popular with everyone."

"Okay," said Suzanne. Her eyes skittered across the crowd, falling on Carmen, who was now overtly flirting with Lester Drummond. "There's another shady character," Suzanne murmured, meaning Drummond.

"Face it," said Doogie, "you really don't like him."

"No, I don't," said Suzanne, gazing at Drummond's

overdeveloped shoulders, which seemed ready to burst from his black leather jacket. "I really don't."

THIRTY minutes later, Suzanne was strolling down Laurel Lane, walking Baxter and Scruff. They'd fallen into a sort of sniff, shuffle, stop, then sniff again routine. A little maddening for Suzanne, but highly desirous to her two canine companions.

"C'mon you guys," Suzanne urged, "I hereby declare that sniff time is over. So let's pick up the pace and focus on the walking portion of the evening. And try to get home and in bed before midnight."

Both dogs stopped to stare at her with furrowed brows and expressions of dismay. Did she not understand the correlation between sniffing and happiness? Did she not understand a canine's primary sensory pleasure?

Pausing in a dark spot to scope out a bed of withered hostas, the dogs tugged urgently at their leashes. Suzanne sighed, then relented, giving them the latitude they needed. While off to her left, a car, running without its lights, slid slowly into the intersection.

Car trouble? Or up to no good? she wondered, tugging hastily on the leashes and quickly shepherding her pups down the street where they could stand under a friendly spill of light from a streetlamp. The car moved slowly on and Suzanne and her charges hurried for home.

Probably not a good idea to be out wandering around, she decided. Especially in the wake of two murders.

Back home, doors locked, lights on, leashes stowed, dogs happy, Suzanne wandered into the kitchen and poured herself a glass of orange juice. Ever since she'd traded words with Sam tonight, she'd been in a state of emotional flux.

Should she get involved with him? Or shouldn't she?

She took a sip of juice, decided for about the hundredth time that after their little snuggle party Tuesday night she was *already* involved.

For better or worse? And all that implied?

Wandering back through the house, still sipping and ruminating, Suzanne was drawn to Walter's old office. Though she was pretty sure she'd be cool about the whole thing, a rush of sadness suddenly swept over her when she stepped inside. Everything that screamed Walter was still in place in this office. His Tiffany pen set, his books on fly tying, photos of him fly-fishing in Canada, even a framed poster from a long-ago Eric Clapton concert.

Maybe, Suzanne decided, it was time to pack some of these things away. Turn this place into a cozy library or music room.

Or a home office for me.

But before she did any packing and redecorating, there was one thing she wanted to look for.

Suzanne sat down at Walter's desk, paused for a moment as the cushy chair yielded to her, then slid open the top drawer on the left. It was Walter's kookaloo drawer, basically a junk drawer, and it was jammed with pens, batteries, sunglasses, old Juicy Fruit gum, a magnifying glass, and even a half-eaten Salted Nut Roll. Suzanne grabbed the petrified nut roll, tossed it into the trash can, and heard it land with a hard thud.

Then she continued rifling through the odd stamps, postcards, and year-old receipts until she found what she was looking for. A white key card. She grabbed it, held it in her hand, then tapped it against the top of the desk. It was a souvenir they'd kept from a weekend splurge at the Edgewater East in Chicago.

Carrying the key card into the kitchen, Suzanne dug around in her own catchall drawer, pawing through twine, old Christmas seals, notepaper, paper clips, and packets of colorful beads, until she found what she was looking for. A small box of tempera paints.

Laying the key card flat on the counter, she took a paintbrush, dipped it into one of the paint vials, and making broad swipes, very carefully colored the key card light blue.

CHAPTER 17

PUSHING open one of the oak double doors of Hope
Church, Suzanne and Toni stepped inside one of the oldest houses of worship in Logan County. Light streamed
through stained-glass windows filling the room with
warmth and a kaleidoscope of sparkling colors. Massive
hand-carved wooden arches spanned the width of the white
plaster ceiling.

An usher, wearing a dark suit and a *Peebler for Mayor*
button pinned to his lapel, hastily handed memorial cards
to Suzanne and Toni.

"Darn," said Toni, as they strolled down the center aisle,
"I wish I'd worn my Peebler button, too. It would have
been a nice tribute."

Suzanne scanned the church, noting that it was barely
filled. "Where do you want to sit?" she asked. "Aisle? Farther in?"

"Not the aisle," said Toni, looking nervous. Like most
folks, Toni preferred to be as far away from a rolling coffin
as humanly possible.

They edged their way into a pew and sat down on a hard
bench just as Agnes Bennet, the organist in the choir loft,
began pumping away. She was a tiny woman, a septua-
genarian who'd been the church organist for almost fifty

years. Even though she seemed the size of a child when seated at the enormous pipe organ, her legs pumped up and down with the athletic skill of an NFL quarterback. Fantasia in C Minor filled the church with a sumptuous sound making it feel as if the Lord himself was bearing witness.

"Not too many people showed up," Toni whispered.

Suzanne glanced toward the front of the church and gave a nod. "Mobley and his flunky Allan Sharp are here," she whispered back.

"Jerks," said Toni. Then, feeling guilty at her uncharitable remark, she quickly dropped her head and made the sign of the cross.

Glancing down at the memorial card she'd been handed, Suzanne stared at the fuzzy photo of Peebler. Under the photo, in a sort of Gothic script, the years of his life were defined by a dash between his birthday and his . . . what would you call it? His death day? Suzanne shivered, just as the doors at the back of the church swung open and something metallic bumped across the sill.

Suzanne and Toni scrambled to their feet, along with the rest of the mourners. Then, from the back of the church, six pallbearers began to wheel the copper-colored coffin, blessedly sealed today, up the center aisle. A spray of white roses jiggled on top, a final floral tribute to the man who probably would have been elected Kindred's mayor.

When the procession reached the altar, Peebler's coffin was jockeyed back and forth and angled next to a half dozen floral arrangements that had been hastily brought over from the funeral home.

"So sad," Toni murmured. "You see that wreath with the miniature . . ."

"Golf club," said Suzanne, nodding. Golf had been

one of Peebler's passions. Now he'd gone to that great fairway in the sky. Or could his poor soul be stuck in a sand trap?

As Suzanne shook her head to clear it, Reverend Strait entered the chancel. His salt-and-pepper hair seemed to reflect the light that seeped through the stained-glass windows on either side of the altar. As he began to intone, "The Lord is my shepherd, I shall not want," his comforting presence seemed to spread out across the room.

After finishing the Twenty-third Psalm, Reverend Strait went on to deliver a heartfelt speech about Peebler's kindness and his dedication to the community. After touching on Peebler's civic pride and love of golf, Reverend Strait then invited others to come up and share their thoughts and recollections.

As community members talked about Peebler in glowing terms, Suzanne noted that no one mentioned Peebler's attraction to strippers or his frequent visits to Hoobly's. Like most tributes to the dead, previous sins were rarely mentioned.

A final blessing was delivered, then the gentle strains of Sarah McLachlan's "I Will Remember You" rolled out from the organ, a cue that the service had concluded.

The casket rolled back down the aisle on clacking wheels, the six pallbearers all looking decidedly serious. Suzanne and Toni waited until the church was practically empty, then stood up and edged toward the aisle.

"You okay?" Suzanne asked.

"Oh yeah," said Toni. "At least the service didn't last an eternity, like some do."

"Interesting choice of words," Suzanne observed. They walked slowly down the aisle and out into a cool, cloudy day where mourners milled about on the sidewalk, talking with each other in a low buzz.

"Too bad Petra had to hold down the fort," said Toni. "She would have liked this, the music and all. And wasn't it lucky that Kit was able to pinch-hit for us?"

"Just as long as Kit doesn't ask us to fill in for her," said Suzanne, as they pushed their way through the crowd.

Toni stared at Suzanne for a long moment, then a wry smile lit her face. "That *would* be something. Us working the stage at Hoobly's!"

"Kit's a good kid," said Suzanne. "I just hope she starts to see the upside of working a regular day job and changes her mind about dancing." They'd reached her car and Suzanne walked around to the street side, ready to climb in.

"It's nice you call it dancing," observed Toni, "instead of stripping. You're always so ladylike and . . ." Her words were chopped off as a rattling pickup truck suddenly careened out of nowhere!

"Suzanne! Watch out!" Toni screamed, as the beater bore down upon her, almost clipping the back end of Suzanne's Taurus.

Then Mike O'Dell jumped from his truck, eyes blazing and his face twitchy with anger. "You crazy witch!" he screamed at Suzanne. "You sicced the sheriff on me!"

Shocked beyond belief, Suzanne took a step backward just as a brave Toni barreled around the front of the car and flung herself at O'Dell. "What are you *talking* about?" Toni demanded.

O'Dell ignored Toni completely. She was nothing more than a buzzing gnat to him as he continued his tirade at Suzanne. "You think just because a man has a crossbow that makes him a killer!"

Suzanne stepped out from behind Toni. "This is neither the time nor the . . ."

But Mike O'Dell was just getting started. "And then you think I'd go and kill a *deputy*? Are you crazy!" Tiny bits of spittle flew from his mouth like a rabid dog. "You take me for some kind of fool?"

Suzanne threw back her shoulders and held up a hand. "Now just back off, mister!" she told him, in a stern voice.

"I oughta sue you for slander!" O'Dell shrilled. "For conjuring up a crazy pack of lies!" He turned on Toni now. "And you! Spreading rumors and lies about Sasha. You're just jealous! Jealous your own husband would rather watch an exotic dancer than spend an evening with you!"

"Enough!" Suzanne yelled. A small crowd of people had begun to gather on the sidewalk, transfixed by the shouting match that was taking place.

Suddenly Sheriff Doogie's voice echoed from across the street. "Hey!" he shouted, his voice sounding like a bullhorn. "O'Dell! What the Sam Hill are you up to?" Then Doogie came steamrolling across the street, his face flushed pink and his anger palpable as he planted himself directly in front of Mike O'Dell. He was so close, Suzanne noted, that the wide brim of Doogie's Smokey Bear hat nearly poked O'Dell in the eye.

"What's your beef?" Doogie asked, putting hands on both hips.

Mike O'Dell didn't back down and he didn't bat an eye. "And *you*, Sheriff! I sure don't appreciate you poking around my farm or asking snide questions all over town, neither. Because I didn't *do* anything!"

"You're disturbing the peace right now," said Doogie, sounding amazingly calm. "Harassing two citizens."

"I got a right to say my piece," snarled O'Dell.

"Not right now you don't," Doogie warned. "Not in front of a church when a man's being buried."

"You gonna arrest me?" O'Dell huffed.

That did it for Doogie. He pulled himself to his full height, hitched up his utility belt, and thundered, "This is your final warning, O'Dell! One more uncivil word, grunt, or snort and I'll run you in!"

Hate blazed in O'Dell's eyes, but he kept his lips pressed firmly together. He shot one final, withering, dagger-filled glance at Suzanne, then careened away and climbed back into his clunker. There was a high-pitched scream as his engine revved, then O'Dell sped away in a cloud of oil.

"That went well," said Suzanne, half gagging from the exhaust fumes O'Dell's car had spit out. "We all kept calm and resolved our issues."

"Suzanne." Doogie waved a warning forefinger in front of her face. "Don't start with the sarcasm." Then he turned and clumped away.

"Zowie," said Toni, "I wish I could get two men to fight over me like that."

"Yeah," said Suzanne, feeling worn out from all the tension, "it's a rare treat."

"Seriously," said Toni, "are you okay?"

"No harm done, but it looks like we attracted quite an audience."

"Aw," said Toni, glancing back at the hastily dispersing crowd, "they're pretty much wandering off now."

But Suzanne did notice Allan Sharp watching them from a distance, a slight smile pasted on his oily face.

Which made her wonder. Was Sharp somehow involved in these two murders? Had he been delighted by her confrontation with Mike O'Dell? Had he viewed it as a possible misdirection that would shift the investigation away from him? And how could she go about prying information— any information—from Allan Sharp?

"Toni," said Suzanne. "I have to make a quick stop. Can you get a ride to the Cackleberry Club?"

"Sure," said Toni. "No problem."

SUZANNE sped down Main Street, practically running a red light in the process. She sat at the light, tapping her fingers against the wheel, impatient to reach city hall. Before she headed for the Cackleberry Club to help with the lunch crowd and this afternoon's Mystery Tea, she wanted to put her plan into action.

Easing her way into a parking spot outside the large sandstone building, Suzanne bolted up the steps to city hall. Her patent leather heels clicked and clacked at they hit the marble steps, then she was striding purposefully down a cavernous hallway. She passed the DMV office and License Bureau. Then she skidded past Parks and Recreation and the City Planner's office, ending up at the reception area, which for some odd reason, was located at the far end of the building.

An old-fashioned, sixteen-foot-wide wooden counter separated inquisitive visitors, also known as potentially angry citizens, from city workers. An original artifact to the old building, the counter would probably one day end up in Arthur Bunch's collection. For now, it merely served as a barrier that helped contain the mounting stacks of paperwork that sat on every employee's desk. The never-ending pieces of paper crept out of dozens of wooden filing cabinets and tall stacks of paper rested between cramped desks and copier machines. Suzanne wondered where all the computers were, then spotted one, buried beneath mounds of paper.

She cleared her throat. "Excuse me?"

Though there were six desks, only one clerk was working behind the counter. The woman turned, gave a perfunctory smile, and came up to greet her. "Help you?" she said, grabbing for a bottle of Purell on the counter and depressing the pump to give herself a good squirt. She looked wary, as if Suzanne might be there to protest one of the inevitable property tax hikes.

Suzanne reached into her jacket pocket and pulled out a key card, the one she'd painstakingly painted blue last night. She flashed it quickly, then closed her hand around it.

"I understand someone might have lost a key card?" she said, trying to sound casual, though her heart was pumping a few beats faster.

"I'm not sure," the woman said, caution shading her voice, as she continued to rub her hands together.

Like a magician once again revealing an important card, Suzanne tapped the key card against the battered wooden counter. "Has one been reported missing? Because I found this, and I'm pretty sure it's from here."

The woman shrugged. "Maybe. I *might* have heard something about it."

"Do you know who could have lost it?" Suzanne asked.

The woman glanced about furtively. "I hate to get anyone in trouble."

"Listen," said Suzanne, trying to look sincere, "I'm not trying to get anyone in trouble, I'm just trying to be a good citizen."

The clerk reached for the key card. "Give it to me and I'll for sure ask around."

Suzanne whisked the key card back into her pocket. "That's okay, I don't mind hanging on to it. Just call me, okay? If one's reported missing?"

The clerk looked slightly suspicious as she grabbed a pen and paper. "And your name is . . . ?"

"I'm Suzanne. Suzanne at the Cackleberry Club."

CHAPTER 18

THE chalkboard said it all, "Basic breakfast today—daily specials cancelled because of funeral. God bless."

No further explanation was needed. Pretty much everyone in town knew that Chuck Peebler had been buried this morning. They were also hip to the fact that he'd been murdered in the Cackleberry Club's backyard. And if all those juicy details had somehow eluded them, the *Bugle*'s front page headline and inside sidebar stories explained it all in exaggerated detail.

"Doggone that Gene," said Suzanne. Toni had shoved the newspaper into her hands the minute she'd walked in the back door and now she was munching a piece of whole wheat toast while fuming and muttering over the story.

"It's not *that* bad, is it?" Petra asked hopefully. She was standing at her prep table, flouring a big ball of dough and kneading it with her capable hands. Toni was running in and out of the café, delivering the last of the breakfasts and picking up dirty dishes.

"Excuse me," said Suzanne, "but did you see this headline?" She grappled with the pages and held them up. " 'The Butchery Behind the Bake Shop: An Expose of Murder in a Small Town.' "

"Oh dear," said Petra, "that does sound awful."

"Smacks of a pulp fiction title," Suzanne snorted. "Gene must be going for the Pulitzer."

"Or a movie deal," said Toni, popping into the kitchen again. "I can't believe Laura Benchley would let him sensationalize the two murders like that."

"Oh," said Petra. "Laura's out of town this week."

"Which means Gene's in charge," said Suzanne. "Lucky us this was the one week he got to play both muckraker and editor."

"I don't know," said Toni, "I thought Gene made it all sound pretty dang exciting."

Suzanne shook her head. "Gene made it sound like we're the murder capital of the world."

"On the bright side, if there *is* a bright side," said Petra, "people are still flocking here like crazy. We were pretty much full for breakfast."

Suzanne glanced up. "How did that go? I mean, with Kit helping out?"

"Good," said Petra, giving her dough a gentle punch. "A few folks were disappointed we didn't offer our usual Foggy Morning Soufflé, but in the end they settled for scrambled eggs and toast."

"And Kit?" Suzanne asked. Rolling the paper up, she set it down with a smack, then grabbed a blue-and-white-pinstripe apron and tied it around her waist.

"She did great," said Petra, as she maneuvered her rolling pin across her dough, rolling it out to about a one-inch thickness. "That girl has a real talent for dealing with people."

"You can say that again." Toni smirked.

"Be nice," cautioned Suzanne. "And how was she dressed?" Suzanne sincerely hoped Kit hadn't come bouncing in wearing Daisy Dukes and a halter top.

"Very appropriately," said Petra. "Still, that girl could walk around in a plus-size burka and men would swoon." She took a circular cookie cutter and began cutting circles in her dough.

"Then let's just hope Kit wants to keep helping out here," said Suzanne.

"You think we're a good influence on her?" Toni asked.

"Well, *you're* more like Lady Gaga than Emily Post." Suzanne laughed. "But Petra and I . . . hey, we're practically model citizens."

"I could tell a tale or two about you, Suzanne," said Toni, crinkling her eyes.

"Don't you dare," Suzanne murmured.

Toni looked impish now. "About this past Tuesday night?"

"What happened Tuesday night?" asked Petra.

"Nothing!" said Suzanne.

Toni grinned. "Bet you're hoping it'll happen again real soon." She snickered, then grabbed a rag and dashed out to wipe tables.

"Hope what . . . ?" began Petra.

"Nothing," said Suzanne. "Nada, nix, nothing. As they say in *The Wizard of Oz*, pay no attention to the man behind the curtain."

"Ah," said Petra, peering at her closely now. "Is this about you and the good doctor . . . ?"

But Suzanne had already escaped into the café.

"DON'T go spilling the beans, okay?" Suzanne asked Toni. Toni was arranging slices of pie in the glass case, Suzanne was putting a final polish on the silverware in anticipation of lunch.

"I didn't know it was so hush-hush," said Toni, still in a playful mood.

"Please," said Suzanne. "I don't want this to get all over town."

Toni made a zipping motion across her mouth. "Mum's the word, girlfriend. Your sordid little secret's safe with me."

"Thank you," said Suzanne, as the tinkle of the entry-way bell interrupted their conversation.

"Hey," said Toni, a wide smile spreading across her face. "It's the Beck sisters."

Only Donna and Nadine Beck weren't really sisters at all. They were sisters-in-law who'd become best friends once they'd both divorced their respective philandering husbands some twenty years ago. Now well into their sixties, they supplemented their Social Security checks by supplying the Cackleberry Club with wonderful homemade foods.

"Whatcha got?" Suzanne asked, as Donna hefted a large, wicker picnic basket onto a table.

"Hope it's pickles," said Toni, peering in.

"Garlic dill pickles," said Donna, who was small, silver-haired, and compact.

"And are they ever garlicky!" exclaimed Nadine, who was small, silver-haired, and pleasingly plump. "You should get a whiff of our kitchen. Even the cat's giving it a wide berth."

"Perfect," said Suzanne. For some reason, oddball goods were always the most popular items. Whip up a batch of cranberry-pear jam and it disappeared from the shelves instantly. Same thing with sprouted wheat bread and potato rolls. So garlic pickles? Sure to please.

"And I brought pies," said Nadine. "Two apple pies, one pumpkin, and another I call autumn harvest."

"Which is?" asked Toni.

Nadine dug in her basket and pulled out the pie. "A mixture of apples, cranberries, pears, and brown sugar."

"Sounds heavenly," said Suzanne, as she led the ladies toward her sputtering, vibrating, maybe-on-its-last-legs cooler.

PETRA strolled out of the kitchen, just as the first of the luncheon crowd was arriving. "Got some specials for you," she told Suzanne.

Suzanne grabbed a piece of chalk and said, "Go."

"Curried egg salad sandwich," said Petra. "Squash blossom soup and a *croque madame*."

Suzanne printed quickly. "And for dessert?"

"Strawberry rhubarb crumble, chocolate cake with coconut sauce, and seven-layer bars."

"Be still my heart," said Suzanne, who considered herself your basic connoisseur of seven-layer bars.

Petra hesitated for a moment, then said, "Toni told me about your little to-do with Mike O'Dell after the funeral."

"The guy went totally postal," said Suzanne. "Good thing Doogie came along when he did."

"You've got to be more careful, Suzanne," said Petra. "More and more people are figuring out that you're running your own investigation."

"I am careful," said Suzanne. "Really." Then, when Petra flashed a questioning glance, she amended her words to, "I'll *try* to be more careful."

"That really was a pretty nasty article Gene Gandle wrote. If you ask me, Gene's adding fuel to the fire."

"Maybe his article will shake something loose," Suzanne suggested, ever the optimist.

Petra considered that for a moment, then said, "Maybe it'll just make the killer angrier."

"DALE," said Suzanne. Dale Huffington slid onto a stool at the counter. He was a big behemoth of a man, a local guy who worked at the Jasper Creek Prison handling security.

"You serving lunch yet, Suzanne?" Dale asked.

Suzanne nodded. "We sure are. What can I get you?" She poured out a cup of coffee as Dale studied the chalkboard.

"You serving frog legs?" Dale asked, beetling his brow.

"Not that I can recall," said Suzanne.

"What's that on the board then?" Dale asked. He shifted around, his bulk spilling over his straining belt. *"Croque madame?"*

"Croque madame is basically a fancy grilled cheese sandwich with a fried egg on top," Suzanne explained.

"Yeah?" Dale looked like he didn't quite trust her.

"It's sourdough bread, Gruyère cheese, ham, and an egg." *See? Nothing up my sleeve, just regular old ingredients.*

Dale gave a loud guffaw. "Shucks, Suzanne, I thought you were trying to pull a fast one on your customers. Like you did with the scones and clotted cream that time. People don't *really* eat clotted cream, do they?"

Suzanne reached across the counter and patted his hand. "Sometimes, Dale, you just have to live dangerously."

CHAPTER 19

"ONE thing's for sure," said Toni, surveying the café, "it sure doesn't look like a man cave."

Suzanne joined in the fun. "No wide-screen TV, no pool table, no pinups . . ."

"No kegerator," Toni added.

"Just perfect decor for today's Mystery Tea," said Petra, as she came chugging out of the kitchen, carrying two crystal bowls filled with Devonshire cream. "I have to say, Toni, you worked wonders in here."

Lunch had been hastily orchestrated and now all the tables in the café were covered with beige linen tablecloths, with chocolate and burnt orange organza sashes swagged around each chair. Carved white pumpkins filled with dried milkweed pods, bittersweet, and autumn leaves served as centerpieces, and were flanked by cinnamon-colored tapers in wooden holders. Place settings were cream-colored china plates with matching teacups and polished silver. Tiny gold-net favor bags held cinnamon sticks, tea bags filled with persimmon and berry tea, and orange-flavored sugar swizzle sticks.

"It's Halloween, but without the black cat and goblin theme," said Suzanne.

"We're saving all that for Sunday night." Toni grinned.

"That's when we go all-out traditional with ghosts, bats, and a scream-a-ganza party!" She gave a little shiver. "A Halloween to die for."

"Let's hope not," Petra murmured, as the front door opened and a half dozen guests spilled in.

"Lovely as always," declared Mrs. Cleo, peering through the black veil that covered her eyes. Mrs. Cleo was Mrs. Cleopatra Sunderd, a staunch member of the community and a woman who adored dressing up for a proper English tea, albeit a Mystery Tea. Her black pillbox hat was teamed with a wine-colored wool suit. The suit was vintage fifties, but Mrs. Cleo hadn't scoured every thrift store in the county to find her prize, she'd just yanked it from the back recess of her closet.

Suzanne checked their guests' names off her reservation list as Toni escorted them to their tables. When the room was about half full, Suzanne suddenly realized that Julie Crane, today's featured author, was standing right in front of her.

"Welcome, Julie," said Suzanne, giving the girl a welcoming hug. She was thin with gorgeous reddish blond hair, and studious looking in a pair of narrow black glasses that looked both severe and fashionable at the same time.

"This is so exciting." Julie bubbled. "My very first book signing. I've always hoped and dreamed about this, but now it's actually happening!"

"And it's well-deserved at that," said Suzanne. "So . . . we'll have you signing at a table in the Book Nook. In fact, I have your books all arranged."

"Oh my gosh," said Julie, following Suzanne into the Book Nook and gaping at the display that had been created, "it looks so . . . so *professional*."

"That's because you are a pro." Suzanne smiled. "No more amateur status for you, my dear."

Julie plunked herself down at the table, pulled two roller-ball pens from her purse, and grinned. "I'm lucky, you know that?"

"How's that?" asked Suzanne, who was busily rearranging books for a second time.

"To even get published," said Julie. "Palette Press generally handles only academic books written by Darlington College professors, but I kind of snuck in the back door. And now they've started to branch out and embrace other genres in hopes of generating additional revenue."

"All businesses have it tough today," said Suzanne. "Restaurants, little retail shops, service industries, you name it." She took a poster she'd whipped up and placed it to one side of the table. "Do you happen to know Jane Buckley, the museum registrar?"

"Oh sure," said Julie, "she's really sweet. Too bad she's been . . . what would you call it? Marginalized?"

Suzanne suddenly snapped to and focused on Julie. "How's that?"

Julie screwed up her face and said, "Unfortunately, the museum is focusing more on exhibitions by their own studio arts professors and students. There's not much on display anymore that you could classify as traditional museum pieces."

"No paintings?" Suzanne asked. "No sculptures?" She remembered attending an art opening at the Darlington College museum a couple of years ago and being blown away by some tasty Early American paintings, Japanese prints, and some very contemporary sculptures. All kinds of things, in fact.

Julie shook her head. "Not anymore. Not unless they're done by professors or students."

"That's awfully sad," said Suzanne, wondering if Jane Buckley could have gotten some sort of crazy idea in her head. Maybe solicit a couple of important donations to score a coup and save her job? Could have happened.

"Oh," said Julie, "and since I got this book deal, I've been asked to teach a creative writing class."

"You know who taught there last year, don't you?" asked Suzanne. "It was . . ."

"Carmen!" Julie gasped, her eyes suddenly skittering past Suzanne and assuming a slightly stricken look.

"What?" Suzanne squawked, spinning around abruptly only to be confronted by the grinning face of Carmen Copeland. Correction, make that a smarmy, grinning face.

"Well, hellooo," said Carmen, oozing her cool brand of charm.

"You're here . . . for the Mystery Tea?" Suzanne asked.

Carmen dimpled prettily. "Not quite. Fact of the matter is, I was hoping to squeeze in an impromptu book signing with my fellow author here."

Suzanne stared at Carmen, marveling at the woman's chutzpah. Now Julie was a *fellow* author. A couple of days ago Carmen had regarded her as a complete nobody.

"I'm not sure how I'm fixed on books," Suzanne stammered. "And there's not much room for two authors."

"Oh, Julie can squeeze over," said Carmen. "Can't you, dear?"

Julie hesitated for a moment, then said, "Sure. Why not? The more the merrier, I guess."

Let's hope so, Suzanne thought to herself as she rushed into her office to grab the ringing phone. Julie may think she could share an author's table with Carmen Copeland, but Carmen had a tricky way of stealing the spotlight.

"Cackleberry Club," Suzanne said, into the receiver.

There was silence for a few moments, then a woman's voice said, "Suzanne?"

"Yes?"

"This is Beth Ann Morrisey from city hall. We spoke this morning? You stopped by?"

"Oh sure," said Suzanne, suddenly recalling the reluctant clerk. "How can I help?"

"I just wanted to let you know that a key card *was* reported missing."

A tingle of excitement shot up Suzanne's spine. "Really?"

"Yes, indeed," said Beth Ann, "there was a memo about it. I didn't notice it at first because we get a lot of memos."

"Do you, um, know which office?" Suzanne asked. "So I can drop it by? I mean, I wouldn't want to bother you."

"No bother at all. But the card belongs to the downstairs storage area."

"The storage area," said Suzanne. The news didn't exactly trip her trigger. Unless . . .

"That's where they keep the voting booths and all?" asked Suzanne.

"I suppose that would be right," said Beth Ann. "The voting booths and other stuff we only use occasionally."

"Okay," said Suzanne. "Thanks so much." She hung up the phone and stared at the top of her desk where a clutter of magazines edged out invoices and recipe cards. And wondered again if Mayor Mobley or Allan Sharp had tried to tamper with the voting booths. Had tried to fix the election.

Would that explain a dropped key card in her backyard?

Better yet, would putting a bug in Sheriff Doogie's ear send his investigation in their direction?

If the key card Doogie had found worked in that city hall location, would it push him into taking a long, hard look at Mobley or Sharp? Maybe. Possibly. Only one way to find out, of course, and that was talk to Doogie.

Suzanne was still noodling ideas around when she emerged into the café. And was thrilled to find every seat in the house occupied and every woman sipping tea and smiling contentedly. Which made her smile contentedly.

"I see the wicked witch dropped in for a spell," said Toni, as she breezed by, hefting a teapot in each hand.

Suzanne dogged Toni's footsteps and asked, "How's it going?"

"Great," said Toni, "they're all loaded up on Petra's pumpkin-walnut scones with gigantic gobs of Devonshire cream, so everyone's pretty much riding a nice sugar high."

"So time to bring out the tea trays?" asked Suzanne. "Dazzle them with Petra's sandwich and dessert artistry while we introduce a little needed protein?"

Toni nodded. "Better hustle into the kitchen and lend a hand if you can."

"Will do," said Suzanne. But when she scurried into the kitchen, Petra already had her three-tiered, silver trays lined up on the butcher-block table and was just arranging her goodies.

"Can I help?" Suzanne offered.

Petra gave a beatific nod as she arranged madeleines, brownie bites, and lavender tea cakes on the top tier.

Suzanne shook her head in wonderment. "This is gonna be great. Again."

Petra nodded. "I just love it when we go all out for tea. Don't you wish we could do this every day?"

"I think we already are," said Suzanne. She stepped to the sink, washed her hands, and said, "What do you want me to do?"

"Middle tier," said Petra. "Sandwiches."

"Okay," said Suzanne. She looked around for the plastic trays Petra normally used.

"There, over on the shelf," said Petra.

Suzanne grabbed the tray and pulled off the plastic wrap. "So . . . we've got salmon and watercress on rye, cranberry walnut salad on buttered crostini, and . . ."

"Cheese and turkey spirals," finished Petra.

Suzanne carefully arranged the small triangles and spiral sandwiches on each tray as Petra gave an approving nod.

"And chicken tartlets on the bottom," said Petra.

"Perfect," declared Suzanne.

Petra grinned. "You think?"

"I know."

"Then let's carry them out."

Together, Suzanne and Petra each grabbed two tea trays, then bumped out through the swinging door.

"Ladies," said Toni, the minute she saw her cohorts appear, "your tea trays have arrived."

At which point, the entire tearoom erupted in thunderous applause.

"Thank you, thank you," said Suzanne, standing front and center, reprising her role from yesterday, as Petra and Toni scurried to deliver the rest of the tea trays. "And I'd like to remind you that Julie Crane is in the Book Nook signing her new book, *Ghostly Lore and Legends*, along with our own bestselling romance author Carmen Copeland."

One of the guests raised her hand. "Are the authors going to do a short reading?" she asked.

"Yes, they are," said Suzanne, deciding that was the perfect way to integrate Julie's mystery book with the Mystery Tea. Along with the wild card Carmen, of course.

Fifty minutes later, tea sandwiches enjoyed and many cups of tea sipped, the guests began to wander throughout the Cackleberry Club. Some congregated in the Knitting Nest while others found their way into the Book Nook.

Much to Suzanne's delight, they sold a respectable two dozen copies of Julie's book, along with another dozen of Carmen's romance paperbacks.

When there was a slight lull, Carmen gazed at Suzanne and exclaimed in a fawning voice, "Such a cute little book our Julie wrote. There's even a positively spine-tingling story about a place in Deer County called Vampire Valley."

"I think I've been there," said Suzanne.

"Julie and I were chatting," said Carmen, launching into magnanimous mode, "and I think it's just *marvelous* that she's going to be teaching creative writing at Darlington College." Smoothing her form-fitting dress, Carmen added, "I simply can't fit pro bono activities into my hectic schedule anymore."

"You're a busy lady," said Suzanne, hoping Carmen would have the good grace to leave it at that.

Of course she didn't.

"Although I do continue to serve on the Darlington College museum board," Carmen announced, in broad tones. "As you've probably heard, I've amassed quite an art collection."

When Julie managed to look vaguely interested, Carmen added, "I started with outsider art and now I'm seriously into photography and contemporary art. People like Chuck Close, Jim Hodges, and Sigmar Polke."

"I'm impressed," said Julie.

Carmen reached over and patted Julie's hands. "Just think, dear, someday you might be successful, too."

That was enough for Suzanne. She retreated behind the counter and proceeded to tally up the afternoon's sales. Unfortunately, she could still hear Carmen prattling away.

"Do you know," said Carmen, "I'm seriously considering opening a coffee shop in downtown Kindred. Right next to Alchemy Boutique. I even have a name for it . . ." She paused for her dramatic reveal. "The Intelligentsia Café."

Gritting her teeth, Suzanne packaged books, made change, made small talk, and finally made it into the kitchen. There, unhappy and slightly offended, she unloaded to Petra and Toni about Carmen's proposed coffee shop.

"What?" said Petra, outraged. "She's trying to one-up you again, Suzanne! When Carmen got an inkling about your plans for a fine dining restaurant called Crepes Suzanne, she spread it around town that *she* was going to open a restaurant, too. Now she's rattling her saber about starting a coffee shop. The woman is totally outrageous!"

"And guess what she wants to call it," Suzanne said in a sour tone. "The Intelligentsia Café."

"Carmen and intelligentsia?" sneered Toni. "There's a concept at odds with itself. Kind of like army intelligence."

"Or educational TV!" Petra added in a huff.

CHAPTER 20

"Is she gone?" Suzanne asked in a small voice. She'd basically hid out in the kitchen for the rest of the Mystery Tea, wrapping up leftover sandwiches, stacking dirty dishes, rinsing teapots, and puttering around, trying to put things back to normal.

"Carmen's gone," Toni said with a sigh, "along with everyone else. So there's no need to exile yourself anymore."

"I'm sorry Carmen was such a pill," Petra said to Suzanne. "But I know all our guests had a wonderful time, so that should serve as some consolation."

Suzanne popped a leftover brownie bite into her mouth and swallowed it whole. "I feel like I'm back in high school, battling my archenemy and getting rejected by the cheerleading squad."

"Sheesh," said Petra. "I got rejected by the projectionist club. Something about not being able to focus."

Toni set down a tray of dirty dishes, fluffed her hair, and placed her hands on her blue jean–clad hips. "Not to flog a dead horse, but you want to know Carmen's parting words?"

"What?" Suzanne asked through tight lips.

"She said, in that high-and-mighty tone of hers, that when she signs books at Barnes and Noble they always give her a muffin basket."

"I'll drop-kick her a muffin," Petra fumed, "right where she deserves it!"

"Whoa," said Suzanne, touching a hand to her forehead, feeling the stirrings of a nasty headache. "Now we're all letting Carmen get to us." She paused, then drew what she hoped was a deep, cleansing, yoga breath. "At least *I* am."

Petra directed a baleful gaze at Suzanne. "You're right. We're all guilty of being cowed and infuriated by Carmen."

Toni nodded. "She did kind of put us off our feed this last hour or so."

"Time to regroup," said Suzanne.

"Reboot the old hard drive," suggested Toni. "Delete the negativity."

Petra spread her arms wide, waggled her fingers, and pulled each of them close to her. "Bless us, Lord, and bring us peace, understanding, and tranquillity."

"Are we good now?" Toni asked, though she was really asking Suzanne.

Suzanne nodded. "Calm as can be."

Petra straightened up, looking content. But when she glanced out the window and saw how dark it was getting, a tiny bit of worry seemed to return. "The Mystery Tea ran longer than we intended. It's going to be dark by the time we get everything cleaned up."

"Let Joey do it," said Suzanne, glancing at her watch. "He should be here in ten minutes or so."

"You think?" said Petra.

"Sure," said Suzanne. "Let's . . . why don't we grab ourselves a nice hot pot of tea and a plate of leftover tea sandwiches and retreat to the Knitting Nest?"

"Veg out," said Toni, liking the idea.

Petra hesitated for a moment, then said, "Does Keemun tea work for everyone?"

SPRAWLED in the Knitting Nest, the three women sipped tea and nibbled daintily at Petra's sandwiches.

"These cheese and turkey spirals are my favorites," said Toni. "Any more left?"

"Probably two dozen," said Petra, "but you'll have to fetch them yourself 'cause my feet are killing me." She slipped off her well-worn Crocs and wiggled her toes appreciatively against the faded Oriental carpet. "Feels good," she breathed.

"I'll grab 'em," said Toni. "No problem."

"What's that?" asked Suzanne. She'd just noticed a green-and-yellow-striped sweater tucked into the knitting basket next to Petra.

"Oh that," said Petra, reaching down to pull it out. "Just something I was working on for Baxter." She held up a dog sweater with stegosaurus spikes running down the back. "I call it a dogosaurus sweater."

"Oh my gosh, it's absolutely adorable!" exclaimed Suzanne. "Baxter's going to love it!"

"'Course now that you have a second dog, I'll have to knit one for him, too."

"You, my dear, are beyond thoughtful," said Suzanne, giving Petra a hug.

Toni was back a few minutes later armed with more sandwiches. "Joey's here and making fabulous progress," she told them. "Our boy is up to his elbows in soapsuds."

"Wonderful," said Petra, snuggling back into her chair.

"When he's finished in the kitchen, I told him to gather up all the decorations, too," said Toni. She took a bite of sandwich, rolled her eyes in appreciation, then added, "Most of the stuff will work for the Halloween party on Sunday, but we're still gonna need a load of pumpkins."

"For cooking and carving," agreed Petra. "And I was thinking of hollowing out some tiny pumpkins to use as soup bowls."

"Cute," said Toni.

Suzanne let loose a sigh. "We'll have to have Junior call in his pumpkin patch marker, after all."

"When would you want to do a pumpkin run?" Toni asked.

Suzanne thought for a minute. "Maybe . . . tomorrow night?"

"Friday's date night," protested Toni.

"My date is Saturday night," said Suzanne, somewhat self-consciously.

"Then Friday night it is," said Toni.

"Your resolve crumbled awfully fast," Suzanne joked. "You sure you don't want to flip a coin?"

Toni gave a shrug. "Nah, the only date I have this Friday is with Brad Pitt. And he's easy. I can pick him up anytime . . . at the video store."

"Good one," said Petra. "Usually you two are . . ." She stopped, frowned, cocked her head to one side, said, "What's that?"

"If Joey broke another dish . . ." Toni threatened.

Suzanne shook her head. "No, something else." She'd heard a noise, too.

"Town siren," said Petra. They sat like statues, listening to the rising wail.

"That's it," said Suzanne, as the insistent noise continued to build.

"Wonder what disaster's about to befall us now?" asked Toni.

"Maybe a fire," said Petra. "Or . . ." This time she was roused to her feet by the sudden, intense clanging of the church bells next door. "What on earth!"

"It's the tintinnabulation of the bells!" Suzanne exclaimed, borrowing a phrase from Poe.

"The what?" Toni asked, confused.

"It's something bad!" said Petra. "I just know it! The siren's still wailing and now the church bells are ringing like crazy!"

A sudden pounding on the front door lent to the wild cacophony!

"Say what?" Toni screamed. But Suzanne had already leapt to her feet and was through the doorway that was draped with hand-knit shawls, hastening across the café.

"Wait for us!" yelled Petra.

Suzanne fumbled with the latch, then pulled open the front door. She was expecting to find Sheriff Doogie, warning them of some imminent firestorm or bizarre accident. Instead she got Reverend Yoder, from next door's Journey's End Church. Tall and thin, clad in black jacket and slacks, he looked like a vision of the grim reaper. Except his kindly gray eyes and gentle demeanor belied that.

"There's been a breakout!" Reverend Yoder gasped.

Suzanne hesitated a split second, trying to wrap her mind around this. "You mean at the prison?"

Reverend Yoder bobbed his head, looking grim.

A chill touched Suzanne's heart. It was everyone's worst nightmare finally come to pass. The Jasper Creek Prison, that most of the town had opposed, held hundreds of dangerous inmates. And now some were on the loose!

Then Suzanne's eyes widened and she suddenly focused on Reverend Yoder. Swaying unsteadily on his feet, he let loose a raspy moan, then lifted a thin, trembling hand and held it to his heart.

Petra, barefoot but with her chef's hat balanced atop her head, caught up to Suzanne and said, "He doesn't look so good," just as Joey came flying out of the kitchen.

"Oh man!" exclaimed Joey, putting both hands on top of his head and looking scared. "Is he okay?"

"Help me," said Suzanne. She wrapped an arm around Reverend Yoder, while Petra got on the other side. Together, they led him, stumbling badly, to a chair.

"I . . . you ladies need to . . ." Reverend Yoder muttered, almost feverishly. Then he seemed to forget where he was.

"I'll get a glass of water," Toni volunteered.

Reverend Yoder's brows knit in pain as he pressed both hands flat against his chest.

"It's his heart," said Suzanne.

"Look at his skin tone, he's positively ashen," exclaimed Petra. "This is not good, not good at all!"

Suzanne knelt down, pulled up the man's sleeve, and placed two fingers on his pulse. It was weak and thready.

Reverend Yoder's eyes fluttered open.

"Reverend Yoder," said Suzanne. "Can you hear me?" No response. "Reverend, I think you're having a heart attack."

His eyes closed, but he managed to nod his head.

"Is he gonna die?" wailed Joey.

"Ambulance," Suzanne snapped to Toni. "Call 911. Reverend Yoder has to get to an emergency room immediately!" She knew the EMTs could administer lifesaving oxygen and chest compressions on the way to the hospital.

Toni sprang for the counter and grabbed the phone. She punched in numbers, then waited. A few seconds later, she screamed, "Doggone! Nobody's picking up!"

"Try again!" Suzanne ordered.

"Nobody's answering because of the prison breakout!" said Petra, her eyes wide with fear.

"No answer!" Toni screamed. "It's like we're completely cut off!"

"The circuits must be overloaded," said Suzanne. "Everybody calling at once, everybody in a blind panic."

"Then *we* have to take the reverend to the hospital," said Petra. "No sense waiting for an ambulance that might never come!"

Grabbing her keys off the back counter, Toni said, "I'll back up my car. It's the fastest and most comfortable."

"Joey," said Suzanne, "get Petra's clogs from the Knitting Nest, then come help us."

Minutes later, the three of them managed to half walk, half carry Reverend Yoder out the door and over to Toni's car. Though her fenders and wheel wells were rimmed with rust and the chassis was edging into beater territory, the engine was tuned to perfection, thanks to the fine hand of Junior Garret.

"Get him in the backseat!" said Toni.

Suzanne and Petra slid Reverend Yoder into the backseat. Though his eyes fluttered open occasionally, his respiration seemed to have gotten worse.

"Everybody in!" screamed Toni.

Petra slid in next to Reverend Yoder, while Suzanne jumped in to ride shotgun.

"What about me?" yelled Joey.

"You lock up!" Suzanne yelled back. "In fact, the smart thing to do is just stay put!" She turned to Toni, said, "Go."

CHAPTER 21

JAMMING the gas pedal to the floor, Toni fishtailed out of the parking lot, tires spinning and spitting gravel like crazy. When she hit paved road, she laid a few yards of rubber, then launched like a rocket.

"Easy, easy," cautioned Suzanne. "Ease it down to mach one. Don't get us all killed!"

"I know what I'm doing," said Toni, pushing her ride even faster. "I started drag racing when I was fourteen."

"You can't get a license until you're sixteen," Suzanne chided.

"Who said I had a license?" Toni replied, managing to come to a quick halt at a stop sign, right before a delivery truck whizzed through the intersection. Then she sped up again and spun her car into a tight turn, bumping down River Road.

"Not many cars on the road," said Suzanne, her eyes casting about. Her voice was tense and terse.

"We're not that far from the prison," said Petra. "Maybe everybody's hunkered in, worried to death."

"You think Doogie is out there rounding up escapees?" Toni asked, grinding gears and hunching over her steering wheel.

"I fervently hope so," said Suzanne. "And just in case

somebody lunges out at us, don't be polite and stop, okay?"

"No stops, no problem," agreed Toni. She peered into the rearview mirror. "How's he doing?" she asked Petra.

"Sleeping, I think," said Petra.

"Or comatose," Suzanne murmured, "from lack of oxygen."

"Oh dear," fretted Petra.

"You think he's always had a bum ticker?" asked Toni.

Suzanne ignored Toni's remark. "Okay, the hospital's just ahead on your right. Go easy on the corner."

"I got it, I got it," said Toni, slaloming into the turn and tap-tap-tapping her brakes.

"Now up that ramp," Suzanne coached.

Toni bounced up the ramp that led to the ER entrance and rocked to a stop. The three women exhaled collectively, then clambered out. Suzanne immediately dashed into the hospital to get help.

Fifteen seconds later, an orderly and a nurse rushed out, pushing a gurney, white sheets fluttering like mad. Reverend Yoder was loaded on and carted inside. The three women, in classic anticlimax mode, headed slowly for the waiting room.

"What are his chances?" asked Petra.

Toni shrugged. "Dunno."

"I have an ominous feeling," said Petra.

"Don't," said Suzanne. "We've had too many deaths already."

They sat there for another three or four minutes. Finally, Toni pulled out an emery board and proceeded to tune up her nails. Petra picked up a magazine.

"What are you reading?" Suzanne asked. She was so nervous, she could barely sit still.

Petra glanced sideways at her. "One of those magazines aimed at *mature* women."

"Menopause and You," snorted Toni.

"Oh yeah," said Suzanne. "I see they got Diane Keaton's picture on the cover, wearing a turtleneck." Suzanne sat for a few more seconds, then stood up so fast her knees made little popping sounds. "I can't stand this anymore. I'm going to go see how he is."

"Do you think we should call someone?" Petra asked, closing her magazine.

"What do you mean?" asked Toni. "Like a wife?"

"He wasn't married," said Petra.

"Well, we know he doesn't have any *kids*," said Toni.

"Maybe . . . a church elder?" asked Petra.

Toni snapped her fingers and pointed at her. "Great idea. You do that while Suzanne and I scope things out."

But when they got to the ER bay, they were met with some resistance.

"You can't go in there," a hospital security officer informed them. He was early twenties, pudgy, with a fringe of dank blond hair that fell into his eyes.

"But we were just *in* there," Toni argued.

The guard shook his head. "Sorry. I've got my orders."

"Hey," said Toni, "we're the good guys, the cavalry coming to the rescue. We brought Reverend Yoder in."

"We just want to check on his status," said Suzanne.

"No admittance," the guard said, this time with more force.

"Give me a break," said Toni. "You think we look like dangerous escaped prisoners?"

The guard glared at her. "I don't know."

"You don't know what convicts look like?" asked Toni. "Sheesh."

"I got my orders," said the guard. "The hospital's worried that escaped prisoners might come here looking for drugs."

"Or they might stop at Hoobly's looking for a date," Toni snapped.

"Suzanne!" called a male voice. It was Sam. Sam Hazelet. And he was striding down the hall, waving at them.

"Thank goodness," said Toni. "Someone who's *really* in charge."

Suzanne and Toni slipped by the guard, who still seemed to regard them with suspicion.

"I heard you brought him in," said Sam. "Good work."

"How's he doing?" asked Suzanne.

"Not so good," said Sam. "But not so bad, either."

Toni peered at him. "So which is it? Maybe yes or maybe no?"

"Is he going to die?" Suzanne asked, cutting to the chase.

"Probably not," said Sam. "You got him here pretty fast, and now he's on thrombolytic drugs and we're considering percutaneous coronary intervention."

"Translation please?" said Toni.

"He'll probably make it, but he's sustained serious damage," said Sam.

"Can we see him?" Suzanne asked.

"Not right now," said Sam. "We're still running tests, looking at serum cardiac biomarkers and various things." When he saw her disappointment, he said, "You know what? You guys did good. You brought him here, and now we're going to take great care of him. So, please, go home and lock yourselves in. Tell your guard dogs to stay alert and keep the phone nearby. I'll call in a couple of hours and give you a complete update. Okay?"

Suzanne nodded. "Okay."

"Everet," Sam called to the guard, "will you escort these ladies to their car?"

"We have to get Petra first," said Suzanne.

"Get Petra and then have Everet walk you out," said Sam. "And, for gosh sakes, be careful driving out there. We don't want you getting carjacked!"

"ARE you up for a glass of wine?" Suzanne asked Toni. They'd dropped Petra at her house, then waited as she scurried in, locked the door, and gave them the high sign. Then Suzanne had driven Toni back to her house where they were going to spend the night together. Safety in numbers, or so the saying went.

Toni leaned back in the chair and placed her hands behind her head. "You're not talking Three Buck Chuck, are you?"

Suzanne's mouth twitched at the corner. "After the day we've had, I think we deserve a lot better. I have a nice bottle of Petite Syrah you might enjoy."

"Let's do it," Toni enthused.

"And some food," suggested Suzanne.

"Now you're talking," said Toni, as she followed Suzanne into the kitchen, followed by Baxter and then Scruff.

Suzanne grabbed the wine from her wine cooler, popped the cork, and took two Riedel glasses from the cupboard. She poured out two fingers of wine in each glass and handed one to Toni.

Toni swirled the red wine in her glass, then said, "We need a toast."

"Okay." Suzanne raised her glass tentatively. "Got a suggestion?"

"Better days?"

"I'll drink to that." Suzanne took a small sip, allowing the wine to slide across her tongue. Excellent. Lush and rich with a hint of oak. "Now for the food. Besides chocolate, what would tickle your tummy tonight? Something light or something heavy?"

"Definitely heavy," said Toni. "I can always diet tomorrow."

"You don't need to diet at all," Suzanne chided. "You need to put on a few pounds."

"You think?" said Toni.

"What's your waist size?"

Toni frowned. "Maybe twenty-five?"

"And your weight?"

Toni shrugged. "Hundred? Hundred and three?"

"See?" said Suzanne. "You got maybe a BMI of eighteen."

"Huh?"

"You have the same body mass index as an underfed gerbil."

"That's good, huh?"

"Are you kidding? That's great."

Toni took another sip of wine, then her grin slowly slipped from her face. "Reverend Yoder was skinny and he had a heart attack."

"You make a good point," said Suzanne, who was already heating water and had just grabbed a package of pasta. "So maybe we shouldn't have fettuccine Alfredo after all?"

Toni grimaced. "But I love your Alfredo!"

"Okay," said Suzanne, "but I'll use half-and-half instead of heavy cream."

"Gotta compromise somewhere," agreed Toni.

JUST as Suzanne was scraping up the last bits of Alfredo sauce in her bowl, the phone rang.

"Sam," said Toni, who was sprawled out on the living room floor, snarfing the last of her supper and dangling cream-coated noodles to both dogs.

Turns out, Toni was right. It was Sam.

"So how are you doing?" he asked. "Locked in all nice and tight?"

"Hopefully," said Suzanne. "So what's going on out there? You hear any news?"

"Just that it was four prisoners who broke out," said Sam, "not an entire cell block, like first reported. Apparently, they stowed away in a delivery van."

"Good security they've got out there."

"And resourceful prisoners," said Sam.

"How's Reverend Yoder doing?"

"Better," said Sam. "Much better, thanks in part to your quick action."

"We did what we had to," said Suzanne. "And Toni will be delighted. She practically qualified for the Indy 500."

"There's an entire contingent from the reverend's church that's here right now," said Sam. "Praying for him." He paused. "Couldn't hurt."

"I definitely concur, Doctor. And how are *you* doing?"

"Tired," he said. "Heading home in another ten minutes."

"One heck of a crazy day," said Suzanne.

"That it was," breathed Sam. "Okay, Suzanne. Take care, love ya." And then he was gone.

Suzanne stood there, gaping at the phone. Had Sam realized what he'd just said to her? Love ya? A tingle rippled through her, then she forced herself to calm down. People said "love ya" all the time to family and friends. On the other hand, love was a really, really good word, right? Sure it was.

"You've got a funny look on your face," said Toni, as Suzanne wandered back into the living room. "Something wrong?"

"Actually, things have been put kind of right."

"Reverend Yoder's better!" exclaimed Toni.

"Toni, lots of things are better."

BY ten thirty they were zonked on pasta, wine, chocolate chunk cookies, and a quartet of *Sex and the City* reruns.

"Man, I love Samantha's saucy attitude," said Toni, stifling a yawn. "She totally cracks me up."

"She's a pistol," Suzanne agreed, getting up to turn out lights. "Dogs were out a half hour ago, so I think it's time we head for bed."

Toni stretched languidly. "I'm so bushed, nothing could keep me awake."

A loud metal clank suddenly echoed from the backyard.

"Wha . . . ?" said Toni, going wide-eyed, as Suzanne held up a hand.

Tiptoeing to the window, Suzanne pulled back the drapery and peered out. Her backyard was silent and empty. Except, of course, for the holes that Baxter had excavated. And that his new compadre Scruff had helped scoop out a little deeper.

"See anything?" Toni asked, padding up behind her.

"No, I . . . doggone!" said Suzanne.

"What?"

"Motion detector light just flashed on. The one over the garage."

"Somebody pussyfooting around out here?" asked Toni. Her voice sounded tremulous and worried.

"Not that I can see." Suzanne pressed her nose to the window, feeling the coolness just beyond the pane of glass. "Oh wait. Something knocked over my garbage cans."

"Something? Or someone?" asked Toni.

"I don't know." Then, when she saw the worry on Toni's face, Suzanne said, "Probably nothing to worry about. Just the neighborhood raccoon looking for a handout."

"Or kids pulling an early Halloween prank?" asked Toni.

"Trying to scare us," Suzanne added, in what she hoped was a soothing tone.

But Toni wasn't buying it. "Huh." She snorted. "They *did* scare us. I probably should have brought my security system along."

"Excuse me?"

Toni grinned. "My trusty twelve-gauge shotgun."

CHAPTER 22

FRIDAY morning may have been Egg Strata Ya Gotta day at the Cackleberry Club, but a sense of unease pervaded the place. Normally the joint was jumping, but today it was a much smaller, more reserved crowd that had piled in for breakfast.

"Everybody's still nervous," said Petra, as she rattled pans and poured pancake batter onto her blackened griddle, "even though two of the prisoners have already been apprehended." They'd heard the news this morning on WLGN radio. Two prisoners had been found curled up behind a Dumpster in back of Paradise Pizza. Apparently, they'd helped themselves to a half dozen or so discarded pizza pies, then fallen asleep from the carbo high. At least that's what they were reporting on the *Bugs and Moe Morning Show*.

"But," said Toni, looking worried, "two guys are still on the loose."

"Probably far away from here," Suzanne said breezily. "Hopped a freight train or something, hightailed it out of the county. Maybe out of the state."

"People still do that?" Toni asked. "Hop freight trains?"

"I dunno," said Petra, "maybe they hopped an Amtrak."

"Dressed in prison pinstripes?" asked Toni.

"You're thinking of prisoners in those old black and white movies," said Suzanne. "I think today they wear orange jumpsuits or something."

"Oh," said Toni. "Trendy stuff."

"Holy smokes," said Petra, "I hope they don't pick up Joey Ewald by mistake. Wasn't he wearing a prison shirt the other day?"

Suzanne rolled her eyes. "Oh man," she murmured, "he sure was."

"Suzanne. Toni," Petra said in a quiet voice. She slid wedges of egg strata onto four plates, added a dollop of salsa, then a tangle of cilantro for garnish. "We have orders to deliver."

"If two prisoners are still on the loose," said Toni, when she and Suzanne convened at the coffeepot, "where do you think they are?"

"Not here," said Suzanne. She gazed out at her customers, eyes pausing to study a few grizzled faces. "At least I don't think so."

"Good thing I took that self-defense class," Toni said, as she filled a pot of coffee, enveloping them in a heady aroma of French roast.

"What was that again?" Suzanne asked. "Jujitsu?"

"Krav maga," said Toni, managing to keep a straight face. "The deadliest fighting art known to man. Only a handful of warriors have actually been initiated. I mean, we're talking *mortal* combat."

"You go, girl," said Suzanne.

"You two sound like you're having fun out there," said Petra, when Suzanne strolled back into the kitchen.

"It's a laugh a minute," said Suzanne.

Petra glanced at her sharply, then said, "Oh you."

Suzanne nibbled at a pumpkin pancake that Petra had decided wasn't quite perfect enough to serve. "Do you think we should call the hospital and see how Reverend Yoder is?"

"I'm sure your doctor friend will keep you tightly in the loop," said Petra. A slow smile spread across her broad face. "Am I right?"

"I suppose," said Suzanne. *Tightly in his arms would be even better.*

"But we should certainly send flowers," said Petra.

"That'd be a nice gesture. Last night, Sam said there was a whole contingent there praying for him."

"Praying for Sam?"

"No." Suzanne giggled. "For Reverend Yoder."

"Then he'll for sure get better, won't he?"

"I'm thinking yes." Suzanne watched as Petra tossed a generous handful of slivered jalapeno and habanero peppers into her cast-iron skillet to sizzle alongside chunks of thick-cut bacon and rounds of diced Yukon potatoes. When everything was golden and brown, she added her whisked egg mixture to the pan. *Très bien!*

"Suzanne," said Petra, who was keeping an eye on three different pans at once, "can you slice up those Granny greens?"

"Sure." Grabbing a silver bowl full of peeled apples, Suzanne balanced a half dozen apples on the cutting block and began slicing them into rounds. "You going to make apple fritters?"

"I thought I might," said Petra. "They're such a nice autumn treat. Good alongside a pork chop, or you can serve 'em with a scoop of vanilla ice cream for dessert."

"You're so creative," said Suzanne.

"Hah," said Petra, "look who's talking. You did the whole menu for the catering gig today."

"Something I'm not exactly looking forward to," Suzanne admitted. In fact, she was pretty much dreading the Cashmere and Cabernet event.

"Carmen Copeland can be a real trial," said Petra. Though she never came out and directly insulted Carmen, Petra did seem to hit the nail on the head.

Suzanne sliced for a few moments, then said, "Petra, you don't think last night's prison breakout could be related to the two murders, do you?"

Petra, who had a wooden ladle halfway to her mouth for tasting, stopped and stared at her. "What are you saying, Suzanne?"

"I don't know. What if last night's scare was engineered to be a . . . what would you call it? A diversion?"

Petra frowned. "A diversion from what?"

"Taking focus away from the two murders? An attempt to make Sheriff Doogie look bad? Reinforcing the need for a law-and-order mayor?"

"That would never have occurred to me! Suzanne, you have a very active and suspicious mind."

"Sorry, but I'm just . . ."

"No, no," Petra said, waving a hand. "You bring up a legitimate concern. Lord knows, things have been kapow crazy all week." She turned toward the large, stainless-steel refrigerator and pulled out a tray of small glass ramekins filled with crème brûlée. "And now that you mention it, the prison break *did* take the edge off the murders." She shook her head. "Now you've got me looking at angles and questioning motives."

"The only sticking point," said Suzanne, "is that it would have to be a fairly elaborate scheme. And Lester Drummond would have to be involved."

"Do you think he is?" asked Petra.

"No clue." Suzanne thought for a few moments. "And the prisoners would have to be sort of dunces, handpicked by Drummond."

"He really bothers you," said Petra.

"I just don't think he's a nice guy," said Suzanne. "Or even trustworthy."

"And he runs a prison," said Petra.

"Go figure," said Suzanne.

Petra was still considering Suzanne's words. "So you think Mayor Mobley and Lester Drummond could be allies?"

"Possible," said Suzanne. "Anything's possible. The thing to figure out is . . . what's the payoff?"

"What do you mean?" Petra asked.

Suzanne popped a bite of apple into her mouth. "Who stands to benefit?"

"Good gizzards!" Toni cried suddenly, as she popped her head through the pass-through. "We just got hit with a spurt of customers!"

"Be right there," said Suzanne.

"I'm going to think about what you said," said Petra.

WITHIN twenty minutes the Cackleberry Club was over-the-top busy again. Suzanne threaded her way from table to table, pouring ice water and topping off coffee cups, while Toni studiously took orders. As Petra cranked out cheesy wedges of strata, scrambled eggs, and French toast, Suzanne and Toni hustled to deliver the orders.

"Hey diddle diddle, it's hot off the griddle," Toni joked playfully.

"Did you hear the one about the Roadkill Café?" Suzanne asked. "From your grill to ours?"

"Good one!" said Toni, whirling like a ballerina, balancing her tray on one hand.

But merriment and mayhem came to a screeching halt when Lester Drummond and Allan Sharp strolled into the Cackleberry Club midmorning.

Lester Drummond, all broad shoulders and shiny bald head, was smiling like Hannibal Lecter after a buffet of fellow inmates. Sharp was equally slimy with a thin, snake of a smile crawling across his face.

Toni flashed Suzanne a *what's up?* glance.

Suzanne answered with a shrug. Something sure looked like it was about to play out.

Drummond strode to the center of the café, hitched up his pants, and broadened his smile. "Ladies and gentlemen," he began.

Customers coughed, forks clanked against plates, and chairs were tilted to catch a better angle. Definite electricity in the air.

Suzanne slammed the register shut but made no motion to interrupt Drummond. He could say his piece, but if he started spouting any type of politics, she'd put a hasty stop to it.

"I know you were all worried about the little incident at the prison," said Drummond. "But I'm pleased to announce that all escaped prisoners have been apprehended and are once again locked securely in their respective cells."

The crowd broke into a round of applause. Murmurs of "thank goodness" and a few hallelujahs were heard.

Incident, thought Suzanne. *That's a nice, benign way to soft-pedal it.*

Allan Sharp beamed, then strode across the room to join Drummond. "At no time was a citizen of Kindred ever in danger," he added. "Our mayor Mobley saw to that."

There was another brief spate of applause, then the two men shook hands, as if they'd single-handedly sloshed through a swamp with a pack of baying bloodhounds and captured the prisoners themselves.

When Drummond and Sharp wandered back toward a table, Suzanne hustled over to greet them. "Great news about the prisoners," she told them, as she filled their coffee cups.

"Thank you," said Sharp, who seemed to have appointed himself grand poobah spokesman and PR muckety-muck.

"My men found them in that old rock quarry out on Driver Road," said Drummond. "They were hiding in a cave."

"So they didn't get very far," said Suzanne.

"Not on my watch," boasted Drummond. "We were able to react almost immediately."

"That's right," said Sharp, like a bad echo, "the warden's own guards apprehended the prisoners. No thanks to Sheriff Doogie."

"I'm sure Sheriff Doogie and his deputies were out looking as well," said Suzanne. "He wasn't just sitting at his desk, twiddling his thumbs and listening to Kenny Chesney albums."

"Still," said Drummond, "we're the ones who got the job done."

"And Mayor Mobley is absolutely thrilled," said Sharp. "The operation couldn't have gone better."

"Sure it could," said Suzanne, dropping menus into each of the men's hands. "Those prisoners never should have escaped in the first place."

"You feeling more optimistic now?" Toni asked Petra. They were all gathered in the kitchen, muddling over Drummond's news and prepping lunch.

Petra nodded. "About the prisoners I do. I'm still worried about Reverend Yoder."

"Suzanne, why don't you call the hospital," Toni suggested. "See how he's doing."

"Now there's a novel idea," said Petra, a definite twinkle sparking her eyes as she stirred a large pot of butternut squash bisque. "Give Suzanne an excuse to call her doctor friend."

"Already did," said Suzanne, as she laid out ten yellow Fiesta ware bowls on the counter. "And he's doing just fine."

"Sam or Reverend Yoder?" Toni sniggered.

"Both," Suzanne shot back.

"Is Sam younger than you are?" asked Toni.

Suzanne blinked. "What?"

"I think he is," Toni said, playfully. "Which officially makes you a cougar."

Suzanne tied a paisley apron around her waist and said, "Honey, *you're* the cougar. Junior is . . . what? Six years younger than you are?"

"I'll be happy when Toni renounces her cougar status," said Petra. "Get that divorce she's always talking about."

"You're talking about me like I'm not here," said Toni. "Like I'm some addle-headed zombie."

"When *is* that divorce going to happen?" asked Suzanne.

Toni was suddenly busy stirring a vinaigrette. "Not sure," she mumbled.

"Oh no," said Petra, "don't tell me you've changed your mind again!"

Toni stuck out her chin. "I have a right. Besides, Junior isn't without certain charms."

"Ah," said Petra, "a man who wears a black mesh shirt is definitely a chick magnet. To say nothing about the grease under his fingernails."

"Junior tries," said Toni.

"Wrong," said Petra, "*you* try while Junior bumbles through life."

"Toni works her kerfloppus off," agreed Suzanne.

"Could we please focus on our customers?" Toni begged. "And drop this particular subject?"

"Gonna come back to haunt you," warned Petra, as Toni bumped through the swinging door and disappeared into the café.

HALFWAY through lunch, Sheriff Doogie stumbled in. With a weary demeanor and wrinkled clothes to match, he looked like he hadn't slept in a week. Which he probably hadn't.

Hoisting himself onto the end stool, Doogie planted his elbows on the counter, stared at Suzanne with bloodshot eyes, and ran a hand across the scratchy gray stubble that covered his cheeks.

Suzanne sprang into action. Pouring a quick cup of coffee, she shoved it across the counter to him. "Nothing personal, Sheriff," she said, leaning toward him and keeping her voice low, "but you look terrible."

Doogie glowered at her. "What's not personal about that?"

Suzanne immediately regretted her choice of words. "Sorry, what I meant to say is I'm worried you're working yourself into an early grave." She flinched again as those words came out of her mouth. There'd been too much emphasis on graves and death lately.

Doogie shrugged. "On my best days I'm not exactly a stud muffin, so I can just imagine what I look like on one of my worst days."

"Is this one of your worst days?" she asked.

Doogie took a sip of coffee before he answered her. "No." He pressed a big hand flat against the marble counter. "Worst day was last Tuesday."

"Wilbur," said Suzanne. "How's that going? Anything?"

Doogie shook his head. "Nope. I'm workin' the case, getting top-notch help from the crime lab guys, but we're mostly coming up empty."

Suzanne thought Doogie might elaborate a little more, but he seemed at a loss for words. "At least the prisoners were caught," she offered.

Doogie shifted his khaki bulk on the tippy stool, causing the metal to screech in pain. "By Drummond's own men. Security guys in blue windbreakers and baseball hats. Made us look like the Keystone Cops."

"The important thing is they were caught," said Suzanne.

"I know that," snorted Doogie. "I'm not an idiot. I swore an oath to protect and serve."

"Okay, okay," said Suzanne. "Take it easy." She walked to the pie saver and grabbed a blueberry muffin. She added two pats of butter, then took it to Doogie. "How about the other case," she asked. "Any new theories on Peebler's murder?"

Doogie's jowls sloshed as he shook his head, then pushed the muffin back across the counter at her. "Nothing new."

Suzanne thought for a minute. "You're looking at suspects."

"Of course I am," Doogie said, sounding downright cantankerous. "And I'm looking hard."

"What if you focused solely on motive?"

He sucked air in between his front teeth and gave a quick grimace. "I'm way ahead of you, Suzanne. I've done that, too. Studied all the angles, turned 'em around and around."

"I take it you went through Peebler's home?"

"With a fine-tooth comb."

"Because if Peebler felt threatened or was trying to follow a trail concerning where his aunt's antiquities disappeared to, there might be some sort of clue."

"I looked awful hard," said Doogie, "and basically came up with squat."

Suzanne thought for a second. "What if you had a fresh pair of eyes?"

Doogie pulled a hanky from his back pocket, blew his nose loudly, then stared at her. "What are you saying? Or, rather, what are you asking?"

Suzanne met his gaze evenly. "I think you know."

Doogie swiped at his nose again and beetled his brows. "Probably not a good idea. Not exactly by the book."

"No, it's not," agreed Suzanne, as Toni came sauntering up.

"Howdy do, Sheriff," said Toni. "You need a refill?"

"Nah," said Doogie, patting his shirt pockets nervously. "Got to get moving. Don't want folks to think all I do is sit around and guzzle coffee."

"Suit yourself," said Toni, moving off.

Doogie dug in his pocket and produced a couple of crinkled dollar bills. He set them on the counter, then slipped off his stool and sauntered away. "Be seeing you, Suzanne," he called over his shoulder.

Suzanne frowned. This was the first time she'd ever known Doogie to pony up for coffee as well as leave a tip. Oh well, first time for everything.

She reached for the money, started to crumple the bills in her hand, then stopped. Hiding under Doogie's dollar bills was a shiny brass key.

CHAPTER 23

"GINGER carrot," said Suzanne, extending a tray filled with luxe little tea sandwiches made with cream cheese, sweet ginger paste, and grated carrots.

The size-four woman picked one up gently and placed it on her small bone-china plate. Moving on, she proceeded to debate over the tray of goodies Suzanne had arranged on the nearby table. Then extended a manicured hand and plucked a single, perfect cherry tomato.

So not fair, Suzanne thought. Holding her tray, dressed in black slacks, white blouse, and long black Parisian waiter's apron, she felt like the ugly stepsister. All around her, skinny, fashionable women were sipping cabernet and swooning over cashmere sweaters, Marc Jacobs boots, and tight blue jeans.

Where did all these fashionable women come from? she wondered. Not from Kindred; couldn't be from Kindred. Women here were normal. They wore regular-sized skirts and blouses and sweaters and ate actual food. They were gracious without being picky and definitely didn't wear the type of filmy, frothy clothes that fluttered expensively on Carmen's display of black-lacquered mannequins.

"Are we having fun yet?" Missy asked. Missy was Melissa Langston, Carmen Copeland's boutique manager and current whipping girl. Missy was a midwestern corn-fed, blue-eyed blond with pale skin and a lush figure. Although lately, that corn-fed figure was looking decidedly more sprouts-and-greens.

"I have to hand it to Carmen," said Suzanne. "She vowed to bring high fashion to Kindred and she did it."

"Alta moda," agreed Missy, who didn't always enjoy working for Carmen, but certainly seemed to love the shop itself.

And who wouldn't? Alchemy Boutique was a tour de force in style. Thick mauve draperies complemented plum-colored walls and the carpeting looked like liquid pewter yet felt like a silk cloud. And the clothes! Oh my, they were something! Think *Vogue* magazine, *Women's Wear Daily*, and Rodeo Drive all rolled into one. There were fluttering silk tops, black cocktail dresses, tight designer jeans from Citizens of Humanity, nipped navy blue blazers, and James Perse T-shirts. There was a display of suede handbags in raspberry red, dove gray, and pale blue. Plus silk scarves to twist casually around one's neck, gigantic cocktail rings that looked like disco balls, leather bangle bracelets, gold chains, and a whole area devoted to flats, boots, and lethal stiletto heels.

Suzanne had already put a few items on her own personal wish list— a pair of camel-colored suede booties with ruffled leather trim at the top, a pair of cigarette-leg Rock & Republic jeans, a raspberry sherbet–colored cashmere scarf. But of course! This was Cashmere and Cabernet, after all!

"Would you like a glass of wine, Missy?" Suzanne asked, suddenly remembering that she was a working stiff today, not little Miss Shopaholic.

"Carmen would kill me," said Missy. "Especially since

I have to honcho the informal modeling in a few minutes, then work the crowd to solicit orders for all the special trunk-show items."

"You sure you enjoy working here?" Suzanne asked. "If you ask me, working conditions seems a little Dickensian."

Missy gave a thin smile. "Oh, you don't think twelve-hour days are the norm?"

"Only if you're the owner," said Suzanne, "working your tail off in a start-up situation."

"Well, I'm not the owner and I'm still working my tail off," said Missy.

"You have skills," said Suzanne. "I'm sure you could go back to being a paralegal."

"Maybe." Missy shrugged.

"It would be better than . . ."

"Missy!" screeched Carmen, suddenly spotting her boutique manager and rushing over to them. Only it was more of a baby steps rush, since Carmen was wearing a tight black turtleneck dress with a black leather corset over it. To polish off her look, Carmen's hair was pulled back severely and her eyes were rimmed in dark kohl.

"Uh-oh," said Suzanne, "looks like trouble."

"You have to get the models dressed!" Carmen hissed.

"Of course," said Missy. "Right away."

Carmen grabbed Missy's arm as she started to dash off. "And don't let the fat girl wear the denim leggings," said Carmen. "Give them to someone they might actually *fit*."

"She's a size six," said Missy.

"Exactly," said Carmen, "way too pudgy for leggings." Carmen switched her focus to Suzanne. "And you," she said, glaring. "Could you *please* pour some wine for my guests?"

"Good gosh, Carmen," said Suzanne, "I didn't realize I was supposed to serve as bartender, too."

"Catering involves more than just standing around holding a tray of sandwiches," said Carmen.

"You think?" said Suzanne. Carmen reminded her of a dust devil, spinning wildly, kicking up huge amounts of dust and debris, but never really going anywhere.

Carmen backed off then, turning a critical eye to the food, the line of sparkling crystal wineglasses, the bottles of ruby red cabernet. "Everything looks perfect, no?" she asked.

"Yes, it does," said Suzanne. "So you should be celebrating your triumph."

Carmen frowned and shook her head. "But such a dismal crowd," she moaned. "I sent out something like fifty invitations, but only thirty-five people showed up." She sighed, grabbed a tea sandwich, and took off like a jackrabbit.

"She's counting the flyspecks in the pepper," Suzanne murmured to herself, then decided to shake it off. Carmen's disappointment and anxiety, whether real or faux, wasn't her problem. And thank goodness for that.

Positioning herself behind the buffet table, Suzanne poured glasses of wine for the guests, used a pair of silver tongs to place miniature quiches and lobster and cucumber sandwiches on their plates, and tried her best to enjoy the event.

As models pranced through the store, showing off the delightful duds, and Carmen and Missy did their best to buttonhole customers and elicit orders, Suzanne grabbed her cell phone and called the Cackleberry Club.

Toni answered on the first ring. "Cackleberry Club."

"It's me."

"How's it going?"

"The clothes are gorgeous, people seem to be spending money, and Carmen thinks it's a flop."

"There you go," said Toni. "That's the difference between Carmen's attitude and ours. We sell eight toad in the holes for breakfast, it's like breaking the bank in Monte Carlo."

"You are so off the hook." Suzanne laughed.

"Of course," Toni said, cheerfully. "So, are you ready to suit up and hit that pumpkin patch?"

"Give me forty-five minutes," said Suzanne. "I'm almost done here, but there's something else I have to take care of."

SUZANNE drove a long, looping, circuitous route to Chuck Peebler's house, even though she knew it was silly to be paranoid. Who would suspect she was going to creepy-crawl his house? Nobody, of course. Still, for Doogie's sake, she was determined to take precautions.

After glancing into the rearview mirror about a hundred times, she'd only noticed one vehicle following her. And that was a Roto-Rooter truck that had peeled off one block back. Somebody's sewer line obviously needing to be roto'ed and rooted.

Suzanne was also well aware that Peebler's house would be deserted. Peebler, being of the divorced persuasion, meant there was no grieving widow left to wander about. So she'd be free to . . . well, wander around.

Crawling down Olive Drive, Suzanne hung a left on Essex Street. There it was, the third Cape Cod from the corner. A simple blue clapboard house, probably built in the fifties, that now looked a little forlorn and deserted. Luckily for Suzanne, the house had mature trees in the yard to help shield her movements from prying eyes. A nice fiery red oak, a grove of five straggly poplars, and two bushy cedar trees that hunkered right along the driveway. So perfect.

Swinging into the driveway, Suzanne nosed up to the garage, getting as close as possible. The better to slip in unseen and avoid any neighborhood snoops who might be gung ho lieutenants in the Neighborhood Crime Watch program.

Suzanne gathered her purse, walked up to the steps, and knocked on the front door. As her left fist rapped sharply, the key in her right hand slipped into the lock. There was a slight hesitation, a subtle click, and then she was in. As the door pushed open, Suzanne smiled and nodded, faking a big smarmy greeting. If a nosy neighbor *had* seen her, it would appear someone was there to let her in.

Stepping inside the dim house, Suzanne shut the door behind her. And locked it, just to be safe. Then she stood in the entryway and squared her shoulders, trying to get a vibe from the house.

Dust motes twirled in the near darkness; a clock ticked in the stillness. Peebler had only been dead for a few days, yet it seemed as if he'd been gone forever. An odor of mustiness permeated the air, and an eerie stillness hung in the house. If Suzanne believed in ghosts, *really* believed, she would have said this house was mourning its owner.

She walked slowly into the living room, flicked on a lamp, and surveyed the room. There was a beige sofa, two brown leather chairs with an old hobnail design around the arms, and a decent-looking walnut cocktail table covered with magazines. Last month's issues of *Time*, *Golf Digest*, and *National Geographic*. She crossed a bright blue oriental rug that was pure acrylic and pulled open the drawer of an end table. It revealed an old *TV Guide*, two remote controls, and a dog-eared crossword puzzle book. Hot times at the Peebler household.

Suzanne made her way into the kitchen, nervously expecting to find Peebler's last meal, half eaten and rotting on the table, blowflies buzzing everywhere. But it was nothing like that. Dishes were stacked neatly in the dish drainer and the counters were remarkably free of the usual cookie jar–bread box–spice rack debris.

A neat, tidy kitchen for a neat, tidy man?

Not quite. Peebler's last evening had been anything but tidy, his argument with Jane ruffling feathers and raising eyebrows. Then his bloody and bizarre murder at the hands of a crossbow-wielding killer. And no clues to point in any direction. So the last evening of his life was not exactly tied up nice and neat with a big red bow. No wonder Doogie had taken her up on an offer of a fresh pair of eyes.

But was she really seeing anything?

No. Not yet. So I better keep moving.

Suzanne left the kitchen, walked down a narrow hallway, and entered a small room that had obviously served as Peebler's office. A campaign poster was starting to unpeel from the wall. Stacks of flyers that had never been handed out, and never would be, sat piled on his desk.

Settling into the swivel chair behind Peebler's desk, Suzanne eased open all of the desk drawers for investigation. She took a pencil and stirred things around in each of the drawers, but nothing popped out at her. She ran her fingertips across files in the deeper file drawer, but they contained mostly household bills, insurance forms, and appliance warranties. Like that.

Finally, Suzanne crept upstairs. With just two bedrooms and a small landing, it felt small, cramped, and warm. One bedroom was unused, obviously a guest bedroom of sorts with a twin bed and an ugly velvet tapestry of a deer in the forest decorating one wall. The other room was Peebler's bedroom. A brown-and-white-checked quilt covered the queen-sized bed, a dresser and mirror hunkered against one wall, and the folding closet doors stood open.

Suzanne figured George Draper had probably dropped by and hurriedly picked out Peebler's best suit for the visitation and funeral.

Now Peebler's lying in that suit, six feet under.

The notion chilled her. Made her want to turn and run pell-mell down the steps and out the front door to escape the claustrophobic aura of a dead man's house.

Instead, Suzanne gritted her teeth and stood her ground. She crossed to the closet, which smelled faintly of mothballs, and searched through the clothes. All conservative stuff, all brown. Just like everything else in the house.

She pulled two boxes down from the top shelf, but they turned out to contain summer shoes. Not much on the closet floor, either. An old shoe-shine kit in a wooden box, a tennis racket with a few strings missing, and an electric fan. No lockbox, no secret compartment, no indication of an overhead crawl space.

Suzanne took a few steps back and stared out a window. A gray car was parked across the street, someone in it. A neighbor? Or had someone tailed her? She pressed her nose to the window, then decided she'd better stick to the business at hand rather than let her paranoia run rampant.

Peebler's dresser held the usual clutter of guy crap. A cheap walnut jewelry tray contained tie tacks, loose change, random buttons and watch batteries, a tarnished silver ID bracelet, and a Jaycees pin.

Looking at the pitiful assortment of stuff, Suzanne's heart sank. Nothing in the house seemed to offer up an instant clue. Maybe this whole endeavor was a waste of time?

She stared at herself in the dusty dresser mirror, wondering why she'd thought she could offer some unique insight. Why she believed her female intuition could ferret out a clue where Sheriff Doogie, a trained professional, couldn't.

Suzanne sighed, frowned, then reached up to place an index finger directly between her brows. She didn't want those worry lines etched any deeper. Her 11's, as they had been referred to in an old issue of *Glamour* magazine that she'd perused at the dentist.

Taking a deep breath, Suzanne gazed at herself again. Better now. Smooth brow, no visible frown lines. Good to catch yourself. Good to . . .

Suzanne's eyes flicked toward a small sliver of yellow stuck in the corner of the mirror. It was right between the glass and the wooden oak frame, the same place one might stick a small photo. She reached a hand out and pulled the yellow sliver from its spot.

Staring at the mini yellow Post-it note, she saw one world scrawled upon it. *Tortuga.*

CHAPTER 24

"YOUR car or mine?" Suzanne asked. She'd arrived back at the Cackleberry Club around five thirty to find Toni waiting for her.

"Jungle Cruiser is bigger," said Toni, cocking a thumb toward the parking lot out front. "It'll hold more pumpkins."

"Done," said Suzanne.

Toni slipped on a worn suede jacket and tucked her jeans into tanned, tooled cowboy boots. "Gonna be cold out there." She wound a knit scarf around her neck.

"Where are we going again?" Suzanne asked.

Toni pulled a crumpled piece of paper from her jeans pocket and scanned it. "Out Hudson Road. By the old Lawson place."

"I have no idea where that is."

"You don't remember old man Lawson? The guy who drops in once in a while, mumbling about fighting Nazis in the Ardennes?"

"Oh sure," said Suzanne.

"And you know where Hudson Road is."

"Kind of," said Suzanne. She had a vague notion that it was north of Kindred, but her own internal Google Earth program wasn't pulling up any sort of detailed map.

"Don't worry," said Toni. "Junior drew a map so there shouldn't be any problem."

"Right," said Suzanne, although it seemed like every day they'd encountered a new problem. Time for something to go off without a hitch? Oh, let's hope so.

They exited the Cackleberry Club, turning out lights and locking the door, then climbed into Toni's car. She cranked the key in the engine, let her car rumble and belch for a few moments, then said, "Ready, Freddy?"

With a few hard tugs, Suzanne managed to yank the frayed seat belt into proper position and snap it in place. "Let's do it."

Toni turned the heater knob to defrost and clicked on a cassette player that looked like it had been recently installed. Red, yellow, and green wires stuck out from below like colorful, techy spaghetti. "Aftermarket," Toni told Suzanne. "It's not exactly a state-of-the-art in-dash CD deck with MP3 and satellite radio, but at least we've got tunes." Toni hit a button and "Girls Just Want to Have Fun," by Cyndi Lauper, suddenly blared from speaker panels in the doors. They grinned at each other, then joined in with Cyndi, bouncing and seat dancing their way out of town.

"So Carmen was a real pain today?" Toni asked, as they rumbled past Pretty Paws Pet Grooming and the Video Hut, heading out of town.

"Carmen's always a trial," Suzanne replied. "I still can't figure how Missy puts up with her."

"Same way I put up with Junior." Toni chuckled. "I never take him seriously." She slowed down as they cruised across a narrow bridge, the boards crinkling beneath them, something clunking in the backseat.

"Speaking of Junior," said Suzanne, "is that his stuff

back there?" She turned slightly, caught sight of a large cardboard box bouncing away on the backseat.

Toni nodded. "Annoying, isn't it?" Every time they hit a little bump there was a metallic rattle.

"What's he got in there?"

Toni shrugged. "I don't know. Car parts. Maybe a carburetor or something."

"Scrap metal?"

"Dunno. Maybe."

"How's that working out for him?" Suzanne asked. "His . . . uh . . . new sideline." She refrained from saying "harebrained scheme," even though that's what it probably was.

"Things are good," said Toni, sounding her chirpiest.

"Seriously?"

"Aw, I don't know," said Toni, her chirpiness crumbling. "Who knows with Junior? At least he's trying. Giving it a whack."

"Planning for the future," said Suzanne.

"Junior's idea of planning for the future is to buy two six-packs instead of one." Toni snorted. "In fact, Junior's so darned immature I worry about finding his face on the back of a milk carton!"

"Funny," said Suzanne, although it was partly true.

Toni popped in a Rolling Stones tape and that kept them entertained for another five miles or so, until Suzanne asked, "How close are we?"

"Pretty close."

Gazing out the window, Suzanne enjoyed the view of rolling fields and blue black starlit sky. Whenever the road dipsy-doodled, she caught a flash of a fast-moving stream. "Does Tortuga mean anything to you?" she asked, suddenly.

Toni hesitated a few moments before answering. "Maybe those islands in the Caribbean? Or, wait a minute, doesn't Tortuga mean turtle in Spanish?"

"I think so."

"Why are you asking?" asked Toni.

Suzanne took a deep breath. "Here's the thing . . . I had a wild idea and did a little snooping today."

Toni glanced at her sharply. "Snooping. Meaning you broke the law? Not that I'm a staunch defender of the law or anything."

"It might have been a criminal offense," said Suzanne, "except I had Sheriff Doogie's endorsement."

Toni giggled. "Seriously?"

"I asked Doogie if he could use a fresh pair of eyes," said Suzanne. "To take a look-see inside Chuck Peebler's house."

Toni's jaw dropped. "Doogie *let* you? You actually snuck in there?"

Suzanne nodded. "All by my lonesome."

"Eeyeew," said Toni. "You creepy-crawled a dead guy's house? I would have been totally weirded out."

"When you put it that way . . ."

"Doogie must be really nervous to let a civilian get in on the act."

Suzanne nodded in the dark. "You saw how depressed he was this morning. And with Deputy Halpern's funeral set for tomorrow, he's really down on himself."

"So where is all this going?" Toni asked. "You found something to do with Tortuga?"

"Oh . . . yeah. Peebler had scrawled the word Tortuga on a Post-it note."

"Maybe he was planning a nice warm-weather island adventure?"

"Maybe," said Suzanne. "Or maybe he just liked turtles."

TEN minutes later, Suzanne was beginning to squirm in her seat. "How far have we come anyway?"

Toni squinted at her dashboard. "According to my handy-dandy trip meter, almost twenty-six miles."

"Long drive just for pumpkins."

"We're almost there." Toni tromped down on the accelerator, edging up to almost seventy miles an hour. For Toni, the posted speed limit was the equivalent of suggested retail price. It could fluctuate widely.

Suzanne watched more woods and fields fly by, thinking back to the other night, when she and Petra had gotten turned around out here. When she'd stumbled upon Wilbur Halpern. "I feel like I was just out this way."

"Aw, these roads all look the same," said Toni. "Farm fields, woods, streams, and stuff."

"I think it's called nature."

Toni slowed her car, rolled past a dark, deserted intersection, then said, "Horse pucky. I think I'm lost."

"Let's stop and look at the map," Suzanne suggested.

Toni eased the car onto the shoulder and clicked on the overhead light. Suzanne held up the map so they could study it.

"What do you think?" asked Toni.

Suzanne puzzled over the hastily drawn map. "It's hard enough to decipher Junior's handwriting, but the map itself is sketchy. Like something the Hardy Boys drew to show the way to their fort."

"Aside from that," said Toni. "Aside from the fact that it looks like a three-year-old did it."

"Nothing's drawn to scale," said Suzanne. "Don't take this the wrong way, but I don't think cartography is Junior's strong point." Her fingernail scratched at the paper. "And what's this humpy-looking line supposed to indicate? Hills?"

"River," said Toni. "Catawba Creek." Toni cocked her head. "Too bad we don't have GPS."

"Instead of JPS," said Suzanne. "J being Junior."

Toni grabbed the map and turned it upside down. "Aw, we're not so far off, ya know? I think the pumpkin patch is down the road we just rolled past."

"You think?"

Toni was already backing up the car. "Sure. We'll be there in a jiffy."

They left the asphalt road and turned down the gravel road, creeping along at ten miles an hour. Rocks crunched beneath their tires, something made a low, guttural sound off in the distance. An owl?

"And here we are," said Toni, pulling onto a flat patch of grass.

"Deserted," said Suzanne, glancing around.

"We follow a short trail through this cornfield, then the pumpkin patch is the very next field."

"We gotta schlep pumpkins all the way back here?" Suzanne asked.

"We'll just scope it out," said Toni. "If the land's flat enough, I'll drive the Jungle Cruiser in and we can load up in ten minutes flat."

"I like your optimism," said Suzanne, as they started down the path.

"Chilly," said Toni, pulling her collar up.

"And dark," said Suzanne. "I can't believe we forgot to bring a flashlight."

They walked for another five minutes on uneven ground.

"Are you . . ." Suzanne began.

But Toni suddenly threw up an arm and said, "Whoa! You hear that? It was like a high-pitched yip!"

Suzanne halted in her tracks. She had heard something.

"Maybe a pack of coyotes?" asked Toni. "We might have to, like, throw rocks at them or something."

"That's our self-defense plan?" said Suzanne. "Throw rocks?"

"I could go back and grab a tire iron."

Suzanne grimaced. "Okay, rocks it is."

But the yips had turned to barking. Loud, insistent barking.

"Dogs?" wondered Toni.

"I think so," said Suzanne. "But more than just a couple. It sounds like a whole pack."

They wandered farther down the path until they came to a weedy area, circular, but with the grass all matted down. Then the moon slipped out from behind the clouds and shone down on a low, wooden building. Now they could hear barks, woofs, and snuffles coming from what appeared to be metal cages.

"It *is* dogs," exclaimed Toni. "Cool. This must be some kind of breeding kennel."

Suzanne was more tentative. "I don't know . . ."

Toni strolled right up to one of the cages. "Or maybe one of those puppy mills you read about." She peered at it, speculatively. "Although these guys look kind of big for puppies."

"Oh man!" said Suzanne, suddenly recognizing the place for what it was. "You know what kind of dogs these are?"

"Cute dogs," said Toni, as she reached a hand out and unlatched one of the cages. "Snuggly dogs."

"They're fighting dogs!" Suzanne yelled, as a brown furry object hurtled from its cage, caroming into Toni and knocking her down. The canine landed in a scramble of legs, righted itself, then paused when it saw Suzanne. The dog moved in a slow circle, tail down, shoulders hunched, its fiery eyes fixed on Suzanne.

"Don't move," Suzanne hissed. "Don't show fear."

"Too late," said Toni, "I think I already wet my pants."

Like a dangerous, fur-covered shark, the dog turned its large head slowly and snarled in Toni's direction. "Good boy?" she said, weakly. The dog didn't adjust his attitude one bit.

"We need to walk out of here very slowly," Suzanne cautioned. "Don't turn your back on him or look directly into his eyes. No challenges; let the dog think he's dominant."

"He'll get no argument from me," said Toni, slowly pulling herself to her knees.

"Easy now," said Suzanne. Gingerly, she took a step backward.

Watching Toni struggle to get up, the canine let loose a low, throaty growl and advanced a step toward her. His muzzle was pulled back in a pile of ugly wrinkles, his eyes were filled with intensity.

"Holy crapola!" said Toni, real fear tingeing her voice. "I think he's gonna . . ."

Suzanne threw her arms up in the air and shouted. "Hey, dog! Get over here, mutt!"

His concentration suddenly broken, the dog swung angrily toward Suzanne. Then he set his muscular legs in a fighting stance and rumbled toward her like a steam locomotive!

Suzanne abandoned her own advice and bolted. Sprinting and scrambling, she knew she wasn't going to make it after the first few steps, then stumbled badly as her toe caught on something.

The earth rushed up to meet her as her open hands slapped hard against a piece of wire mesh. Quick as a snapping turtle, Suzanne staggered back to her feet, holding up the discarded mesh as a kind of shield. The dog lunged at her, but Suzanne fended it off. "Easy," she told the dog. "Just take it easy."

The dog rushed at her a second time and this time Suzanne pushed the mesh firmly against its muzzle. Then, still positioning the mesh as a barrier between herself and the dog, Suzanne slowly maneuvered across the dry grass to grab Toni.

"Don't let him bite me!" Toni chattered, clutching Suzanne's arm in a vise grip as the dog jumped and barked at them.

"We're gonna be okay!" Suzanne shrilled as, together, they crab-stepped backward.

"Doesn't he know we *love* dogs?" asked Toni.

"I don't think anybody's ever shown this guy love," said Suzanne.

"Well, if he'd just be nice . . ." said Toni.

But the wily dog continued to snap and dart at them, driving them at a crazy angle, causing them to retreat deeper and deeper into the nearby woods.

"But my car's thataway," said a frantic Toni. "What are we gonna do, climb a tree?"

"Then we'll just be treed game," said Suzanne. "No, look for a stick or some kind of club."

"You want to club him? Doesn't that constitute animal cruelty?"

Think of it as extreme self-defense!" said Suzanne. She was a dog lover, but she loved her own hide, too.

"Listen," said Toni, her hands still clutched around Suzanne's waist, "you hear that burbling? We're going to end up at the creek."

"That's not good," said Suzanne, wishing they could find a hunk of wood or piece of metal to club the dog with and render it senseless.

"Okay," said Toni, "my boots just hit mud."

"I feel it," said Suzanne, as dampness started to seep into her shoes.

"Gonna be kind of cold for swimming," Toni warned.

"Unless . . ." Suzanne took her eyes off the slavering dog to look around quickly.

"Not even a dock," mourned Toni.

"But there's a canoe!"

"What?"

"Just to your left, an old wooden canoe."

"Holy moley!" said Toni.

They edged their way left, until Toni was able to reach out and touch a hand to it.

"Think it floats?" asked Suzanne.

"We'll cross that stream when we come to it!"

"Flip it over," Suzanne urged, still fending off the dog. "Try to get it partially into the water!"

Toni bent quickly to her left, let loose an inelegant

grunt, and flipped the canoe right side up. She grabbed the two paddles, tossed them into the canoe, and with a mighty push, sent it halfway into the river.

"Got it!" Toni yelled, as she struggled to hold the canoe in place against the fast-moving current.

"You jump in first," said Suzanne, "then I'll push off."

Toni made a leap of faith, landed squarely in the middle of the canoe, then struggled her way to the bow. "I'm in!"

Suzanne backed up into ankle-deep water, took one last look at the angry canine, then in one swift move, thrust the screen at him as she jumped in, too.

Grabbing a paddle, Suzanne pushed off hard, just as the dog splashed in after them.

But the current of the Catawba River caught them, mercifully spinning them around and pointing them down-river. In seconds they were carried swiftly away.

As they floated down the Catawba River, buffeted by the various eddies and swirls, Toni glanced back nervously and asked, "Can dogs swim?"

CHAPTER 25

"YOU'RE lucky you didn't get rabies," Petra scolded.

They were all three sitting on a hard wooden church pew in Pilgrim's Church, waiting for Wilbur Halpern's funeral to begin. Wilbur's family had elected to forego a funeral home and have a final viewing at the church.

"I guess the dog's bark was worse than his bite," said Suzanne, trying to make light of what had been a harrowing situation.

"How did you two even get home?" Petra asked.

"That was the easy part," said Toni. "Eventually we just floated into town. When we hit Bluff Creek Park, we ditched the canoe and walked home."

"What about your car?" Petra may have been worried, but she was also curious.

Toni grinned. "I called Junior and told him to go out there and tow it." She paused. "And pick up some pumpkins, too."

"Good thinking," said Suzanne.

"You called Doogie?" Petra asked. "Told him about the dogs?" She glanced toward the front of the church where Sheriff Doogie, sitting ramrod stiff in his dress uniform, shared a pew with Wilbur Halpern's family. They were, in turn, surrounded, by other sheriff's deputies, state patrol officers, police officers, and firemen from the tri-county area and beyond who had shown up this morning to bid farewell to a fallen brother.

"I spoke to one of his deputies first thing this morning," said Suzanne. "He promised to tell Doogie as well as rustle up animal control and the local humane society. He said they might even try to stake it out—figure out who owns those poor creatures, since dogfighting is a felony."

"Shh," said Toni, putting a finger to her lips. "The funeral."

The double doors in the back of the church suddenly creaked open, a cue for the organist to hit the first bars of the "Funeral March" from Beethoven's Sonata no. 12. Mourners scrambled to their feet, shuffled, and turned to watch the sad procession file in.

Six uniformed sheriff deputies, looking both stricken and solemn, wheeled the flag-draped mahogany casket down the aisle.

"Oh dear." Petra lifted a crumpled hanky to her mouth.

Toni oozed a silent tear.

Suzanne thought, *Doggone, if I'd only gotten to Wilbur five minutes earlier.*

Reverend Falk came out to meet the coffin. He laid his hands gently upon it, watched as the pallbearers seesawed it into place, then launched into his opening benediction.

Suzanne folded her arms across her black funeral suit and hugged herself tightly. Today, Wilbur Halpern was being celebrated as a true hero. A man who had died in the line of duty. But what a terrible price to pay for that honor!

Suzanne wanted to cry, but didn't. Crying was a fine release of emotions and endorphins, of course, but it did nothing to help bring about justice. And that's what Su-

zanne was most interested in for Wilbur. And for Chuck
Peebler, too. Capture whatever madman was lurking out
there and bring him to a swift and awful justice.

Letting loose a silent sigh, Suzanne saw that Toni was
digging in her purse for Kleenex. In fact, there didn't seem
to be a dry eye in the house. Except for her. This funeral
was a necessary tribute, of course, but she was more anxious for closure in the form of arrests, sentencing, and
prison terms.

Harsh, but true.

As Wilbur's uncle took the podium to talk about Wilbur's life and devotion to family, Suzanne's mind continued to race. She thought about Chuck Peebler again. About
his sad, empty house and his strange note about Tortuga.
She thought about poor Scruff, the dog she'd picked up the
night she'd discovered Deputy Halpern. Scruff must have
been one of a number of hapless dogs tossed into the ring to
tangle with the fighting dogs. A sort of sparring partner—
except poor Scruff, who was a docile, gentle guy, had been
expected to lose!

Doogie's cough, meant to clear his throat, brought Suzanne back to the moment at hand. Doogie stood poised
at the podium now, gazing at Wilbur's casket as he nervously unfolded a single sheet of paper. Smoothing it out,
he glanced about the church, then began his tribute to Wilbur Halpern. He spoke of Wilbur's patriotism and civic
pride. Of how proud Wilbur had been to serve as a deputy
and how he'd glowed with happiness at earning his various medals. How Wilbur had gone out of his way to help
people, even driving a couple of elderly residents to the
Westvale Medical Clinic when they couldn't find a ride.

Suzanne was surprised at the dignity and gentleness of

Doogie's tribute. But when he began to relate a story about Wilbur going on patrol, Doogie's voice turned hoarse and papery, and he began to choke.

Reverend Falk improvised expertly. He thanked Doogie for sharing his fine words and memories, then gazed out over the crowd of mourners, requested that everyone kindly stand, and launched into the Lord's Prayer.

That was pretty much the signal that the service had concluded. The organist played "Dust in the Wind," which had apparently been one of Wilbur's favorite songs. The pallbearers snapped to attention and wheeled the coffin down the aisle and out into the thin October sunlight.

"So sad," said Petra, blotting at her eyes. "I just can't imagine the agony Winnie is going through." Winnie was Wilbur's mama.

Suzanne reached out and grabbed Petra's hand, then Toni put one of her hands on top of theirs. Huddled together like that, they listened to the music and watched the family shuffle past, followed by at least fifty men in uniform.

DOOGIE was standing by his cruiser when Suzanne walked up to him. His gray eyes looked tired and sad, but his shoulders were back and there was some pride in his carriage. He knew he'd be leading the funeral procession up to Resurrection Cemetery where Wilbur would be laid to rest.

"It was a wonderful service," Suzanne said, quietly.

"He deserved it," Doogie responded.

"You're leading the procession?"

Doogie nodded. "We're even doing a twenty-one-gun salute."

"I think Wilbur would be pleased," said Suzanne.

"The day after he was murdered," said Doogie, "I issued a Sheriff's Commendation."

"That was nice of you."

Doogie shook his head. "What would really be nice is if I could find his doggone killer."

"Sheriff," said Suzanne, "we need to talk."

Doogie nodded. "I hear you. I got your message about the fighting dogs. I plan to follow up on that right away. According to my calculations, that dog kennel is something like two miles as the crow flies from where Wilbur was killed."

"I thought it might be close," said Suzanne. "But we also need to talk about my little foray into Chuck Peebler's house."

Doogie's eyes swept the crowd, then he dropped his voice. "I figured if you found anything, you'd let me know."

"I'm letting you know."

Surprise registered on Doogie's face. "Hah?" Clearly he hadn't expected her to find anything at all.

"On the mirror in Peebler's bedroom," said Suzanne. "I found a yellow Post-it note."

Doogie stared at her more intently. "Okay."

"The word *Tortuga* was scrawled on it."

Now the sheriff just looked confused.

"Tortuga," Suzanne repeated. "It means turtle in Spanish. You didn't see the note when you were sifting through his house."

Doogie canted his head. "Apparently not."

Suzanne stared at him. She wasn't sure how she'd expected him to react. Praise her for her eagle eye observation and catlike skills? Pat her on the back for a job well done? Or just stare with quizzical stoicism.

"Tortuga," Doogie said, finally, shifting his weight from one leg to the other. "I gotta tell you, in the scheme of things, it doesn't exactly unlock any big mysteries for me."

"Maybe not," said Suzanne, as she felt heat rush to her face. "But it's what I've got, okay?"

TODAY was also the morning Suzanne filled in at radio station WLGN.

"Amazing," said Suzanne, gazing at her reflection in the glass partition that separated her radio booth from the control room. "I look like a real DJ." Then she glanced down at a sound board with hundreds of dials and gauges. "Uh-oh."

"Now all you have to do is act like one," Wiley Von-Bank, the engineer, told her. He stood next to her, adjusting levels, pointing out the various call buttons and dials.

"Crap," said Suzanne, "I knew there was a catch."

"And when we go live in a few minutes," said Wiley, "*crap* may not be the best word to use with our callers."

"Gotcha. So what exactly do I do?"

Wiley got down to business and gave Suzanne a quick lesson about the board, the various dials, and what buttons to push.

"And remember," said Wiley, "broadcast tends to depress the emotions, so you need to be extra bright with your speech. Try to project over-the-top enthusiasm."

"Enthusiasm," Suzanne repeated, a look of sublime panic on her face.

"Don't worry so much," Wiley told her. "I'll do the lead-in and control most of the broadcast from the studio next door. If there's anything else you need to push or switch, I'll let you know. But basically, job number one is to sit in that chair, be chatty and friendly, talk to callers, and not touch your cans."

"Watch it!" said Suzanne.

"No," Wiley said with a laugh, "your headphones. You gotta wear 'em so I can talk to you. Get inside your head."

"Like I said, watch it."

"One minute," said Wiley. Returning to his studio, he smiled at her through the glass, then pulled his microphone close to his mouth. "This is WLGN, your good neighbor in Logan County. It's partly cloudy right now, but we're hoping the sun will peep through. Sixty-one degrees in beautiful downtown Kindred, sixty-three over in Jessup. And time, once again, for *Friends and Neighbors*."

Wiley hit a button and produced a ten-second spurt of upbeat music that was a cross between salsa and country, then he pointed directly at Suzanne, giving her the cue to jump in.

Suzanne took a deep breath, then went with the opening she'd practiced all morning . . . "Good mornnnnnning, Logan County!"

With any luck, she figured she sounded like a passable morning DJ.

"This is Suzanne Dietz," she said, trying to sound bright, chirpy, and pitch-perfect, "filling in for the fantastic and vacationing Paula Patterson on your favorite Saturday morning talk show, *Friends and Neighbors*. As always, we'll chat about whatever's on your mind or whatever's happening around our lovely county. Plus, I'd like to share a recipe or two from the Cackleberry Club. And in case you don't know . . ."

One of the call lights lit up immediately.

A little shocked, Suzanne said, "Maybe you *do* know about the Cackleberry Club." She quickly pushed the call button, exactly as Wiley had instructed her.

"You've reached *Friends and Neighbors*," Suzanne said. "And you're on the air!"

"Paula?" an elderly female voice quavered.

"No, this is Suzanne. Paula's on vaca—"

Click! The caller had hung up and none of the other lines were lit.

Suzanne glanced over to see Wiley holding his sides, laughing hysterically.

"While I'm waiting for your calls to pour in and light up this switchboard," said Suzanne, "let's talk about soup. As you know, there's nothing better on a chilly autumn night than squash bisque with toasted croutons."

Suzanne gave a few quick details about the recipe and was pleased to see a call line light up. And then a second line.

"Lots of calls coming in now . . . let's see who this is." She punched button number one.

"Suzanne," said a male caller, "I had that soup at your restaurant once and it was fantastic."

"Thanks so much," said Suzanne, "love to hear that." She pressed the second call line. "Hello? You a soup lover, too?"

"I need some advice," came a woman's voice.

"We do our fair share of advice here," said Suzanne, hoping for an easy question. "What can I help you with?"

"My husband's retired," said the caller, "but I still can't get him to do any chores around the house. Do you know any tricks?"

Hah, Suzanne thought. *Do I dare? Why not?*

"The best way I know to get a guy to do something," said Suzanne, "is tell him he's too old to do it."

Canned laughter suddenly echoed in Suzanne's ear and she noticed that Wiley was nodding and smiling encouragement at her now.

"Next caller," Suzanne said, breezily, her confidence growing by leaps and bounds.

"Halloween's coming," said another woman caller, "and my ten-year-old son wants to come to your Cackleberry Club party as a character from that vampire show, *New Moon.* What do you think?"

"Not sure," said Suzanne. "But if you cross a vampire with a snowman you get frostbite." More canned laughter echoed in her ear as Suzanne gave the thumbs-up sign to Wiley.

Next caller was a man. "I need your advice," he said in a slightly muffled voice.

"Okay," said Suzanne. "We've been doling out lots of free advice this morning."

"I know this woman and she's really quite nosy."

"I know a few folks like that myself," said Suzanne. "Is she a neighbor?"

"Not exactly," said the man, "but, man, is she getting on my nerves."

"How so?" asked Suzanne, suddenly wondering if this call was really legit.

"She's poking around where she doesn't belong," said the man. "Even sneaking into empty houses."

Suzanne straightened in her chair and a tingle ran down her spine. "The owner's deceased?" she asked, her throat suddenly tightening up.

"That's right," continued the man. "And the thing is, I need to warn this woman. She's got to learn how to mind her own business."

"Sounds like a plan," said Suzanne, her nervousness turning to anger as the call continued.

"Because," said the man, "the next step I take might be an actual, physical threat."

"Better be careful," Suzanne said into the microphone, "because she might just threaten you back!"

Wiley suddenly broke in. "And that's our first crank caller of the day!" he enthused. "So tell me, Suzanne, how do you like hosting so far?"

CHAPTER 26

GRABBING a butcher knife, Suzanne lifted it high above her head, then brought it crashing down with brute force.

"Whoa there," Toni cautioned, "ease off. That's just a poor defenseless carrot!"

Suzanne continued to whack the heads off the rest of the carrots lined up on the cutting table. "Don't mind me, I'm just taking my frustration out on a lower form of life."

"Go for it," said Petra, who was waiting to toss the sliced veggies into the soup pot.

"I guess you're still whipped up over that crazy caller this morning," said Toni.

"You think?" asked Suzanne. She'd tried to get Wiley to trace the call, but no dice.

"Sure you are," said Toni.

"As if encountering a pack of wild beasts wasn't enough," Petra said with a sigh, "you had to tiptoe through Chuck Peebler's house, too. And from the gist of that strange call this morning, somebody *saw* you going in!" Petra was unnerved by Suzanne's confession of creepy-crawling Peebler's house and finding the Post-it note.

"I thought I was doing Doogie a favor," said Suzanne.

"What's that weird saying?" asked Petra. "No kind act goes unrevenged?"

"That *is* convoluted," said Toni.

"But maybe a little true," Suzanne admitted.

"I have a terrible, gut-wrenching feeling someone knows you're seriously on the hunt for the killer," said Petra, looking worried. "Maybe even the killer himself!"

"It's possible," Suzanne admitted, though she didn't really want to go there. Trying to track down a murderer sounded so much better in the abstract!

"And it's all my fault," said Petra. "I was the one who initially asked you to help clear Jane!" She threw her arms up, looking colossally unhappy. "And now everything's snowballed!"

"You didn't know things would get this crazy," said Toni. "How could you know?"

"Tell me, Petra," said Suzanne, "what does Tortuga mean to you?"

Petra wiped tears from the corners of her eyes and shook her head. "I don't know. Turtles."

"That's what I said," said Toni.

"Are you thinking the note is some kind of anagram or riddle?" asked Petra.

"Yeah," said Suzanne. "Maybe."

"And maybe I should go wait on customers?" said Toni.

Petra leaned forward and took a quick peek through the pass-through. "Please do get your fanny out there." She turned back to the stove, flipped over a pair of grilled cheese sandwiches, and said, "Tortuga. Maybe it was some kind of cue or prompt."

"Excuse me?" said Suzanne.

"You know, slow as a turtle," said Petra. "Peebler was running for office against an incumbent, so maybe he was just reminding himself that slow and steady wins the race."

"But Peebler was ahead," said Suzanne. "He was the hare."

"Maybe he wasn't ahead when he *wrote* it," said Petra. She slid her spatula under the cheese sandwiches, lifted them off the grill, and expertly set them atop a lovely green sweep of lettuce. Then she added a dill pickle spear and a mound of salty kettle chips.

"You might be right," Suzanne said, just as the phone shrilled. She spun about, grabbed the phone from the hook, and said, "Cackleberry Club."

"Suzanne." It was Sam Hazelet.

"Hello there," she said, her voice going up an octave, a smile lighting her face. She snicked open the door of the pantry and slid in. Better that way. More privacy.

"I just had an interesting conversation with Sheriff Doogie," said Sam.

Oops. "You did?"

"Don't play cute, Suzanne," said Sam, his voice serious verging on terse, as if he was about to deliver an unwelcome medical diagnosis. "You know exactly what I'm talking about."

Do I really? Are you talking about ransacking Chuck Peebler's house, getting cornered by a slavering dog, or being threatened by a crank caller this morning?

"Um," she said, stalling.

"The dogs," said Sam. "Or should I say *fighting* dogs."

"Oh that. Those."

"According to Sheriff Doogie you stumbled into a nest of pit bulls. Highly *dangerous* pit bulls."

"And here I thought they were teacup Chihuahuas."

"Sometimes you scare me to death, Suzanne," said Sam. "This having been a particularly harrowing week in Kindred, although it probably seemed normal for you." He sounded upset, just this side of angry.

Breaking-up angry? She hoped not.

"Believe me, I don't run around looking for trouble," Suzanne told him.

"Maybe not, but trouble certainly seems to find you in its crosshairs."

"Could we please change the subject," Suzanne asked, "now that I'm thoroughly chagrined?"

He was silent for a few moments. "I suppose."

Suzanne crossed her fingers. "Did you by any chance catch my radio show this morning?"

"I'm sorry I wasn't able to catch it. I had to stop by the hospital."

"Too bad," Suzanne cooed. Although she was really thinking, *Excellent, then you didn't hear that nasty, threatening phone call I received.*

"Are we still on for our date tonight?" Sam asked. Now there was a questioning tone in his voice, as if he might be worried about coming off too harsh or overbearing.

"Absolutely, we're on," said Suzanne.

"Just burgers and beer? You won't be disappointed?"

She wanted to say, *I don't think you could ever disappoint me.* Instead she said, "Sounds delish."

"How are we set for tomorrow night?" Suzanne asked Petra.

Petra had just finished toasting almonds for her *Fave dei Morti* almond-flavored cookies. Done in the shape of beans, they were traditionally eaten in Italy on Day of the Dead. She was about to toss her almonds into the food processor, whir them to bits, then add them to her sugar cookie dough.

"You mean with the food, the tent, or the decorations?" asked Petra. "Because there's a *ton* of stuff that still needs doing."

"You just worry about the food," said Suzanne. "Let Toni and Junior deal with the tent, fire pits, and decorations."

"I know they offered," said Petra, rolling her eyes, "but Lord help us."

"He will," said Suzanne.

Petra wiped her hands on the front of her apron. "The food is for sure under control. I'm going to bake up these cookies, then sort of prep, as best I can, the rest of the stuff."

"That being . . . ?"

"Hot dogs and buns, baked beans, deviled eggs, apple strudel cider . . ." She stopped in midsentence. "I'm forgetting something. Oh, the s'mores."

"Can't forget those."

Petra's normally guileless eyes took on a mischievous glint. "Except I'm going to do s'mortuaries. They're like s'mores, only deadlier!"

"Petra, I never thought I'd say this, but you are off the chain, girl!"

"She sure is," said Toni, wandering into the kitchen again. She was futzing with some of the orange rubber bracelets they were going to give to their guests Sunday night, stacking them on her wrist. "What's the cover charge going to be for the Halloween party?" she asked.

"Ten dollars," said Petra.

"I thought it was going to be fifteen," said Toni.

"That's what we talked about," said Petra, "but after I

figured our food costs, it looks like ten is a more reasonable number." She glanced at Suzanne. "After all, these are tough times."

Toni looked up from her wrist. "What?"

"Because of the recession," said Petra. "People don't have a lot of extra money right now."

"Huh," said Toni, "and all along I thought it was just me."

"SUZANNE, if you don't start visiting us more often, I'm going to have to change the name of our salon from Root 66 to Root 66,000. Because you've put lots of miles on between touch-ups." Gregg, one of the salon owners, stood behind Suzanne, clucking his tongue and gazing balefully at her in the mirror as he ran his hands through her silky, silvery blond hair.

"Sorry," said Suzanne, "I've been busy."

"What else is new?" snipped Gregg. "You always say that."

Tall, blond, and ethereal, Gregg and his partner, Brett, were the most popular hairstylists in town.

Suzanne smiled back at him in the mirror. "Nice to see you, too, Gregg." It was three o'clock Saturday afternoon in the salon on Kindred's main street, and the place was packed. Women in black smocks were being shampooed, trimmed, blown-out, and touched-up, as well as manicured and pedicured.

"You all set for your big party tomorrow night?" Gregg asked, as he slipped on vinyl gloves and began mixing hair color.

"I wish," said Suzanne. After she left here she was going to zap back to the Cackleberry Club and carve pumpkins. Then rush home to get ready for her date with Sam, hoping and praying she didn't get pumpkin goo stuck in her soon-to-be newly blonded hair.

"We're planning to be there," said Gregg, glancing at his partner, Brett, who was busy cutting the hair of the woman in the chair next to them. "Aren't we."

"That's right," said Brett. He was the polar opposite of Gregg, short and dark, a dynamo with a long ponytail draped down his back. "And if we don't get our act together and figure out a costume, we'll be forced to come as gay hairdressers. Heaven forbid!"

"At least we have dates," said Gregg. "I hope our Suzanne here has been eyeing the local rogue's gallery for potential male companionship."

"Don't worry about me." Suzanne laughed.

Sensing a shift in Suzanne's dating status, Gregg, ever on the prowl for good gossip leaned closer to her. "Who is it, sweetie? Someone we know?"

"Sam Hazelet," said Suzanne. She couldn't help smiling at her reflection in the mirror.

"I heard that!" said Brett. "And may I just say the man has *no* business whatsoever being a doctor."

"Excuse me?" said Suzanne.

"Because," said Brett, "the man is drop-dead gorgeous. He should be a movie star at the very least!"

"I'll tell him you said so." Suzanne laughed again.

Brett suddenly looked worried. "No, don't! Forget I said anything at all!"

* * *

"SPACE alien." Gregg laughed some twenty minutes later. "If I leave the foils in your hair you can go as a space alien tomorrow night."

"Too bad I already have a costume, though it needs a bit of tweaking," said Suzanne.

"Are we going to wax your brows today?" Gregg asked, as he untwisted the foils. "Or better yet, let me tint them? They are a tad light. Darkening them would give you better definition. Of course, so would a shot of Botox between those nonexistent brows."

"No, thanks," said Suzanne. Her eyes flicked toward Gregg. "Gregg, what does Tortuga mean to you?"

He shrugged. "I don't know. Turtle?"

"That's what everyone says."

"Well, is that the right answer?"

"I don't know," said Suzanne. "It's something I'm still puzzling out."

Gregg pulled out the last foil. "It also makes me think of tattoos," he added.

Suzanne crinkled her brows. "Really? How so?"

"You know, a tattoo as a symbol." He thought for a moment. "Like a tribal thing, you know? Tribal motifs are very popular right now."

"I never thought of it that way," said Suzanne, "but I suppose a turtle can be quite symbolic."

"Sure, like in Native American culture," Gregg pointed out.

"Then it might even be spiritual," said Suzanne.

"What's spiritual?" asked Brett, as he eased his way over to steal a scissors.

"A turtle. Or a turtle tattoo," said Gregg.

"Oh sure," said Brett. "Like that big guy has on his arm." They exchanged knowing glances with each other.

"What are you talking about?" Suzanne asked.

"He means the guy from the prison," said Gregg. "The big, bald guy."

That answer pretty much rocked Suzanne's world. "Lester Drummond?" she said, her voice rising in surprise. "The warden?"

Gregg smiled back at her in the mirror. "That's it!"

CHAPTER 27

SUZANNE glanced into the rearview mirror and checked herself for about the twentieth time. Makeup? Fine. Lips? Thinly veneered with L'Oréal's Berry Burst lip gloss. Hair? Deliciously honeyed thanks to Gregg's fine hand.

She'd parked her Ford Taurus on the street directly across from Schmitt's Bar and knew that Sam was already waiting inside. His BMW was both sandwiched and dwarfed between a Ford F-150 and a Chevy Silverado right in front of the place.

Grabbing her bag, Suzanne climbed out of her car and jogged across the street, feeling upbeat and a little jazzed, hoping she looked casually chic in her suede jacket, designer jeans, and low suede boots.

As she pushed open the door to Schmitt's and stepped inside, the aroma of beer and sizzling burgers enveloped her immediately, and she was treated to the sound of Trace Adkins playing on the jukebox accompanied by the plinkety-plink backbeat of pinball machines.

Sam was already seated in a wooden booth, a frosty mug of beer in front of him. "Hey there," he said, when he caught sight of her. He stood up to greet her, put a hand on her shoulder, then leaned forward and gave her a quick peck. "You look great." He beamed like a guy on a first date.

Suzanne's hand instinctively crept up to her hair. "Thanks," she said.

"I . . ." She was about to tell him she'd just had her hair done, then caught herself. Changed her words to, "I was afraid I'd be late." She slid into the booth across from him and shrugged out of her jacket. Gave him what she hoped was a dazzling smile.

"You want a beer?" he asked.

"Sure."

"Food, too?" he asked. "The ubiquitous greasy burger basket?"

"Of course. With plenty of crunchy onion strings."

"We'll throw caution to the wind and forget about HDL tonight." Sam laughed. He lifted a hand and waved at Freddy, the bartender. Freddy caught his wave and nodded back, loping around the bar, digging a pen and order pad from his bartender's apron.

"What's your pleasure, Ms. Dietz?" Freddy asked.

Suzanne grinned in spite of herself. Freddy was a laconic sort, who wore old-fashioned round John Lennon glasses and sported a braided goatee. He was also a student of poetry and philosophy and had once won first prize in an amateur poetry contest the VFW had sponsored as a tribute to World War II veterans.

"Burger basket with everything," Suzanne told him.

"Same here," said Sam.

"And to drink?" Freddy asked.

"Beer for Suzanne, another one for me," said Sam. When Freddy was gone, he hunched forward and said, "Man, you look terrific."

Suzanne grinned until she felt her face would crack. She was scared, hopeful, and excited, all rolled into one. She was also aware that this was their first public appearance together. Their debut. In a small town like Kindred, a Saturday night date, humble though it may be, pretty much announced to the universe that you were a couple.

"People are going to start connecting the dots," Sam told her, glancing around.

"People tend to do that," Suzanne agreed.

"You're not worried?" asked Sam.

Suzanne reached across the table and put a hand on top of his. "I'm a little worried about you," she said.

Sam furrowed his brows. "How so?"

"I mean, you're new in town and it's . . . um . . . awfully early to start a relationship."

Sam lifted a thumb and rubbed it gently against her hand. Suzanne thought it felt warm and smooth and really quite wonderful.

"If you ask me," said Sam, "we're already *in* a relationship. In fact, I think it pretty much commenced Tuesday night."

Suzanne blushed and ducked her head. "I suppose you're right."

"I know I'm right," said Sam. "And I'd pretty much love to shout it from the rooftops." When he saw her stricken look, he added, "But I won't. We'll take it slow and easy. Let decorum be our watchword."

"Whew," she said, doing a pretend cartoon swipe of her forehead.

"So nothing to be nervous about."

"Glad we cleared that up," said Suzanne.

"Except for one thing . . ."

Suzanne took a deep breath. She pretty much knew what was coming.

"Last night," said Sam. "The dogs. A very bad situation."

"Terrible," Suzanne agreed. "What kind of inhumane person would . . ."

"I'm talking about you."

"Excuse me?"

"Don't go all wide-eyed and innocent on me," Sam cautioned. "You know exactly what I'm talking about. In fact, we touched on it this morning. It chills me to know you were the one who discovered Wilbur Halpern shot to death and that you got yourself into another problematic situation last night with those dogs." When Suzanne started to launch a pro forma protest, Sam grabbed her hand again and said, "Listen, sweetheart, I don't want to be called to the emergency room and find out the patient I'm treating is you."

"I don't relish the idea of ending up there, either," said Suzanne, wondering if she should spill the beans about her little foray into Chuck Peebler's house. Maybe some things were better left unsaid?

But when the burger baskets arrived, the need to tell him burned strong. Suzanne wanted to be completely straight with Sam. Deception was never a smart way to begin a relationship. Just look at Toni and Junior.

"There's something else I need to tell you . . ."

Sam glanced at her, midbite in his burger. "Is it serious?" His words came out, "Is it sherioush?"

"I think so."

"Oh boy." He chewed quickly and swallowed.

"Here's the thing," said Suzanne. "You know I've been worried about Sheriff Doogie."

"Okay."

"Doogie's been taking a lot of flack about not coming

up with a suspect in Peebler's death, plus he's extremely ripped up over Deputy Halpern."

"Sure," said Sam, "it's what you'd expect. Logical human emotions."

Suzanne continued. "So I offered to help him."

"In what way?" Sam asked, suddenly on the alert.

Suzanne shrank back in the booth. "I offered to go into Chuck Peebler's house and look around? See if I couldn't find some sort of clue?"

"Offered?" asked Sam. "Or did."

"Did," said Suzanne. "Yesterday afternoon, right before Toni and I went looking for pumpkins and ended up finding dogs."

Sam gazed at her in horror. "You're telling me you went into the deserted house of a murder victim?"

"Well, Doogie did give me the key."

"He what!" Sam ducked his head and said, "Doogie's off his rocker! He's completely lost it!"

"I kind of nudged him," Suzanne admitted.

"You're really something," said Sam. He grabbed a paper napkin, blotted at his lips.

Suzanne thought she might be off the hook, but Sam suddenly turned deadly serious.

"How did you know someone wasn't waiting for you inside that house?" Sam asked. "How do you know someone didn't see you go in?"

Suzanne shook her own head in disbelief. "I guess I didn't. I don't. My mind didn't go in that direction at all." She paused. "But I did find something that perked my interest."

"What?" Sam asked. He was still sitting back from the table, as if he was slowly digesting everything Suzanne was telling him.

Suzanne dug in her purse and pulled out the Post-it note. "This," she said, extending her hand and sticking the note on the back of Sam's hand.

He peered at it speculatively, like an entomologist might peer at a bark beetle. "Tortuga?"

"It was tucked in the frame of Peebler's bedroom mirror."

Sam's eyes darted toward her again. "You went in his bedroom?"

"It was an *investigation*," she said.

"Still . . ."

Picking up her burger, Suzanne said, "There, now you know everything. No secrets, no hidden agenda, everything on the up-and-up." She took a nibble. "A clean slate."

"So what's the meaning of Tortuga?" Sam asked.

"No idea, but I found out that Lester Drummond sports a turtle tattoo."

"The prison warden?" Sam looked thoughtful. "And you think there's a connection?"

Suzanne smiled to herself. "That's what I'd like to find out."

"You're incorrigible," said Sam.

"Sorry," said Suzanne. "That's me. It's a package deal."

He gave her a wink. "Some package."

They relaxed and ate their burgers then, relegating the two murders and Suzanne's investigation to the back burner for the time being.

And they talked. About Suzanne's plans for the Cackleberry Club and her dream of someday opening Crepes Suzanne, a small fine-dining restaurant. Sam told her about his residency at Massachusetts General and then they traded small talk and onion strings.

"This is a great place," said Sam, leaning back, looking relaxed. His red plastic burger basket was heaped with paper napkins. "Greasy, but nice." He glanced up at a battered metal sign that said, Your Burger Is Ready When the Smoke Alarm Goes Off, and grinned.

"Nobody does a burger basket like Schmitt's," agreed Suzanne.

"Not even the Cackleberry Club?"

"We do burgers, but they're of the chicken and turkey variety."

"Ah," said Sam, "the healthy stuff."

"Petra says she doesn't want to be responsible for causing coronary thrombosis or myocardial infarctions all over town."

"Nice of her, though it does impact my business."

"She also says . . ." A loud whump suddenly rattled the front windows of the bar, then bright orange flared in the street. "What was that?" Suzanne cried.

"Fire?" said Sam. "Explosion?"

Everyone in the bar seemed to jump up at once and scramble for the front door, causing a good deal of panic and an alcohol-fueled traffic jam. By the time Suzanne and Sam elbowed their way out, flames were shooting thirty feet into the air!

"That's my car!" Suzanne screamed, gazing at the angry fireball that, forty minutes earlier, had been her beloved Ford Taurus. The one she'd sometimes called Cynthia. "My car!" she cried again, as she tried to rush toward it.

Sam caught Suzanne by the shoulders and pulled her back with a firm grip. "Don't," he said. "It's gone."

"But . . ." Her arms fluttered futilely.

Within a matter of minutes they heard sirens. Then an enormous fire engine roared down Main Street, its horn making flat blats. As it rocked to a stop, four volunteer fire-men jumped from the cab. Hoses were unfurled, wrenches clanked against fire hydrants, and great gluts of water began to surge. But it was all too little, too late. All the oil and grease and gas had burned like a cheap cheeseburger on Freddy's grill.

"Poor car," Suzanne mourned.

"Better we should go back inside," said Sam.

Suzanne shook her head. No. She wanted to watch. "I'm . . . I'm in shock," she told him.

Sam did a quick check of her pulse, respiration, and skin pallor. "Emotional shock," was his final diagnosis.

The wail of another siren caused everyone to crane their necks.

A maroon-and-gold sheriff car careened up, stopped in the middle of the street, and Sheriff Doogie hopped out. Dressed in civvies, he wore blue jeans and a gray sweatshirt that said, *This isn't a beer gut, it's a liquid grain storage fa-cility.* Stalking over to the burned-out car, Doogie surveyed the wreckage, then stomped back toward Schmitt's Bar, trying not to stumble over the tangle of fire hoses. When he caught sight of Suzanne, he said, "Isn't that your car?"

"It *was* my car," said a glum Suzanne.

"What the hale holy hector happened?" Doogie de-manded. Then, without giving Suzanne time to answer, said, "You start smoking again, Suzanne?"

Suzanne shook her head. "Hardly."

Doogie looked puzzled. "You notice any burning smell when you parked that thing? Any engine lights come on? Or maybe the muffler was shot?"

"No."

"This looks fairly suspicious," Doogie said, as one of

the firemen continued to pour water on the smoldering wreck. "Could have even been intentional."

"Gee," Suzanne said, under her breath. "You think?"

"What?" said Doogie, staring into the crowd, as if he might pick out a guilty face or two. "Huh?"

"You don't think it was random vandalism?" Sam asked.

"Not sure," said Doogie, "although if I was a kid who wanted to cause a heck of a commotion I might have set my sights on this BMW here." He gestured with an upturned thumb at Sam's car.

"Thanks a lot," said Sam.

Suzanne didn't want to leave, of course, but the crowd was piling back into Schmitt's Bar, the really big excitement concluded for the night. Finally, Sam convinced Suzanne to climb into his car. By that time she was shaking from the cold and looking more than a little lost.

"I'll take you home," he told her, in a voice that was both sympathetic and tender.

"You'll stay over?" she asked.

"Yes," he said. "Of course. If that's what you want."

She leaned against his shoulder. "That's what I want."

He turned the key, cranked up the heater, and pulled away from the curb slowly. As they drove past the smoldering remains of Suzanne's car, Sam said, "Do you think it was random?"

Suzanne stared at the burned-out hulk. "No, I don't," she said in a whisper.

Sam put an arm around her and pulled her closer. "Deliberate?"

"Yes."

"But why pick on you? On your car?"

"Because," said Suzanne, "it was meant to be a warning."

CHAPTER 28

SUZANNE woke to crumpled sheets, warm memories, and an empty bed.

She let out a gasp. *Oh no!*

It crossed her mind that her romance, her fling, her whatever wonderful thing it might have been, was suddenly ancient history. Then a dazzling man wearing a tight T-shirt and an even tighter pair of jeans appeared in her bedroom doorway holding a steaming mug of coffee.

"This could become a habit," Sam drawled. He smiled at her in the morning light, his hair tumbled and mussed, looking more youthful than ever.

"The coffee?" Suzanne asked, modestly arranging a sheet around herself.

"No, you." Sam sauntered over to her and handed her the coffee.

Suzanne accepted it, took a sip, and glanced at the clock on the nightstand. "Ten thirty! I can't believe I slept so late!"

"You were in dire need of restorative sleep," said Sam. He sat down next to her on the bed and gently kissed her forehead.

"We didn't get to sleep *that* early," she told him.

He grinned. "No, we didn't."

The dance card of last night's bizarre events flashed through her brain. "Did you call . . . ?"

"Shelby's." He nodded. "They'll tow your car to the garage. What's left of it."

"I don't think hammering on a new fender or ironing out the front bumper is going to do the trick."

"No, but they can put together an estimate for your insurance company."

"Ah," she said, "that's how that works." Suzanne savored his closeness as she thought for a few moments. "I better call Toni and see if I can get myself a loaner for a couple of days."

"Toni owns a used car lot?"

"Junior has a collection," said Suzanne.

"Sounds like a plan then. And while you're busy with that, might I inquire where you keep the kibble? You have two canines who are demanding room service, *s'il vous plaît*."

"Red plastic barrel in the pantry off the kitchen," she said, as she reached for the phone.

Toni answered on the sixth ring. A sleepy, "Hello?"

"Happy Halloween!" was Suzanne's greeting.

"You're chipper this morning." Toni yawned.

"I got my full eight hours of sleep," said Suzanne. *Well, maybe seven and a half.* "Listen, does Junior have an extra car I can borrow?"

"What's wrong with your car?"

"Somebody barbequed it," said Suzanne. "Outside Schmitt's Bar last night."

"What!" came Toni's shrill bark. "Are you serious? Can it be repaired?"

"We might be able to salvage the engine block and turn it into an end table."

"Holy smokes," breathed Toni.

"So I was hoping," said Suzanne, "that Junior could loan me a car. Or rent me one."

"For you, it's gratis," said Toni. "And, yes, Junior has an entire fleet of available junkers. He's your basic nightmare used car dealer who can't bear to part with anything."

"Excellent," said Suzanne. "At least it'll give me a set of wheels until I square things away with my insurance company."

"Not to worry," Toni promised. "I'll have Junior run one of his classics over to you right away." She paused. "Only one problem."

"What's that?"

Toni cackled wickedly. "The tires are probably gonna be a lot like Junior, overinflated and going bald!"

"I love that sound," Sam told her. He was sitting at the kitchen table, sipping coffee, moving a sugar bowl around in circles.

Suzanne dipped another slice of French baguette into her mixture of eggs, milk, cinnamon, and vanilla, then plopped it into a heavy cast-iron skillet bubbling with butter.

"You mean the sizzle of the French toast?" she asked.

"I'm talking about the sound of someone fixing breakfast for me," said Sam. "All the little tips and taps and clicks and clacks of home cooking."

"Happy to do it," she said, grabbing a bottle of Vermont maple syrup from the refrigerator. "And could you pop this in the microwave to speed things along, please? Oh, take the metal cap off first."

"And set the table?"

"Sure," she said, sounding a little surprised. "If you don't mind."

"Mind?" said Sam. "I'm usually puttering around by myself in the morning, eating three-day-old Entenmann's Crumb Cake. This is a rare treat."

Hopefully not too rare, she decided. *Hopefully an event that will be repeated again and again.*

Suzanne focused on her French toast, while Sam set cheery orange plates on linen placemats, then peered in a couple of drawers until he found the silverware.

"Fantastic!" Sam declared, when they finally sat down to eat.

"If I'd had the right kind of goat cheese, I would have made stuffed French toast," Suzanne told him.

Sam closed his eyes and let his fingertips do a light pitty-pat dance against his chest. "Be still my heart."

Suzanne managed to eat three slices of French toast, while Sam downed five slices. As well as another mug of coffee, a glass of fresh-squeezed orange juice, and great puddles of syrup.

Finally, after they'd eaten, chatted, and marveled at how sticky their fingers were, Sam hunched forward across the table and said, "You're sure somebody torched your car on purpose?"

"Pretty sure. I mean, how often do you see cars just blowing up?"

"In Bruce Willis movies," said Sam, "a lot."

"But in real life?" Suzanne asked.

"Hmm," said Sam. "Hardly ever."

"Exactly my point."

"And you think it was a warning," said Sam.

"Had to be," said Suzanne. "Somebody got wind that I've been doing a little sleuthing."

"Snooping," Sam amended.

"No," said Suzanne, "snooping is being nosy for amusement purposes only. Sleuthing is trying to connect clues to an actual crime."

"Did you just make that up?" Sam asked. "Or did you read it in a Nancy Drew mystery?"

Suzanne shrugged. "It just came to me on the spot."

"You're really quite brilliant, you know that?"

"No," said Suzanne, "I really don't." *But I sure don't mind hearing it. From you, that is.*

"This is great," said Sam, stretching his legs out. "I wish we could sit here all day and just eat and talk." He peered at her. "But I'm guessing you have to take off for the Cackleberry Club fairly soon?"

"We're officially closed today, so no breakfast or brunch to prepare. But I do have to head over and help with preparations for tonight."

"Are you looking forward to your big Halloween party?"

"I am, although two murders have kind of taken the edge off things. That and my exploding car."

"I predict this evening will be smooth sailing," said Sam. "No problems, just your magical little goblin fantasy party."

"I hope you're right," said Suzanne, reaching for his plate. She stopped, gave him a speculative gaze. "You have to wear a costume tonight, you know."

Sam looked startled. "I do?"

"Sure. It's a costume party."

Sam didn't look convinced. "You're not just saying that,

are you? I mean, if I show up dressed like a Klingon, you're all not going to be in street clothes laughing at me?"

"It's a funny idea," said Suzanne, "but no. It really is a costume party."

"What are *you* going to wear?" Sam asked.

She gave him a conspiratorial wink. "Don't tell anyone, but I'm going as the Headless Horseman."

Sam was momentarily charmed. "So you're going to ride your horse, too?"

"Mocha's part of it, sure," said Suzanne. "And when the moment is right, I'll gallop through the party and scare the living daylights out of everyone!"

"I love it!" Sam declared. "So I *do* have to dress up. But what should I wear?"

"Maybe go as a doctor? Wear scrubs or something."

"No, no, no, I get enough of that every day."

Suzanne thought for a minute. "Maybe . . ." She held up an index finger. "Wait right here, I have an idea."

Suzanne returned a few minutes later to find Sam standing at the sink, up to his elbows in sudsy water.

"An employed male who isn't afraid of soapsuds. Almost as good as a multimillionaire who loves to shop." She grinned at him. "Come on over here and sit down. I want to try something."

Sam wiped his hands, then obediently followed her to the table and plopped down.

"Now tilt your head back," said Suzanne. Using red lip liner, she drew a lightning bolt scar on Sam's forehead. Then she balanced a pair of round, wire-rimmed reading glasses on his nose and wound a long scarf around his neck. Finally, she rumpled his hair and brushed it forward.

"You have a dark tweed jacket?" she asked.

Sam nodded.

"Perfect."

"What am I?" Sam asked.

"Welcome to my Halloween party, Harry Potter!"

That sent him skittering to the mirror. He came back, moments later, looking quite pleased. "You're a very crafty lady," he told her. "In more ways than one."

"Really?" Suzanne responded. "I think you're the crafty one, maneuvering another sleepover."

Sam spread his arms wide, the better to envelop her. "What could I do? You were a damsel in distress."

TRUE to Toni's promise, Junior had parked a red Chevy Impala in front of her house. Correction, eons ago, it had rolled off a showroom floor as red. Now the car's color was pretty much an oxidized liver brown spackled with demarcations of rust. In some spots, even the rust had blisters of rust. But it was here, so it must still run.

Suzanne grabbed the keys that dangled from the rearview mirror and held her breath as she cranked the engine. First the car shimmied, then it rattled like it was being buffeted by an F6 tornado. *Maybe an exhaust system hanging on for dear life? A transmission ready to implode?*

Suzanne pulled away from the curb, chuckling, wondering if the neighbors were getting an eyeful. And when she stopped at the corner, Junior's clunker belched like a flatulent old man, then actually bucked!

But she made it to the Cackleberry Club, where Toni and Petra were already scurrying around like mad.

Junior was there, too, dressed in a black T-shirt that said

Carpe Noctem across the front and his usual pegged jeans, pounding in the last stake that held up a ginormous white tent that was open on three sides.

"How's it running, Suzanne?" was Junior's greeting. He pulled a pack of Camel straights from his rolled-up sleeve and lit one. "Purring like a kitten?"

"More like a salsa dancer with indigestion," she told him, with a wry smile.

Junior grinned like a maniac, loving her analogy. "Ha-cha!"

Toni came bounding up to them, in blue jeans, a chambray shirt tied at the waist, and a red bandana containing her wild fluff of hair. "When you finish pounding tent stakes, Junior, I want you to set up the tables and chairs."

"Yeah, yeah," mumbled Junior. Toni could be a tough taskmaster.

But Toni wasn't finished. "Then you gotta haul those hay bales . . ." She pointed at a stack of hay bales that had magically materialized from Ducovny's farm. "And arrange them in concentric circles. That's where we'll set the fire pits for roasting hot dogs and s'mores."

"What's concentric?" Junior asked, tossing his dark forelock of hair back and pluming out a stream of smoke.

Toni rolled her eyes. "Round."

"Oh," said Junior, catching on, "yeah."

"He's like a fourth grader who needs remedial help with geometry and a juvenile delinquent all rolled into one," Toni told Suzanne, when Junior finally stumbled off to his next task.

"But he's working," said Suzanne. "Which is what I need to do."

"We're actually in pretty good shape," Toni told her. "Joey Ewald was here earlier, so he schlepped most of the heavy stuff for us. Of course, Petra's going crazy inside."

"It's not high tea," said Suzanne, "it's hot dogs and beans."

"Try to tell her that," said Toni, as they headed inside.

"Hey," said Suzanne, "does Junior know what's on his T-shirt?"

Toni giggled. "Naw. He thinks *Carpe Noctem* means fishing at night."

"SUZANNE!" cried Petra. "I heard what happened last night!" She came flying from the kitchen, deep concern etching her broad face, and grasped Suzanne in an expansive bear hug. "I feel awful! More repercussions!"

"I think so," said Suzanne.

"I'm going to say a special prayer," said Petra, "so your guardian angel watches over you extra carefully today. Oh, and poor Cynthia!"

"Who's Cynthia?" asked Toni.

"Her car," said Petra. "Cynthia was her car."

"You name your car?" Toni asked, scratching her head. "I thought only I did that. And Junior."

Petra let loose a mock shudder that almost caused her chef's hat to topple. "I hate to think what names Junior dreams up."

"Dodie," said Toni, "he calls his Mustang Dodie."

Petra grabbed Suzanne's hand and pulled her into the kitchen. "And I have an update on Reverend Yoder."

"Good news, I hope." For some reason, Suzanne felt guilty for not asking Sam how the good reverend was doing. Then again, she really didn't want to mix business with . . . pleasure.

"He gets out of the hospital tomorrow," said Petra. "Too bad he couldn't make it to the party tonight."

"You really think a minister wants to rub shoulders with people dressed like witches and ghosts?" asked Toni.

"Mmm," said Petra, reconsidering, "though it's all in good fun, you make a good point. He might not appreciate it."

"Maybe more than his heart can take," Toni muttered.

"Oh my gosh," said Suzanne, gazing at a huge silver tray, "you made your special bedeviled eggs." Petra's bedeviled eggs included hot peppers, diced pimento, onions, and homemade mayo.

"Honey," said Petra, giving an offhand wave, "that's just the tip of the iceberg. There are two more trays in the cooler."

"This has to go down in the annals as a Cackleberry Club specialty," said Suzanne. She glanced around the kitchen. "What else?"

"Beans are on the stove," said Petra, pointing to an enormous vat of bubbling brown liquid. "I'm going to toss in more molasses and brown sugar, then shove 'em in the oven to finish off."

"Yum," said Toni.

"The bakery came through with a special delivery of hot dog buns," said Petra, "and I ordered bratwurst instead of hot dogs." She shrugged. "Tastier, I think. Meatier."

"Our wurst is our best," Toni joked.

"Oh," said Petra, "and Junior gave me his recipe for deviled ham."

"Junior has a recipe?" asked Suzanne. This from a man whose idea of haute cuisine was Old Country Buffet?

"Petra said we could whip it up," said Toni, jumping in. "I guess it's not too complicated."

"No," said Suzanne, "I doubt it is."

They worked together for the next twenty minutes, prepping the rest of the food, discussing the best way to arrange the buffet table, and trying to figure out how many fire pits they'd need for making s'mores—or S'mortuaries, as Petra insisted on calling them.

Just as they decided that Petra would oversee the cooking of all the brats on the outdoor grill, Junior strolled in. He grinned, grabbed a sugar cookie that was shaped like a bat and decorated with chocolate icing, and promptly bit off its head.

"You're here to help us set up, Junior," said Toni, trying to snatch the cookie away from him. "Not eat."

Junior danced out of reach. "Yeah, but think of all the free consulting work I've given you."

"Consulting work?" said Suzanne.

"Sure," said Junior, looking earnest. "Coming up with ideas on where to put the tent, figuring how many chairs you'd need, deciding where to put the band. You guys didn't even *think* about the band."

"You're right," said Petra, "we didn't. Have another cookie, Junior."

"Don't mind if I do," said Junior, grabbing an entire handful of cookies. "You can't let a musical group dominate festivities," said Junior, "but they still need to be front and center. For entertainment purposes."

"Where'd you learn this stuff, Junior?" asked Petra. "How did you get to be such a crackerjack party planner?"

Junior shrugged, looking pleased. "Jeez, I don't know. Going to stock car races, I guess. Hanging around in the pits, where they have music and beer tents and sexy tire models and stuff."

"Well put, Junior," said Suzanne. "Well put."

"Done with your break?" Toni asked as she pinched his arm hard. "Because we've got *lots* of decorating to do."

"More work?" whined Junior.

"And then you have to set up the games," Petra reminded them.

"Oh man," he groaned.

CHAPTER 29

IT took a lot of sweat and effort, but by the time the sun sank low on the horizon, turning the sky a perfect Halloween orange, the parking lot in front of the Cackleberry Club had been transformed into a veritable Halloween land. Filmy white chiffon ghosts fluttered from tree limbs. Life-sized witches hunkered over cauldrons filled with steaming dry ice. A grinning glow-in-the-dark skeleton clicked and clacked ominously from his perch in a large oak tree. Entire cadres of black vinyl bats dipped and swung from the tent's rafters. And realistic-looking tombstones tilted crazily in the yard.

"This looks spectacular," said Suzanne. She and Toni were doing a quick reconnaissance. Junior had set up the tables and chairs, some under the tent, some under the stars. The buffet station and large grill had been moved into the tent. Hay bales were arranged in circles and an area for the band had also been marked with hay bales.

"All we need to do is haul out a few more pumpkins," said Toni. She pointed at a row of stakes that had been pounded into the ground. "You see that? I'm gonna plant a grinning, glowing jack-o'-lantern on top of each stake."

"Very effective," agreed Suzanne.

"We just need to carve a few more."

"You need my help?" Suzanne asked.

"Naw," said Toni, "Kit's gonna come by and help me finish up."

"Glad to hear she's not dancing tonight," said Suzanne.

"She's not," said Toni, then gave a mischievous grin. "At least not at Hoobly's."

Suzanne suddenly had a mental picture of Kit showing up in her red bra and panties. "She's not going to wear her usual costume, is she?"

Toni shrugged. "Search me. Or better yet, search her."

"Not with those skimpy clothes," said Suzanne. "No place to hide anything!"

They both chuckled, Suzanne a little uneasily, then turned to look as a rattling truck and trailer chugged its way into their lot.

"Junior," said Toni. "With the fire pits."

Junior hopped from the cab of the truck and grinned. Spreading his arms wide, he twirled around, the better to show off his red devil costume. Then he reached back into the cab and produced a sparkling, silver pitchfork.

"Good gravy," Suzanne breathed. Now she really was glad Reverend Yoder wouldn't be around to catch this act.

"Like my costume?" asked Junior. "It's guaranteed authentic."

Suzanne lifted an eyebrow.

"And it's made of genuine polyester," Junior added.

"Don't get too close to the fire," Toni cautioned, "you'll go up like a moth in a flame!"

"Where did you find it?" Suzanne asked. Honestly, where did one purchase a perfectly hideous red polyester devil suit that had the same basic construction as a pair of long johns?

"Dollar store," said Junior.

"Such a deal," said Suzanne.

"And I got your fire pits," said Junior. "Come on and take a look."

Suzanne and Toni followed Junior to the trailer and peered in. He was as good as his word. Three low, round fire pits, almost like flattened-out cauldrons, squatted in the trailer.

"You made these?" Suzanne asked, trying to ignore the truck's mud flaps, which featured silhouettes of reclining naked girls.

Junior nodded. "Welded 'em using a couple of oil drums."

"From your scrap metal business," said Suzanne.

"Um, sort of," said Junior, shifting nervously.

"Well, they look just great!" Toni exclaimed. "Perfect for toasting marshmallows and roasting chestnuts. Look! They've even got legs."

"I always figured that welding class I took in reform school would come in handy," said Junior, practically crowing over his handiwork. "It's amazing what kind of art you can create with an acetylene torch."

"So here's how it's gonna work," explained Toni. "Ten dollars buys an orange bracelet, which gives customers unlimited access to our food, cider, s'mores, games, prizes, music, and the costume contest."

"And how many people are we expecting?" asked Petra. They were crowded in the kitchen, making last-minute adjustments.

"Maybe a hundred," said Suzanne. "Although I suppose it could even run to a hundred and fifty."

"The Cackleberry Club is the most popular venue in town!" Toni said, with glee.

"So maybe even two hundred people," Petra fretted. "I wonder if we have enough . . ."

"Knock, knock," came a woman's voice at the back door.

"You'll have to go around front," Toni screeched through the screen. Then did a fast double take and said, "Kit?"

Kit Kaslik grinned as she pushed her way into the kitchen. Dressed in a white silk minidress, Kit had plastered Priority Mail stickers all over her dress. On her head was a veil made of bubble wrap.

"I get it!" Toni squealed. "You're a mail-order bride!"

"Oh, that's so creative," Petra enthused. "And here I'm just going to be plain old Raggedy Ann."

"What's your costume, Toni?" asked Kit.

"Cowgirl," Toni said, proudly. "What else?"

Kit gave Suzanne a shy smile. "How about you, Suzanne?"

But Suzanne was surprisingly mum.

"She's not talking," said Toni. "It's some kind of big hoo-ha surprise."

"That's right," said Petra, "You'll just have to wait and see. And be around when I do my special introduction."

"This is intriguing," said Kit.

"Have to wait and see," said Suzanne, a sparkle in her eye.

TONI pushed two tables together in the café and laid out newspapers. Then she and Kit rolled up their sleeves and went to work on the pumpkins.

"We don't have much time left," Suzanne cautioned. The food was prepped, the cauldrons were lit, chestnuts were roasting. In another thirty minutes their guests would begin to arrive.

"We're only going to carve seven," said Toni. "Special ones to, you know, sit on top of those wooden stakes."

"I like what you've got going there," said Suzanne, studying one of Kit's pumpkins. It was a goofy face with a crooked grin.

"Thanks," said Kit. Then she gave a wicked laugh. "I modeled it after one of the customers at Hoobly's."

Hoobly's, thought Suzanne. *Where Sasha O'Dell also danced. And where her crazy husband, Mike, probably looked on with some trepidation. Or was he feeling vindicated now? Could he have killed Peebler and Wilburn Halpern and gotten away scot-free?*

"How's your friend Sasha doing?" Suzanne asked.

"Good," said Kit, scraping away pumpkin pulp. "In fact, I told her to stop by tonight."

Suzanne frowned. "Seriously?"

"Yeah, I asked her to help me with the games," said Kit. Then she made a nervous gesture. "I think she might bring her husband, too."

Mike O'Dell, Suzanne thought again. *I hope he's not in costume so I can keep an eagle eye on him. The last thing we need tonight is some kind of . . . accident.*

"How many games did we end up with?" Toni asked. She glanced over at Suzanne, who was filling out gift certificates to be used for prizes.

Suzanne tapped her pen against the table. "We've got Pin the Tail on the Werewolf, Wheel of Misfortune, Vampire Ring Toss, and a Witches Pond, which is really a sort of fishpond for the kids. Oh, and the costume contest. I guess you could count that as a game."

"Know what we should do next year?" said Toni.

"What?" said Suzanne.

"Have a zombie crawl," said Toni. "Get a whole bunch of people to dress up like zombies and then have everybody lurch through downtown."

Kit chuckled. "They already do that. Every Saturday night after last call!"

Toni glanced out the window, suddenly taking notice of a battered minivan. "Hey, our band just arrived. We should go out and show them where to set up."

"Got it," said Suzanne, pocketing her pen and tamping her gift certificates into a nice, neat pile.

Toni looked at the pumpkins as she wiped her hands on her jeans.

"You go," said Kit. "I'll finish up here."

"You sure?" asked Toni, but Kit nodded sagely.

"Who's the band again?" Suzanne asked, as they tromped outside.

"Buckshot Benoit and the Ring Tones," said Toni.

"I'm not familiar with them," said Suzanne, somehow doubting that this group's musical repertoire had ever made it to serious ringtone status.

Junior came hustling up as they threaded their way through hay bales, heading for the band. "Where does the Wheel of Misfortune go again?" he asked, waving his pitchfork, looking a little weary.

Toni heaved a sigh and took off with Junior, leaving Suzanne to go it alone with the band.

But the band turned out to be a friendly lot, with the band's leader greeting her effusively.

"Buckshot Benoit," said a tall, bespectacled man in overalls, as he offered a hand. "Pleased to make your acquaintance, and thanks so much for inviting me and the boys to play."

"I hope you have enough room here," said Suzanne. There seemed to be five musicians in all. Two guitar players, two fiddle players, and a drummer. They were all men, all of an indeterminate age owing to various beards, goatees, ponytails, piercings, and tattoos.

"We're just fine." Buckshot grinned.

"What kind of music do you play?" Suzanne asked. She hadn't vetted the group and had relied solely on Toni and Junior's recommendation, so she wasn't sure what brand of rompin', stompin' music they'd pump out.

Buckshot picked up his guitar and plucked a string. "Rock, disco, old-timey, we play it all."

"Eclectic," said Suzanne.

"Electric?" said Buckshot. He shook his head, sadly. "Naw, we just got regular old acoustic guitars."

FIVE minutes later, Suzanne slipped into Junior's clunker and chugged her way across the back field. It was time to saddle up Mocha Gent and then ride him back across to the Cackleberry Club. After all, she had a grand entrance to make on horseback!

But as she bounced across the rutted field in the dark, Suzanne's party mood began to slip. Low hanging clouds had filtered in, blotting out what should be a full moon. They hunkered low and fretful, giving the night an eerie feel. Adding an element of . . . danger?

Suzanne thought about all the costumed revelers who'd

soon show up at the Cackleberry Club with one thing in mind—dancing, eating, and playing games, as if they didn't have a care in the world.

As if nothing had happened in Kindred.

But that wasn't the case. Two murders remained unsolved. A killer was still running loose. And tonight, the trusting folks of Kindred might even mingle unknowingly with him.

A killer who was, quite possibly, hiding behind a mask.

CHAPTER 30

SUZANNE, Toni, and Petra crowded into the back office, giggling and elbowing each other as they changed into their costumes. Toni was a slam dunk, of course. She just tucked a gaudy, embroidered Pepto-pink cowboy shirt into form-fitting jeans and donned boots, hat, and string tie.

"Cute," said Petra, as she struggled into her Raggedy Ann costume.

"Holy buckets," said Toni, "you're wearing red-and-white-striped stockings, too?"

Petra stopped and gazed at her. "Do I look stupid? I look stupid, don't I?" She seemed like she was ready to cry. "And I shouldn't be wearing a polka-dot smock, it's just too weird."

"It's adorable," Toni assured her, but couldn't seem to restrain her giggles.

"Aw crap," said Petra. "I *knew* it." All the last-minute preparations had frazzled her confidence.

"No," said Suzanne, "you look cute."

"Cute?" asked Petra. "Or cutesy? There's a difference, you know."

"What can I tell you," said Suzanne. "It's a great costume."

"Really?" Petra asked, fingering her bonnet. "You wouldn't just say that?"

Toni was nodding her head like mad. "That bonnet lends an extra special touch."

"Group hug," Suzanne declared. "Everybody take a deep breath and think only happy thoughts. Then let's go out and have fun."

"Doggone," said Toni, wiggling her hips like a hula dancer. "My six-guns are flapping."

"That's what you get for having big guns," Suzanne cackled.

"Oh you!" said Toni, punching Suzanne on the shoulder as she shrugged into her black, high-collared jacket. "Hey, what are you dressed as *really*?"

"Have to wait and see," Suzanne cautioned.

"A Revolutionary War character?" Toni asked.

"Maybe," smiled Suzanne.

"John Paul Jones?"

"No."

"Sergeant Pepper?"

"Try again."

Toni stomped a foot. "I hate it when you get all coy!"

NIGHT was full on now, with flames dancing in the fire pits, a breeze stirring the ghosts in the trees, the band playing a blend of country and rock, and the drifting scent of burning pine and apple wood hanging like incense in the air.

"Yowza," said Toni, surveying the scene, "everything looks spectacular."

"Spooktacular," added Petra.

Suzanne had to agree. The Cackleberry Club's front lot had indeed been magically transformed. And just when things couldn't get any better, like leaves tumbling in on the night wind, their guests began to arrive.

There was a clown, a pirate, an astronaut, Darth Vader, and a whole troupe of vampires.

"Look," said Petra, pointing, "even Spider-Man came."

"So did Hugh Hefner," said Toni.

"He's got the requisite smoking jacket and pipe," said Suzanne, "but no bunnies on his arm."

"This is gonna be a madhouse," said Petra, as more people arrived.

"Don't you love it?" asked Toni.

They scattered in a rush, then, Suzanne dashing over to greet their guests, only to find that Junior had put up a sort of rope entrance. "What's going on here?" she asked.

"Me and Kit are taking tickets," said Junior, in a self-important tone.

"You don't have to make a big deal of it," Suzanne told him. "Just give each guest a plastic wristband and let them in."

"You sure?" asked Junior.

"Yes, I'm sure," said Suzanne. "And lose the rope. "What do you think this is? Studio 54?"

PETRA busied herself with grilling brats, while Toni served up hot cider. Buckshot Benoit and his gang cranked out tunes like mad and even inspired some vigorous dancing.

A caveman, a French maid, and a ghost came waltzing in, and then, just as Suzanne was beginning to wonder where the heck he was, Harry Potter arrived.

"You look great," Sam said, hugging her.

Suzanne shook her head. "This is only part of the costume."

"I wasn't talking about the costume," Sam said, pulling her closer. They swayed together, arms entwined, bumping hips, watching the festivities heat up around them.

"Limousine coming," observed Sam.

"Not for this party," said Suzanne.

"It's stopping," said Sam.

Suzanne gazed at the glistening black stretch limo as a driver in hat and coat jumped out, then dove for the back door. It yawned open and Carmen Copeland, their local author *terrible* slowly emerged.

Carmen was dressed as a sorceress in a stunning purple velvet dress. It was hooded, floor length, and slit up one side. A dangerously plunging neckline was modest only by dint of a stunning crystal pin that thankfully covered a large expanse of skin.

"She looks like some exotic character out of a Jackie Collins novel," Sam commented. "And making a grand entrance to boot."

"Carmen's the queen of grand entrances," Suzanne told him.

"Tell me about it," said Sam. "Carmen comes into the clinic, it's like she expects us to roll out the red carpet."

"Well, do you?" asked Suzanne, a hint of jealousy creeping into her voice.

"Are you kidding?" said Sam. He clutched her hand tighter. "No way."

Suzanne wasn't expecting him, but Sheriff Doogie showed up, too. She didn't think he was on duty, but he was wearing his uniform.

"Nice costume," said Toni, as she flitted by him. "What is that? French Foreign Legion?"

"Very funny," said Doogie, as he headed for Suzanne, looking slightly grim.

"Evening, Sheriff," said Sam, who threw a meaningful glance at Suzanne, then slipped away quietly.

"Sheriff," said Suzanne, greeting Doogie, "everything okay?"

Doogie answered with a shrug.

"If you're looking for suspects," she said, "it appears the whole town has turned out here tonight."

Doogie nodded. "Kind of what I expected."

"But you're not expecting anything else, are you?" Suzanne asked. "Like trouble?" She glanced over at Petra, who was talking with an animated Jane Buckley, and wondered if Doogie was still hounding Jane. Maybe. Maybe not.

"I'm just surveying the crowd," Doogie told her. "Keeping the peace."

Suzanne did a quick check to make sure they wouldn't be overheard. "Did you find out anything about my car, yet?"

Doogie shook his head. "Only that it's still a smoldering piece of metal."

"How about the fighting dogs?"

"Got something on that," Doogie said, brightening. "I dug around county records and came up with the owner of the farm where the dogs were kenneled."

"Did you pay the owner a visit?"

"I did," said Doogie. "At first the guy didn't want to talk, but I can be a fairly persuasive fellow, so he finally admitted that particular piece of land was leased to Parnassus Enterprises."

"What's that?" Suzanne asked.

"Funny you should ask," said Doogie. "Because then I had to do some *more* digging and finally discovered it was a subsidiary of Obsidian Inc."

Suzanne frowned. "I never heard of them, either."

"It's a shell company."

"Shill?"

"No," said Doogie, "shell. But never mind that. Guess who's one of the corporate officers?"

Suzanne considered this for about a second. "Mayor Mobley?"

"Nope," said Doogie. "Lester Drummond."

"The prison warden?" Suzanne squealed. "Are you serious? Lester Drummond is raising fighting dogs?"

Doogie gave a nod. "Looks like."

"Illegal," said Suzanne.

"A felony," said Doogie.

"Do you think . . ." Suzanne's mind was racing a mile a minute now. "If there's a clandestine dog fighting ring around here, do you think it could be linked to Chuck Peebler's murder as well as Deputy Halpern's?"

Doogie gazed into the crowd. "Possible."

"What if Peebler found out and disapproved to the point of turning Drummond in?"

Doogie nodded. "That's one possibility."

"And your deputy caught on to it," Suzanne added.

"Again, a decent enough supposition," allowed Doogie. "Now we just need some actual *proof*."

JUST when Suzanne figured the party couldn't get any more crowded, Mayor Mobley and Allan Sharp showed up. They weren't in costume per se, although their bad golf shirts and shiny double-knit slacks probably counted as a kind of small-town politico costume.

"You see that?" asked Petra, sidling up to Suzanne. "They're passing out campaign buttons. Doesn't that just frost your pumpkin?"

"But look," said Suzanne, as a woman laughed at Mobley and turned away, "people are pretty much ignoring them. They know it's a Halloween party and not a political rally."

"And thank goodness for that," said Petra, taking a sip of amber liquid.

Suzanne's mouth crinkled in a quirky smile. "And just what are you drinking, my dear?"

"Hennessy," said Petra, with a look of feigned innocence. "Junior gave it to me, said it would help calm my nerves."

"Or have you partying like a rap star." Suzanne laughed.

"Still," said Petra, "it's kind of tasty." She dropped her voice. "Did you see that Sasha and her husband, Mike, showed up?"

Suzanne nodded.

"Think there's going to be trouble?"

Suzanne thought for about half a second. "The potential certainly exists."

"Oh dear. And I thought all I had to do was keep Doogie away from Jane."

"That and feed everyone," said Suzanne.

Petra took another small sip. "Probably time to set up my dessert bar."

"Need help?"

"That'd be great," said Petra. But when they got inside

the Cackleberry Club, Suzanne noticed that more than a few people had made their way into the Book Nook. She hadn't expected book business tonight, but no way was she going to complain. Slipping behind the counter, she reminded herself that all book sales would be a welcome addition to their bottom line.

"Who are you supposed to be, Suzanne?" asked Lolly Herron. Even though Lolly was dressed as a witch, she slid a very non-witchy cookbook across the counter for purchase. *Pasta for Deux*.

"Big secret," Suzanne told her. "All will be revealed later."

"Do you have any more of these alphabet books?" Snow White asked, as two of her dwarfs, really children, clung to her voluminous skirt.

"I do," said Suzanne, "but I'll have to dig them out. Can you give me a few minutes?"

"No problem," said Snow White. "We'll go bob for apples and come back."

Suzanne rang up a copy of *Blackwork* and a copy of *The Teaberry Strangler*, loving the extra business, but worrying about who was entertaining Sam. Not Carmen, she hoped.

When there was a break in the action, she dashed into her office to try to unearth that children's book.

As she pawed through a carton of books, Suzanne noticed a man in a Davy Crockett costume sidle slowly into the Book Nook. Since his back was turned toward her, she couldn't quite make out who it was. But, out of the corner of her eye, Suzanne noticed the man select a book, then browse through it for a few moments. Then he glanced around, set the book down, and slipped away. It was doubtful he'd even noticed her watching.

But something about the man's furtive gesture had registered with Suzanne. She drew a breath and hesitated.

Something about him . . .

Maybe she was jumping at shadows, but a low-level vibe had insinuated itself in her prefrontal cortex.

Suzanne thought for a few moments, then clambered to her feet and hurried over to grab the book the man had just abandoned.

She stared at the cover—*Spain's Gilded Riches*—and opened the book, glancing quickly at color photos of armor, helmets, breastplates, gold chalices, and coins. Treasure to be sure.

What the . . . ?

And like a slow-moving galleon, the word *Tortuga* swam into her brain.

Suzanne blinked, spun toward her computer, and typed in *Tortuga*.

CHAPTER 31

AND came up with something like four million hits. There were Tortuga T-shirts, Tortuga rum cakes, and Tortuga maps, as well as games, knick-knacks, and hundreds of Tortuga resorts scattered all across the Caribbean.

So an impossible search, really.

But Tortuga was the note Peebler wrote to himself and Tortuga seems to synch nicely with Spanish armor and coins, doesn't it?

Suzanne chewed on that notion for a few minutes, wondering where it might lead her.

To Lester Drummond, with his turtle tattoo and stash of vicious fighting dogs? Had Drummond murdered Chuck Peebler?

Or was Jane Buckley involved, after all? During his rant at the read dating event, Peebler had pressed Jane about stolen antiques. And Jane worked at a museum, so she had firsthand knowledge about antiquities. Was mild-mannered Jane really a stone-cold killer?

And what about Mayor Mobley and Allan Sharp? Were they so obsessed with winning that they'd kill an opponent? But how did antiques come into play?

And then there was Mike O'Dell, the man with a crossbow and a wife who'd been hassled by Chuck Peebler. Was

O'Dell a spurned man or a common thief? Could he have stolen antiques from Peebler's aunt and then fenced them?

Suzanne felt her mind spinning like a centrifuge. Where was she going with all of this? Where were the answers?

She pressed the book to her chest, as if she could absorb critical information through osmosis. And puzzled some more.

The next step was so simple it made her laugh.

Find Davy Crockett.

Maybe if she found the man in the buckskin jacket and coonskin cap, she'd also find a semblance of an answer. Or at least a clue.

Rushing outside, Suzanne was startled to see that Petra had already started the costume contest. She was standing on an orange crate, head and shoulders above the crowd, holding a microphone and introducing the evening's finalists.

Suzanne glanced at her watch. Petra would be introducing her shortly. So . . . first things first. She'd better stay on schedule and do her Headless Horseman thing. Then she'd grab Doogie and go on a Davy Crockett hunt.

Ducking back into her office, Suzanne scrunched up her jacket and inserted a couple of foam shoulder pads, making her shoulders high enough and broad enough to rival any NFL linebacker. Then she tied a black do-rag over her hair and hiked up her collar so it came just below her eyes. She checked herself in the mirror. With the black scarf covering her head, it really would appear as though she was headless. So far, so good!

She pinned on a black wool cape, perfect Sleepy Hollow couture, and grabbed the fake head that was sitting on her desk. It was really a plastic foam wig head she'd purchased from a beauty supply store. But with a bit of brown spray paint, it now looked like a head that had just flown in from a sunny weekend in Boca Raton.

Suzanne slipped through the kitchen and out the back door.

Mocha was tied to a fence at the back of her property. He turned his handsome head and nickered when he saw her approach, almost as if he'd been waiting for her. Knew in his horsy mind that the two of them were going to make a grand entrance at tonight's big party.

With a tingle of anticipation, Suzanne untied the reins, put her left foot in the stirrup, and swung up onto Mocha's broad back.

And that's when the world tilted crazily on its axis.

That's when Arthur Bunch came strolling out of the woods wearing his coonskin cap and buckskin jacket. Suzanne would have laughed out loud at how authentic Bunch looked—except for the gray snub-nosed pistol he held in his hand—the pistol that was pointed directly at her heart.

"Bunch!" she cried, startled.

"Get down, Suzanne," Bunch said through clenched teeth. "We need to talk."

"Talk?" said Suzanne, suddenly realizing Arthur Bunch was deadly serious. "Sure, Arthur, whatever you say. Just don't point that thing at me, okay? Go easy." She knew for a fact she wasn't going to get off her horse. Right now, her horse was the only advantage she had.

An evil grin lit Bunch's face. "Scared, aren't you?" He seemed to revel in his power over her.

"You bet I am," Suzanne gibbered, using her apparent fear to buy her time to think. "So just take it easy, I'll do whatever you say."

"I thought you might," Arthur said, a thin smile on his face, his attention relaxing for just a split second.

That's when Suzanne dug her heels into Mocha's flanks and drove her horse directly at Bunch.

The big horse's chest struck the man hard, spinning him around. Bunch, his arm suddenly flung up over his head, fired one shot into the sky, then the pistol flew from his hand. Still driving at him, one of the horse's metal shod hooves ground down hard on top of Bunch's left foot, eliciting a scream and sending Bunch reeling in pain.

"How do you like that, Bunch?" Suzanne taunted, suddenly grabbing the upper hand. "Want to mix it up some more? Want to tell me why you killed Charlie Peebler? Why you shot Wilbur Halpern?" Still hanging on to the wig head, she threw it at him with all her might.

But Arthur Bunch wasn't having it. He ducked the flying head and flung himself away from Suzanne and her horse. Stumbling, cursing at her, he picked himself up and took off running around the side of the Cackleberry Club.

"Doggone!" cried Suzanne. The last thing she wanted was for Arthur Bunch to find refuge in the big crowd that mingled out front. He could easily grab a different mask or costume and melt into the crowd. Or worse yet, try to take someone hostage!

Suzanne kicked Mocha again and took off after him. Cantering around the side of the building, the horse's hoofbeats rang out in the still, cool air.

"Do you folks hear that?" asked Petra's voice over the microphone, right on cue. "Do you think we might have a special visitor this Halloween night?"

Coming at full gallop, Suzanne rounded the corner, just in time to see the crowd part for her and Arthur Bunch duck past the tent. She spurred her horse on as she bent low, galloping swiftly past the row of flickering jack-o'-lanterns that Toni had planted on wooden stakes.

Grabbing the last jack-o'-lantern, Suzanne galloped through the crowd, holding the lighted pumpkin high, her cape trailing out behind her. There were appreciative oohs and aahs from the crowd.

Raising the pumpkin high above her head, Suzanne flung it with all her might. The orange missile went tumbling through the air, sparks flying, glinting jack-o'-lantern eyes winking, crooked pumpkin mouth grinning at the crowd. Then the pumpkin struck Arthur Bunch in the middle of his back, knocking him to the ground as it exploded into a hundred pieces, splattering everyone nearby with orange pumpkin goop!

"Holy bull dingers!" Doogie cried. Darting toward Suzanne, he held his hands up as if to stop her, as the crowd roared its approval at such a dramatic tableau.

"Grab him!" Suzanne yelled, as she reined her horse back hard. "Grab Bunch. He's the one who killed Charlie Peebler and Wilbur!"

CHAPTER 32

BUT the crowd's instantaneous burst of applause blocked the sound of Suzanne's plea to the sheriff! She sat atop the dancing horse as the crowd surged around her, staring out at Sheriff Doogie's quizzical face, feeling terrified and enormously frustrated.

"Bunch!" she cried again. "Grab him!"

Doogie spun about, but was trapped by the crowd and unable to make a move or get a bead on Bunch. He whipped his head back and forth frantically, but to no avail.

Suzanne, perched atop Mocha, could see Arthur Bunch just fine. The rogue killer was still on the ground writhing in pumpkin goop, gripping his knee in pain.

"Stop him!" Suzanne shouted again. "Arthur Bunch is the *killer*!"

Struggling to his feet, Arthur Bunch seemed dazed but determined to make his escape. He flashed a look of triumph at Suzanne and began limping away.

"No!" Suzanne shrilled.

That's when a comical red figure with white pearly horns stuck on the sides of his head jumped out from the crowd and poked Bunch in the backside with his pitchfork.

"That's it, Junior, do it!" Suzanne screamed.

Abruptly poked and jolted, Arthur Bunch fell forward and landed flat on his face.

"Got him!" screamed Junior, letting loose a high-pitched war cry.

The crowd turned, en masse, to witness Junior poking his pitchfork in Bunch's rear end and roared their approval!

"What an act!" someone yelled.

"Like vaudeville!" cried a voice.

"Wonderful," another voice cried. "I didn't know these gals had it in them!"

Then, as if Arthur Bunch and Junior Garrett were an acting troupe, as if the Cackleberry Club was the new theater-in-the-round, the crowd surged forward and formed a circle around the two men.

Buckshot Benoit's group struck up the first couple bars of *Devil Went Down to Georgia* and the crowd screamed again, loving it.

"Hang on to him!" Doogie yelled, as he thrashed his way through the crowd of revelers.

"Junior, be careful!" cried Toni. She was on the sidelines, hopping up and down.

"I got him, I got him!" yelled Junior, as he prodded Bunch one more time, shoving him to the ground.

The crowd, still thinking it was a wonderful slapstick play, cheered wildly. Even Carmen Copeland was laughing and giggling like a schoolgirl.

Junior, playing broadly to the crowd now, planted his right foot on Bunch's rear end and held the writhing man firmly in place. Then he grinned wickedly, brandished his pitchfork, and took a deep bow.

"Thank you, thank you all," shouted Suzanne, pulling

off her head scarf with a flourish and suddenly gaining the attention of the crowd. "I'm so glad you all enjoyed our little theatrical presentation," she said, winging it. "And now, if you'll kindly follow Petra into the Cackleberry Club, we'll be serving dessert and hot cider for everyone!"

Looking slightly stunned and unsure at what had just transpired, Petra gamely led the crowd inside for dessert. Amazingly, the crowd moved after her, still chattering about the wonderful show.

"YOU miserable piece of filth!" Suzanne screamed, as she jumped from her horse. She dashed up to Arthur Bunch and angled one cowboy-booted foot at him. "I ought to kick your . . ."

"No, Suzanne," cautioned Doogie. "We've had enough of that for one night. I'll take care of him."

Bunch groaned miserably on the ground.

"He's a stone-cold killer," Suzanne cried, unable to curb her anger. "He even pointed a gun at me!"

"What!" said a stunned Sam, as he suddenly rushed up to join Suzanne.

"Threatened me," Suzanne muttered, aiming a foot at Bunch again. This time Sam pulled her away.

Doogie grabbed a set of handcuffs from his belt and quickly secured Bunch's hands. Then, grabbing Bunch by the scruff of his neck, Doogie yanked him rudely to his feet. "You and I are going to do some talking!" Doogie commanded.

Junior was suddenly jumping around, waving his hands

in everyone's faces. "Can I help drag him to the car? Can I? Huh?"

"You can drag him into the swamp and leave him there for all I care," snorted Doogie. Then he pulled himself together and said, "Okay, Junior, tonight you're a deputy."

"Deputy devil," muttered Toni. "Seems fitting."

Sam was still staring at Suzanne. "He threatened you? With a gun?" He shook his head in amazement. "Holy Christmas."

TWENTY minutes later it was all over. Bunch had spilled his guts. Well, most of them anyway.

Doogie climbed out of his cruiser and stumped over to where Suzanne, Sam, Toni, and Junior were standing.

"You were right about that Tortuga thing," said Doogie. "Bunch talked the old lady into donating an old conquistador helmet and some gold coins to the historical society. Then Bunch turned around and sold them to some outfit in Florida. Tortuga Trading Company, he says."

"Tortuga," said Suzanne, feeling vindicated.

Sam let out a low whistle. "Those kind of antiques must have been worth a fortune."

"I'm thinking that's exactly right," said Doogie.

"So Peebler was on to him," said Suzanne.

"Peebler must have found some kind of donation papers in his aunt's house after she died," said Doogie. "As well as some reference to Tortuga. And I suppose Peebler's first thought was of Jane Buckley."

"When it was really Arthur Bunch," said Suzanne.

"But Bunch knew Peebler would keep nosing after the

antiques," said Doogie. "So before Peebler could do anything more, Bunch shot him."

"Did Bunch kill Wilbur, too?" asked Toni, wide-eyed at this tale of greed and murder.

"Bunch hasn't copped to that one yet, but my guess is yes," said Doogie. "Since I was the one who sent Wilbur over to Peebler's house to investigate."

"And Bunch didn't realize Wilbur hadn't found anything," said Suzanne.

"Bunch gave Wilbur the benefit of the doubt and then killed him for it," said Doogie, his voice tightening. He swept his hat off his head, murmured, "Doggone it."

"But it's over," said Toni. "That's what's important." She turned toward Junior, still in his devil costume, and gazed at him with unabashed love in her eyes.

"It's over for now," said Doogie. "Thanks to Suzanne and, I guess, Junior."

Grinning from ear to ear, Junior thrust his pitchfork above his head and crowed, "The devil made me do it."

Gazing up at the sky, breathing a sigh of relief, Suzanne saw that the clouds had lifted and that the church spire next door was silhouetted against a full moon. She smiled, slipped her hand into Sam's, and whispered, "But it's the angels who lend wings to our prayers."

Favorite Recipes
from the Cackleberry Club

Bedeviled Eggs

12 eggs, hard-boiled
⅓ cup mayonnaise
2 tbsp. spicy mustard
¼ cup pickle relish
Hot sauce
Hot paprika
Salt and pepper to taste

Cut eggs in half and remove the yolks. Mash the yolks with the mayonnaise, mustard, pickle relish, hot sauce, and paprika. Sprinkle in salt and pepper to taste. Now fill eggs using a tiny spoon, or pipe filling in using a pastry bag for a more elegant look. (Note: you can substitute 2 tbsp. horseradish for the mustard if you're a horseradish fan!)

Eggs in a Basket

1 can refrigerator biscuits (8)
8 eggs

Grease a muffin tin, then press a biscuit into each opening to create a small basket. Put a fresh egg into each basket. Bake at 400 degrees for 10 to 20 minutes, until eggs are solid. Garnish with crumbled bacon, shredded cheese, or hollandaise sauce—or eat on their own!

Petra's Pumpkin Pancakes

1 egg
1 cup of milk
¾ cup white flour
¾ cup whole wheat flour
½ cup cooked pumpkin (canned okay)
1 tbsp. sugar
2 tsp. baking powder
¼ tsp. cinnamon, ground
Pinch of nutmeg, ground
2 tbsp. vegetable oil

Combine beaten egg, milk, white flour, wheat flour, cooked pumpkin, sugar, baking powder, cinnamon, and nutmeg in mixing bowl. Stir until well blended. Pour vegetable oil into fry pan or on griddle, then pour out pancakes. When bubbles

form and break around edges, they're ready to be flipped over.
Serve with butter and your favorite syrup.

Chicken Divan

8 chicken breasts, boneless
8 slices Swiss cheese
1 can cream of chicken soup
½ can milk
¼ cup sour cream
1 cup bread crumbs
¼ cup melted butter
Salt and pepper to taste

Place chicken in 9-by-12 baking dish. Top each piece with
a slice of cheese. Mix together soup, milk, and sour cream,
then pour over chicken. Sprinkle on bread crumbs, add salt
and pepper to taste, and drizzle with melted butter. Cover with
foil and bake at 350 degrees for 30 minutes. Then remove foil
and bake for another 30 minutes. Serves 6 to 8.

Sam's Breakfast Egg Pizza

1 can (8 oz.) refrigerator biscuits
½ lb. pork sausage, crumbled and browned
½ cup red pepper, chopped
¼ cup onion, chopped

2 eggs
2 tbsp. milk
Salt and pepper to taste
1 cup Colby or cheddar cheese, shredded

Place refrigerated biscuits on round pizza pan and press flat to create a pizza crust. Make sure seams are joined together well and you have a small ridge around the outside. Add browned sausage to crust, then layer on red peppers and onions. Whisk the eggs, milk, salt, and pepper together in a small bowl, then pour over the pizza. Add the cheddar cheese on top. Bake at 375 degrees for 20 to 25 minutes. Make sure the eggs are set and the crust is golden brown. Serves 4 for breakfast.

Hot Mama Frittata

1 cup fresh mushrooms, sliced
3 green onions, finely chopped
1 cup cooked ham, cubed
2 tbsp. butter
8 eggs
¼ cup water
¼ cup Dijon mustard
½ tsp. Italian seasoning
¼ tsp. garlic salt
1½ cups cheddar cheese, shredded
½ cup tomatoes, chopped
1 can diced green chili peppers (7 oz.)

Sauté mushrooms and onions in butter until tender. Add ham and heat. In mixing bowl, beat eggs with water, mustard, Italian seasoning, and garlic salt. Stir in the mushroom and onion mixture, cheese, tomatoes, and diced chili peppers. Pour into shallow greased baking dish. Bake at 375 degrees for approximately 25 minutes. Yields 4 servings.

Crabby Omelets

4 eggs
1 tbsp. milk
Salt and pepper to taste
1 tsp. olive oil
1 cup cheddar cheese, shredded and divided
½ cup crabmeat or imitation crab, divided
Prepared hollandaise sauce, mix or jar

Beat eggs, milk, salt, and pepper in a bowl. Heat olive oil in a 9-inch skillet over medium heat. Add the egg mixture. Then, as the omelet begins to set, lift edges so uncooked mixture can flow beneath. Sprinkle with ½ cup cheese, then add crabmeat. Add another ½ cup of cheese and fold omelet in half. Cover and cook for an additional 1 to 2 minutes. Top with hollandaise sauce.

Miniature Crustless Quiche

4 large eggs
¾ cup milk
¼ cup onions, chopped

¼ *cup red peppers, diced*
¼ *cup mushrooms, diced*
1 *tbsp. olive oil*
½ *cup cooked ham, diced*
½ *cup cheddar cheese, grated*
1 *tsp. flour*
Salt and pepper to taste

Sauté onions, red peppers, and mushrooms in olive oil, then set aside. Whisk together eggs, milk, ham, cheese, flour, salt, and pepper. Grease a muffin tin (or use muffin cups) and add vegetables in the bottom, dividing portions equally. Add egg mixture on top, again dividing equally. Bake at 350 degrees for about 20 minutes, until firm and slightly puffy. Serve with toast, English muffins, or hash browns. Yields 6 to 8, depending on the size of your muffin tin.

Hazelnut Scones

1 *cup roasted and chopped hazelnuts*
2½ *cups flour*
1 *tbsp. baking powder*
½ *tsp. salt*
½ *cup butter*
⅓ *cup brown sugar, packed*
1 *cup milk*

Mix flour, baking powder, and salt in a large bowl. Cut in butter until mixture resembles fine granules. Add brown sugar and hazelnuts. Stir in milk and mix until dough forms a soft ball. Scoop up ¼ cup portions and place on ungreased baking sheet, about 2 inches apart. Bake at 425 degrees for about 15 minutes. Cool slightly before serving with pear butter.

Pear Butter

3 large pears
½ cup apple cider
¼ tsp. ground cinnamon
Dash of lemon juice
½ tsp. vanilla extract

Peel pears, removing seeds and stems, and cut into large pieces. Place pears in saucepan and add apple cider, cinnamon, and lemon juice. Cover and bring to a boil. Reduce heat to medium and cook 15 minutes or until pears are tender. Remove from heat and cool slightly, then puree the mixture in a food processor. Cook over medium heat again, bringing pears to a boil. Add in vanilla extract and allow mixture to thicken. Cool and serve. Makes about 2 cups.

Apple Strudel Cider

Powdered sugar
Cinnamon stick
6 oz. apple cider
Apple, sliced
Caramel apple dipping sauce

Rim a mug or glass with powdered sugar and add cinnamon stick. Heat apple cider and pour into mug. Dip an apple slice into caramel apple sauce and drop in mug as a garnish. Enjoy!

Junior's Deviled Ham Dip

½ cup sour cream
1 pkg. cream cheese (8 oz.)
1½ cups cheddar cheese, shredded
1 can green chilies (4 oz.), diced
1 small can deviled ham
¼ cup minced onion
1 large round of bread, sourdough or your favorite bread

Mix together sour cream and softened cream cheese. Add cheddar cheese, chilies, deviled ham, and onion and mix well. Hollow out the center of your bread, reserving those small pieces for dipping. Now fill your bread with the deviled ham dip, cover with foil, and bake at 300 degrees for about 45 minutes. Arrange bread dip on platter with small bread pieces. Note: You can also add crackers, pretzels, celery sticks, and sliced red peppers for dipping.

S'mortuaries

(Like s'mores, only deadlier!)

Graham crackers
Chocolate bars
Banana, sliced
Marshmallows
Caramel syrup
Chocolate chips

Lay out graham crackers and top with chocolate bar pieces and banana slices. Toast marshmallows, then place on top of chocolate bar and bananas. Drizzle on caramel syrup and add chocolate chips, then top with another graham cracker. Smoosh together and enjoy!

Turn the page for a preview of the next
Tea Shop Mystery by Laura Childs . . .

Scones & Bones

Coming March 2011 in hardcover
from Berkley Prime Crime!

A smirking human skull, all hollow eye sockets and pronounced parietal bones, grinned diabolically at Theodosia. A second skull, this one with crooked teeth clenched in an agonized grimace, wasn't quite as mirthful.

"Some of these images are a little bizarre," Theodosia murmured to Drayton.

"Jolly Roger flags were meant to frighten," Drayton replied. "The pirates who flew them wanted their designs to inspire fear and dread."

Theodosia took a step backward and gazed at the diverse collection of antique pirate flags that hung inside the shallow glass case. There were skulls and crossbones, full-sized skeletons, even skeletons dancing a jig.

"Actually," said Theodosia, a smile twitching the corners of her mouth, "they're just the kind of thing today's graphic designers and tattoo artists would groove on."

It was Sunday night at the Heritage Society in Charleston, South Carolina, and the grand opening of the Pirates and Plunder show. Theodosia Browning, proprietor of the Indigo Tea Shop, had been cajoled into attending the event by Drayton Conneley, her master tea blender and all-around Heritage Society booster.

"Take a look at this drinking cup," said Drayton, nudging her with the shoulder of his tweedy jacket. "It's the one that was featured in the Charleston *Post and Courier*'s arts and entertainment section a few days ago."

Theodosia moved to a freestanding glass display case to gaze at what was certainly a bizarre curiosity—a genuine human skull that had been transformed into a drinking cup. The cranium had been pared away, a silver web surrounded the skull on four sides, and a silver handle jutted out. But the *pièce de résistance* was the enormous diamond snugged beneath the skull's chin. A diamond that, to Theodosia's curious eyes, had to weigh at least ten carats, if not a whopping twelve.

"This piece was owned by a pirate as well?" Theodosia asked. She pushed back her tousle of auburn hair and bent even closer to get a good look. Set on a black velvet cushion, the skull cup was horrifying, sensational, and awe-inspiring all at the same time.

"I assume this bizarre little beauty belonged to a pirate," said Drayton, "though a diamond of such magnitude was no doubt plucked from the necklace or bracelet of some hapless noblewoman who ventured onto the high seas." He straightened up and gave a quick smile.

"Gives new meaning to the phrase 'killer diamond,'" Theodosia responded. She could just imagine standing on the foredeck of one of His Majesty's clipper ships, bound for Charles Town and a new life in the New World. Then gray mists parted, a giant black galleon rose up, and screaming pirates bore down upon you. Grappling hooks clamped the rails, murdering brigands swung onto your ship to . . .

Theodosia shook her head, aware that her overactive imagination had carried her far, far away, into a different, high-adventure realm. Then again, Theodosia looked like she might have slipped in from an earlier century. Her abundance of auburn hair could have inspired Raphael, her fair English skin seemed tempered by the cool, rainy weather of the Salisbury Plain. Theodosia's blue eyes sparkled with barely contained energy, and her face, with its high cheekbones and full mouth, was agile and expressive. Theodosia never bothered to keep a tight rein on her passions, whether they be ire or mirth. She wore her heart and her feelings on her sleeve and crashed through life at full tilt.

Drayton slipped on a pair of tortoiseshell half-glasses and inclined his dignified, graying head. "Let's read the description card for this oddity," he mumbled to himself. He was a sixty-something history buff who loved nothing better than to delve into the provenance of an obscure object.

"What's it say?" asked Theodosia. She smiled to herself at Drayton's bounding enthusiasm. He was an almost-partner, dear friend, and quirky sidekick. Not necessarily in that order.

"Whoa ho," said Drayton, nodding his head with approval. "This wasn't just owned by a pirate, it *is* a pirate!"

"Excuse me?"

"Says here it's reputed to be Blackbeard's skull." Drayton took a step backward and blinked in surprise. "My goodness."

"Are you serious?" said Theodosia. Blackbeard was, after all, the big daddy of pirates. A man with dozens of grisly legends attached to him and a fierce and fascinating character who'd entertained and inspired for practically two centuries.

Growing up in Charleston and the surrounding low country, Theodosia had heard endless tales about the swashbuckling pirates and brigands who'd plied the Carolina coast right up until the nineteenth century. Many had roamed all the way from South America up to Canada, terrorizing merchant and passenger ships and enjoying a wild, freewheeling life on the high seas. Some had been captured by U.S. Navy ships and met their fate on a gallows just a few blocks from here, on the Battery near White Point Gardens. Of course, the gallows was long since gone, while the gardens were now a frothy riot of magnolias and dogwood.

"I had no idea Timothy possessed such an amazing collection of pirate memorabilia," said Theodosia. Timothy Neville was the director of the Heritage Society, a crusty octogenarian who had a knack for twisting donors' arms and a keen, calculating memory that could recall exactly which old skeletons lay in uneasy repose in which Charleston attics.

"Although the Heritage Society owns a few of these pieces, most are actually on loan," Drayton explained. "Cajoled from antique dealers and private collectors."

"Really quite spectacular," said Theodosia, leaning forward to admire gold doubloons that spilled from an old wooden chest, a parchment map that depicted the Carolina coasts and shipwreck locations, and other maps that hinted at where treasure might still be buried. And, of course, there was that ubiquitous collection of pirate flags.

"I'm also told," said Drayton, "that this show was inspired by one of the curators stumbling upon an interesting stash of pirate memorabilia in the downstairs storage rooms. Items they didn't even realize were in their possession!"

"This show really does have the wide appeal of a museum blockbuster," said Theodosia. "I mean, who doesn't like pirates?"

"They *are* fascinating," agreed Drayton.

"Blackbeard and Bluebeard," said Theodosia. "And Captain Jack Sparrow." She chuckled as she glanced around. Though Theodosia had been immediately swept up in pirate legend and lore, most of the guests here tonight seemed much more focused on the champagne and hors d'oeuvres that were being served by tuxedoed waiters out in the great hallway.

As if to underscore her thoughts, a piercing shriek suddenly echoed through the almost-empty gallery.

"Good grief!" said Drayton.

Theodosia and Drayton turned in unison to find Delaine Dish and her crazy sister, Nadine, running playfully toward them. Close on Nadine's heels was Bill Glass, the scummy editor of an even scummier weekly tabloid known as *Shooting Star*.

"Theo*do*sia!" Delaine demanded, in her strident, pay-attention-to-me voice. "You're missing all the fun!" Delaine was the owner of Cotton Duck clothing boutique and a confirmed social gadabout. With her heart-shaped face, swirl of dark hair, and piercing eyes, Delaine was a striking beauty. Yet her appeal was undermined by her abrasiveness and constant need to know.

"You're missing the show," Drayton replied in a curt tone.

Delaine gave a clumsy shrug, splashing a few drops of champagne onto her pale yellow suit. "Oops. Clumsy me," she said, obviously a little tipsy.

Nadine, who was dressed in a bright purple suit, giggled loudly. "Maybe you should give us a quick lecture, Drayton. After all, you're on the board of directors here."

"Yeah," said Bill Glass, gesturing offhandedly at one of the displays, "tell us about these crazy black-and-white flags."

"The Jolly Roger," said Drayton, pulling himself to full height, "is derived from the French phrase *jolie rouge*, meaning pretty red."

But they really weren't listening. Instead, Delaine had her nose pressed tightly against a glass case, gazing starry-eyed at a glittering array of gold doubloons.

"Pirate's booty," she murmured.

At which point Bill Glass slung his arm around Nadine's waist and gave a wolfish grin. "*This* is my idea of booty!"

This was followed by shrieks of uproarious laughter from both Delaine and Nadine.

That did it for Drayton. Disorder and double entendres in the hallowed halls of the Heritage Society were high treason to him. He clenched his jaw so tightly the muscle quivered and his brows shot up. With a stoic yet pained expression, he turned to Theodosia and said, "Time for a refreshment?"

Theodosia immediately agreed. "My thought exactly."

"A terrific show," Theodosia told Camilla.

"Very impressive," offered Drayton.

Camilla Hodges, the Heritage Society's office manager-slash-secretary-slash-membership director, gave an appreciative smile. "Thank you," she said, "it took a fair amount of work to pull this off." Camilla was sixty-something with a waft of white hair and thighs that were permanently encased in Lycra. She was also enveloped by a constant cloud of perfume, but always a classic scent, like Shalimar by Guerlain or Joy by Jean Patou.

"You received some great publicity, too," said Theodosia. Before she stepped off the business merry-go-round to become chief bottle washer and proprietor of the Indigo Tea Shop, Theodosia had worked as an account executive in a large Charleston marketing firm. She'd waged constant war to snag her fair share of publicity and newspaper articles, so she knew how important the photo and accompanying blurb in the *Post and Courier* had been for the Heritage Society.

"Thank you," said Camilla, raising her champagne glass and clinking it against Theodosia and Drayton's glasses. "Now that our budget's been snipped yet again, I think they've added the title of PR director to my already long list of responsibilities."

"Well, you did a masterful job," said Drayton.

Camilla reached out and grabbed the arm of a young man who was standing nearby and pulled him into their circle. "This is Rob Commers," she told them. "One of our history interns and all around good guy who pretty much functioned as my right-hand man."

Rob, a string bean, earnest-looking college kid who couldn't have been a day over twenty, blushed furiously.

"You're getting your degree in history?" Theodosia asked him.

"I am," said Rob. He had short, cropped dark hair and long, dark eyelashes, the kind Theodosia would have killed for. "And since I've been interning here, I found out how much I don't know." He gave a rueful grin. "Which means I should probably go on for my master's."

"Nothing wrong with that," said Drayton.

"Rob was an enormous help in organizing this show," Camilla continued. "He did a fantastic job at handling the mailing list and invitations."

"It worked," said Theodosia. "Because you got a great turnout." Indeed, they were standing elbow to elbow in the great hallway.

"I just wish more guests were looking at the displays," said Camilla. Her brows puckered in a frown and she shrugged. "What can you do?"

"I'm afraid it's see and be seen," said Theodosia. Much as she loved Charleston, it was largely populated by social animals. Folks who wanted to go out, rub shoulders with others, be recognized, and get their photo in the society section. Nothing wrong with that, of course, except for the fact that you could end up rubbing shoulders with the same old shoulders week after week.

"Maybe we could somehow cajole a few guests to take a quick peek in the gallery?" suggested Drayton.

"Better wait until Delaine and Nadine come out," said Theodosia. Then she caught sight of Delaine's heart-shaped face and flashing violet eyes and said, "Oh, here she comes now."

"What if we turned down the lights in the gallery?" suggested Rob. "Make it a little more sexy and inviting."

"Not a bad idea," said Theodosia. "Just have the over-head pinpoint spots on." She recalled the spectacular jade exhibit in Chicago's Field Museum where the lights were positively cocktail lounge low. But the moody, intimate atmosphere packed visitors in like crazy.

Camilla grabbed Rob's elbow and said, "We'll be back in a minute. As soon as we find the rheostat."

"We'll save you a lobster roll," said Drayton, eyeing an approaching waiter who carried an overflowing tray of appetizers.

"And maybe a cream cheese wonton," said Theodosia, as the waiter stopped and tilted his tray toward them.

"Fantastic!" exclaimed Drayton, helping himself to a small, golden roll.

"Better yet," said Theodosia, grabbing a bright blue toothpick, "I'm going to have one of these lovely pink shrimp." But just as she stabbed a giant cooked shrimp, there was a loud shatter of glass followed by a bloodcurdling scream!

Don't miss the next Cackleberry Club Mystery

Stake and Eggs

A bizarre murder leaves the townsfolk of Kindred badly shaken. And inquiring minds want to know—will the ladies of the Cackleberry Club jump in to solve this one, too?

**Watch for the next Tea Shop Mystery
also from Laura Childs and Berkley Prime Crime**

Scones & Bones

As Charleston's Food and Wine Festival gets under way, Theodosia and the Indigo Tea Shop gang introduce the hottest new culinary trend—tea and cheese. But with a shocking murder, raft of suspects, and a bungled investigation, something smells funny. And it's not just the Gorgonzola!

And the next Scrapbooking Mystery

Skeleton Letters

Business is humming at Memory Mine as Carmela offers lessons in calligraphy and plans an extravagant wine tasting party. But when a friend is murdered and a valuable crucifix stolen from a church, the intrepid scrapbooker takes matters into her own hands.